This Family Life

First published in 2015

To Charlotte and Jack, who made this book possible.
Daddy loves you.

About the author

JON RANCE writes novels about love, family, relationship, and all the messy bits in-between. His novels have been described as hilarious, romantic, heart-warming, and perfect for fans of *Mike Gayle* and *Beth O'Leary*. His first book *This Thirtysomething Life* was a self-published Amazon top-ten bestseller and subsequently published by Hodder and Stoughton. Since then, he has written numerous novels including, *Sunday Dinners*, *About Us*, *Dan And Nat Got Married*, and *The Notecard.*

Jon grew up in England and studied English Literature at Middlesex University, London, before travelling the world and meeting his American wife in Australia. He now lives in California with his wife, two kids, and a dog called Pickle, where he writes full-time and drinks far too much tea.

Also by Jon Rance

This Thirtysomething Life
Happy Endings
A Notting Hill Christmas
Sunday Dinners
Dan And Nat Got Married
About Us
The Summer Holidays Survival Guide
The Notecard
Good Grief
One Lie

January

Tuesday 1 January 7.00 a.m.

New Year's Day

In the lounge watching William sleep. Emily's asleep upstairs. It's drizzling with rain. All quiet on the Wimbledon front.

Last year was generally a bit shit. I almost had an affair with my old sixth form ex-girlfriend Jamie but didn't. I almost lost Emily as a result but didn't. I almost lost my job, but luckily my evil Headmistress Miss Simpson was fired before me, and so I didn't. I was also accused of raping Emily's grandmother, but that was just a misunderstanding. The one bad thing that did actually happen was that Grandad died.

There was of course, the one amazing, brilliant and wonderful thing that happened last year, and has completely changed my life. William. He's four and a half months old now and I'm still in complete and utter awe of him. He has Emily's face, her dark eyes, and her slender nose. He has the cutest little baby body and as my mother always points out, such adorable little fingers and toes (or 'piggies' as she calls them), although he does seem to have my knees (the poor bugger). He's definitely a handsome little fella, although from somewhere in the darkest recesses of our family gene pool, he's got the world's craziest hair. It's dark like Emily's, but as patchy as fuck and because it's long in some parts and short in others, he has a sort of 'old man comb over'. I don't care though. He could look like a baby Adolf Hitler, and I'd still love him more than anything in the world. Saying that, I do wish he'd have the decency to have a lie-in once in a while.

I'm thinking about last year because I'm making some resolutions for this new one and I don't want to fuck this up. Having almost lost Emily once, I can't go through that again and most of all, I want to be a good dad to William.

After some thinking, a strong cup of coffee, and three (that's right, three) Shredded Wheat, I come up with this:

New Year's Resolutions:

Don't do anything really fucking stupid

This should just about cover everything.

Despite last night being New Year's Eve (the biggest party night in the world and usually an alcohol-fuelled orgy of disgracefulness) Emily and I were tucked up in bed by ten-thirty. We couldn't even stay up for Jools Holland's Hootenanny.

It was just after ten and Emily was falling asleep on the sofa.

'I can't make it,' she said.

'Just another hour.'

'I can't.'

'But the Hootenanny, Em.'

'Sorry,' she said and trudged off upstairs.

I tried to stick it out, but I fell asleep shortly afterwards and then went to bed. For the first time since I was about ten, I didn't see in the New Year, and I missed the Hootenanny. The stench of middle-age wafts pungently around the Spencer household.

Something else that's wafting pungently around the house is William's nappy. He just did something evil in it. I've been a father for over four months now and I'm used to William's poos, and so without even looking, I know this one is bad.

The Poo Index

1. Rabbit droppings. Small, hard and harmless
2. Pebbles. Larger than rabbit droppings, but still fairly

firm. Low to medium on the whiff factor

3. The Curry. Messy. Stinky. A pain to clean up and leaves a lingering stench

4. Throw up. Poo that looks like puke. Runny and grainy with traces of food

5. Not as smelly as the curry, but a higher chance of leakage

6. The Monster. Does exactly what it says on the tin. It's messy, the smell hits you right away and won't go away for days, and the clean-up requires gloves, a mask, and preferably an incinerator

7.15 a.m.

Nuclear. I just added this to the list after William's poosplosion. I think the name says it all.

1.00 p.m.

Emily plodded downstairs at ten o'clock and announced she's getting fit. Actually, she made it perfectly clear that we're getting fit.

'I've made some resolutions,' she said, sitting down at the breakfast table and unfolding a piece of paper.

'It looks very official.'

'That's because it is,' she said with a wry smile. 'Have you made any?'

'Just one. Not to do anything really fucking stupid. It's all encompassing,' I said proudly.

'I'm not sure that's technically a resolution, Harry. Although let's hope you can stick to it.'

'So what's yours?' I said quickly changing the subject.

'I think now we have William we need to be more careful about what we eat. He's going to be on solids soon and I don't think ordering from The Spice of Wimbledon twice a week is sending out the right message.' And then she said the four words I feared the most: 'So I've been thinking ...'

I love Emily dearly. She's the love of my life, but whenever she starts sayings things like, 'I've been thinking,' or 'It's time we made some changes,' I know my life is about to get infinitely harder. 'And don't take this the wrong way, Harry, but the problem is you.'

'Oh.'

'And unless you agree to the changes I'm suggesting, I think we're all going to be deeply unhappy.'

'No pressure then.'

'Number one,' said Emily looking at me with a confident smile. 'Only one takeaway per month.'

'A month!'

'They're very bad for you. Plus, now I'm a stay-at-home mum, I can make you curry from scratch. I got that new Jamie Oliver cookbook for Christmas.'

'It isn't the same though.'

'Because it's healthier. It will be fine once you get used to it.'

'You said that about tofu.'

And whole wheat bread (it just isn't the same as white) and don't get me started on 1% milk.

'Number two. We're joining a gym.' I was about to jump in with my perfectly reasonable reasons why joining a gym is a terrible idea (we'll probably stop going after a few months and end up paying for it for the rest of the year, I don't want to be the sort of person who says 'just off to the gym' and lastly, there's always at least one naked old man in the changing room drying his wrinkly old balls with no shame - no amount of fitness is worth this), but Emily put up her hand - I was literally talking to the hand. 'And before you say anything, we're doing this. I'm going to get us membership at the gym around the corner.'

'The one with all the muscle guys who ponce about in front of the mirror?'

'They have classes too. They have Zumba, Yoga, Pilates. It might be fun.'

'So while the world's strongest men lift small cars in the

man zone, I can stretch it out with the ladies and the geriatrics?'

'Exactly,' said Emily with a smile. 'And they even have a crèche for William. Number three,' she said looking at me, suddenly serious. 'You have to quit smoking.'

'Now hang on a minute, Em.'

'You were going to quit before you were twenty-five. Then it was before you were thirty. Then it was definitely before we had kids. You're thirty-four now Harry and we have William. It's time. No more excuses.'

I wanted to defend myself, but I couldn't. She was right, it was time. I've thought about quitting before and there's always been a reason to put it off. The truth though is that I like it, I'm an addict and it's easier not to quit. However, we have William now and I don't want to set a bad example. I don't want him growing up thinking that it's all right to smoke.

'I need a day,' I said.

'A day?'

'One day at the pub with Rory and after that I'll quit. Promise.'

'It's a deal,' she said giving me a kiss before she bounced away and popped the kettle on. I'm going to go to the pub with Rory, get drunk, smoke until I can't smoke anymore and then I'll be done. I'm going out with a bang or, more likely, a severe cough.

3.00 p.m.

In the shed. Eating the last of my Christmas chocolate orange. Emily inside feeding William. Raining.

I rung Rory Wilkinson (Art teacher at school and stand-in best mate since proper best mate Ben left for Australia last year with new wife Katie). We're meeting on Thursday at The Alexandra for an all-day session.

Off to Waitrose to procure the last of the food for tomorrow's Bank Holiday BBQ bonanza. We're having both sets of parents over, which is obviously a terrible idea. The reason we try so hard to keep our parents away from each other is that my dad and Emily's dad don't get on. This is Emily's attempt at making it all right. I predict a riot.

Wednesday 2 January 9.00 a.m.

In the lounge. William on his blanket. Emily on the phone to her mum. Sunny (ish). The BBC weatherman has predicted 'some very heavy rain' on the way.

There is a decidedly unpleasant smell coming from William. He probably needs a nappy change. If I wait and pretend to ignore it, Emily will change him when she gets off the phone. Payback for last week when I knew she knew he'd done a really bad one, but she ignored it until it was time for me to put him down for his nap. This stinky mess has her name written all over it. Oh, here comes Emily.

'What's that smell? Have you done something bad in your nappy little man?' She looks down at William and he gives her a knowing smile. 'And Daddy's pretending not to notice.'

'Oh, what's that?' I said.

'The disgusting smell coming from William's bottom.'

'I hadn't noticed,' I lied.

'Right, of course.'

Time to take the mini quiches out of the fridge.

11.45 p.m.

In bed. Emily's parents in the spare room. My parents on the sofa bed in the lounge.

The dads were frosty at first. Monosyllabic conversation over sausage rolls, but a few pints and a cigar in the garden later and they were getting on like a house on fire. I popped out to join in with the male banter while the girls were inside drooling over William.

'We're looking at Tenerife,' said Emily's dad, Derek.

'Helen and I were there in 2001,' said Dad. 'Lovely.'

'Tenerife for what?' I said.

'A holiday home,' said Derek.

'Oh, that would be nice,' I replied.

Derek shot me a look which I'm sure said, 'But you'll never see the inside of it, sunshine'. Despite everything that's happened and even since William was born (which Emily claims has softened him), Derek still treats me like the unwanted, stray dog of the family. Maybe it's because he's an ex-copper, but I always feel like I'm being interrogated for a crime I didn't commit.

'Still talking about it,' said Derek. 'Pam wants to look at Lanzarote, even though we already agreed on Tenerife. Women,' tutted Derek with a knowing look at Dad.

'I know what you mean,' said Dad. 'I want to get a new car. The Ford's been a decent runner, but I want to get something a bit jazzier.'

Had Dad actually used the word, 'jazzier'? Derek nodded as though he knew exactly what he meant. Apparently, among late fifties men, 'jazzier' is a known word.

'Something like a Saab?' said Derek.

'Or an Audi,' said Dad.

'Nice car, the Audi,' said Derek.

'I'd get one tomorrow, but you know ... women,' tutted Dad.

'Women, right?' I tutted.

'That's my daughter you're tutting about,' said Derek with a disdainful look.

'Have some respect,' said Dad shaking his head and I scuttled back inside.

Most of the afternoon was spent fending off my mother.

'Can I do anything? Are those sausages cooked? I want to ask Pam how she's feeling about the HRT. Do you know about the HRT? Is William all right? He looks a little on the thin side. Emily says you're going to the gym. Is that true because you know what happened at secondary school sports day? The doctor called you a 'sickly child', remember that? Are you sure I can't help with something?' And so it went on.

Then there's Emily's mum Pam. The only thing worse than being alone with Mum, is being alone with Pam. We have nothing to say to each other. Whenever I'm alone with her, I'm forced to resort to the same tried and tested questions. I ask how she is, about her knitting and her brother Sam, and that's all we have. Then follows a lengthy silence. Today, after an unlucky turn of events, I was left alone with Pam for a while and so after our usual silence, I had to say something else.

'Derek was talking about the holiday home in Tenerife. That sounds nice,' I said trying to be chatty. However, it quickly became apparent I had spoken out of turn. Pam's usual gloss of ambivalence turned sharply to prickly annoyance.

'Oh, Derek mentioned that did he?'

'Well ... I …'

'I can't believe he's still talking about Tenerife. Agh!' said Pam then she stormed off.

'Why's Mum shouting at Dad in the shed?' said Emily a few minutes later.

'No idea.'

Derek found me a bit later.

'Pam said you mentioned Tenerife?' said Derek, looking at me with a disturbing twitch in his right eye; his large frame, and ex-copper expression which said, 'I know you're guilty,' turned my knees to jelly.

'Well …I—'

'What's wrong with you?!' he shouted.

'Why's Dad shouting at you?' said Emily.

'No idea.'

As the afternoon turned to evening things got better. Actually, we all got a lot drunker. William was put to bed after performing his rolling from front to back party piece for the fiftieth time, and that's when the fun really began. Derek demanded some 'proper music' and I managed to find a sixties compilation CD. Before long the old folk were dancing like it was 1969 all over again. Pam threw her cardigan suggestively across the back of the sofa. Dad was gyrating and moving around the lounge like Mick Jagger on speed. Mum was kicking her legs in the air and knocked over the last of the sausage rolls. And Derek was down to his vest unnervingly quickly.

'This isn't what I had planned,' said Emily.

'If you can't beat them, join them,' I said and started dancing too.

The crowd cheered, and the evening went a bit barmy from there on. Dad and Derek started doing karaoke using props from around the house, and before long Derek was on the sofa singing his lungs out to Street Fighting Man by The Rolling Stones with one of my old ties around his head (à la Keith Richards), and Mum and Pam were doing a never-ending conga around the house. Eventually, around midnight, as people were starting to fall asleep in unusual and uncomfortable places, we all trundled off to bed. Which leads me on to What Happened on the Landing. I was in bed, about to roll over and go to sleep when I realised I needed a wee. I walked out onto the landing and that's when I saw him. Derek. Naked as the day he was born, although he still had my tie around his head.

'Jesus Christ, Derek!' I said, unable to hide my obvious shock and embarrassment.

'This is a bit awkward.'

'Just a bit,' I said incredulously.

The thing was, he wasn't doing anything to cover himself

up. He just stood there, truncheon on parade (to use a police metaphor) without a care in the world.

'It's the Scotch.'

'Right, well,' I said, attempting to end our conversation and go about my business.

'The nakedness, Harry. The Scotch. I can't help myself. Still, all forgotten in the morning, eh?'

'Definitely,' I said with a vague smile. 'Night then.'

'Night,' said Derek and that's when it happened. That's when the world I knew came crashing down around me. Naked Derek hugged me. I can still feel him on me now and I can still smell the Scotch. Oh, the Scotch. 'See you in the morning, son.' And then he called me son for the first time. Yuk.

Thursday 3 January 12.15 p.m.

In the pub waiting for Rory. Forty cigarettes and a pint in front of me on the table. No sign of the 'very heavy rain' the BBC weatherman predicted. This is it. The day I quit smoking. The end of an era.

Emily never fails to amaze me. I was about to leave when she said,

'I'm so proud of you, Harry.'

'Because I'm about to leave you for the day and get slaughtered at the pub?'

'No, silly, because you're quitting smoking. I know how hard it must be for you. I just want to say thank you, on behalf of me and William.'

'You're welcome,' I said, and I thought about telling her about her dad and his late-night truncheon parade on the landing, but the words, 'your dad and his wrinkly old penis' just didn't seem to want to come out.

'Try and be quiet when you stagger in.'

'Will do,' I said and gave her a kiss goodbye.

Rory is running late. He texted me and said there was trouble brewing with his better half Miranda. Here he is, and he looks miserable.

Friday 4 January 1.00 p.m.

On the sofa. Emily and William visiting her friend Stella in Kingston-upon-Thames. Still no sign of a downpour. The BBC weatherman looked a bit down today.

Why did I smoke forty cigarettes?

Why did I drink enough alcohol to quench the entire population of Belgium?

I am a fool.

At least the last thing I want at the moment is a cigarette.

I'm worried about Rory. He turned up last night looking as though he had the weight of the world on his shoulders. He sat down, I got him a pint, and I asked him what was going on.

'It's Miranda and me. You know we've been trying for a baby for a while now, but nothing's happening. She wants us to go to the doctor. She's worried we can't have kids.'

'It can take a while sometimes and it's only been a few months.'

'I know that, and you know that, but Miranda's gone a bit mental about it. I'm worried about her. She didn't want me coming out today and drinking ten pints because apparently alcohol makes sperm swim slowly.'

'Maybe they're just bad with directions,' I said trying to lighten the mood, but Rory was really down about it.

'It will be all right, won't it mate?'

'Of course,' I said. 'Now let's go and have another smoke.'

And so we drank and smoked our way from midday all

the way until closing time. Eleven hours of drinking, smoking, eating, and talking absolute nonsense, but at eleven-thirty sitting in Wimbledon Kebab, two things became clear: Firstly, it was only a matter of time before Rory and Miranda conceived their first child, and secondly, I wasn't sure I could quit smoking.

'It's for the kids, Harry. It's all for the kids,' slurred Rory.

'And I love William more than life itself. I just don't know if I have the will-power.'

'And I don't know if my balls work,' said Rory and we burst out laughing, even though neither subject was particularly funny, and both were actually quite serious.

Lying on the sofa in the harsh light of early afternoon, I realise I need to try my best to quit. Emily's right. I need to do this for her and more importantly, for William.

Saturday 5 January 11.00 a.m.

About to go to the park with William and Emily. Cloudy, but no sign of rain. I think the BBC weatherman might be going through some sort of crisis. He looked very withdrawn today.

Derek rang me and wants to play golf tomorrow. I panicked and said yes. I'm terrified. I don't want to talk about what happened on the landing. Emily is pleased. She thinks we're finally bonding. If only she knew the horrible truth. I think I'm going to tell her.

Off to the park. I'm going to take William in the Baby Bjorn. I wonder if it ever gets confusing in Sweden because they could have a baby called Bjorn in their Baby Bjorn.

12.30 p.m.

Back from the park. Emily making us a 'low fat' ploughman's lunch.

We met our new neighbours on the way to the park. Since Mrs Crawley (ex-Head of the Neighbourhood Watch committee, almost certainly a racist and definitely a scary old lady) moved out last year, whoever bought her house has taken a while to move in (it's had a 'Sold' sign up since last October). There's a tall, dark-haired man about my age called Mark, who's an investment banker in The City and has a bit of the Colin Firths about him, his very attractive wife Sophie; blonde, big breasts and legs that go on forever, and their five- year-old daughter, who is apparently named Lexus. 'But not after the car,' said Mark sternly after he introduced her.

We shook hands and said we'd have to get together soon. To be honest, I was too busy worrying about tomorrow's game of golf with Derek, but Emily said we'd love to and on the way to the park they were all she could talk about.

'They seemed nice. Didn't they seem nice? Did you see the ring on her finger? Lexus, what a cute little thing and such a pretty name.'

'She's named after a car, Em.'

'Mark said she wasn't. Anyway, people are using all sorts of interesting names nowadays. If we have another and it's a girl, I'd like to call her either Petal or Blossom.'

'Are you being serious? We're not calling our next kid after a part of a flower.'

'And I suppose you want something more traditional?'

'What's wrong with that?'

'It's just a bit old school. I think we should think outside of the box for the next one - like Mark and Sophie.'

I have an awful feeling I'm going to be hearing that a lot from now on. But I have more pressing issues to deal with though, like my impending eighteen holes with Derek. I really could do with a cigarette.

9.00 p.m.

'Em, there's something I have to tell you,' I said.

We were on the sofa watching TV. Emily muted the telly and turned to look at me.

'Sounds serious.'

'It is. I don't quite know how to say this.'

'Just tell me, Harry,' said Emily looking worried.

'The night your parents were here, something awful happened. I just don't know how to say it.'

'What, Harry?'

'I was in bed. You were fast asleep. It was late. I had to get up to go for a wee and so I walked out onto the landing, and that's when it happened.'

'What happened?'

'Your dad, he was ... naked.'

'What?' said Emily, her face suddenly changing, the beginnings of a smirk starting to appear.

'He was stood there with no clothes on. I saw his penis.' Suddenly Emily started laughing. 'It's not bloody funny, Em. I saw his wrinkly old balls.'

'Is that why you're playing golf tomorrow?' she said trying to hold back more giggles.

'I don't know, Em. I don't want to talk about it anymore.'

'Right, yes, of course,' said Emily still laughing. 'Just one thing.'

'What?'

'Did you offer to show him yours?' she said bursting into laughter.

I wish I hadn't told her. She thinks it's hilarious. I'm scarred for life.

Sunday 6 January 5.05 p.m.

Home. Tired. Plasters on most of my fingers. Emily making a low fat, low calorie and I assume tasteless dinner.

Unbelievable. It's the only word I can think of to describe today's golfing debacle. Putting aside that it took us nearly four hours to do the full eighteen holes, I lost most of Derek's balls and I may have done some permanent damage to my fingers, the worst part of the day was on the ninth hole. Derek wanted to talk about What Happened on the Landing.

'The thing is, Harry, it happened. We can't pretend it didn't.'

'Or we could pretend it didn't.'

'We need to talk about it.'

'Do we though?'

'I was drunk. It shouldn't have happened. You can't tell a soul.'

'Right,' I said wishing I hadn't already told Emily.

'Especially Emily and Pam. They can't know what happened.'

'My lips are sealed,' I lied, and I thought that was it.

'Just one last thing. It's a bit delicate.'

'Sure.'

'Did you notice anything … unusual?'

'Unusual?'

'Down there?' he said nodding towards his groin.

'I don't think so,' I said hesitantly.

'Been having some problems, you see, Harry. Penis problems. I can't tell Pam. Don't know what to do about it and then after you had a good look at it—'

'I wouldn't say a good look,' I protested.

'Still you saw it and there was nothing unusual about it. Nothing out of the ordinary?'

'Like I said, I wasn't really looking, and it was dark.'

'It was,' he said. 'Very dark.'

'Maybe you should go to the doctor.'

'Right, yes, of course.'

'Should probably, you know, take my next shot,' I gestured at my ball.

'Right, yes. Remember, head down, eyes on the ball.'

I tried, swinged, and missed. I'm fairly sure the worst piece of advice in golf is to keep your head down and eyes on the ball. Then, after the ignominy of having to face Derek, I had to return home to a still smirking Emily.

'How was golf?' she asked.

'Terrible.'

'It wasn't … strip golf, was it?' she said laughing.

'Oh, very bloody funny. Clothed, obviously. You can't tell him you know. I'm sworn to secrecy, and he already hates me.'

'He doesn't hate you, Harry,' said Emily giving me a kiss. 'Maybe this will bring you closer together. Your little secret.'

'It's not funny, Em. Can we just not talk about it?'

'Of course,' said Emily, although I clearly saw her grinning as she carefully placed two meatballs on my dinner plate. I'm never going to live this down.

It's the first day of school tomorrow. I am dreading it, but not for any of the usual reasons. I have to leave Emily and William. I've loved being home with them. Now I'll only see William for a couple of hours a day. I'll miss so much of his life. It wasn't something I really thought about before we had him, but now he's here the thought of being away from him fills me with dread.

Monday 7 January 11.15 p.m.

In bed. Eating a rice cracker (yuk). Four days without a cigarette (ugh).

I got to school and was immediately called into the Head's office. Since Miss Simpson was fired and replaced by the burly and Welsh Mr Jones, school has been brilliant. Mr Jones is strict, but fair and for some reason seems to quite like me. Today was the cherry on the cake though because I've been made Acting Head of Department (AHOD), which means more work, but also a slight increase in salary. Apparently, Eddie Collins (previous HOD) was found face down in a pool of his own vomit outside Toys "R" Us on Saturday morning.

'It was very upsetting for the children,' said Mr Jones.

'Obviously.'

'He's in no state to return to work, at least for a few weeks, and even then I don't think he can resume his Head of Department role. So that leaves a slot open for Acting Head of Department until the end of the year. What do you say?'

'But what about Clive or Chris? They've been here a lot longer than me.'

'Clive isn't the sort of person I'm looking for. Too many issues with other departments, if you know what I mean?' I had no idea what he meant, but I nodded anyway. 'And Chris is just too, what's the word? Oh yes, stuck in his ways. I'm going with youth. A clean slate. I want you, Harry.'

'Then, I suppose, yes.'

'Brilliant,' said Mr Jones. 'The actual title has been changed to Acting Subject Manager or ASM. It was almost Acting Subject Leader or ASL, then it was Acting Department and Subject Manager or ADSM, but that felt too long and so now it's just plain old ASM. I hope that suits?'

'Yeah, I suppose.'

'You're going to have to jump in headfirst, pardon the pun, but I know you're up for it. Mrs Jarvis will give you the full rundown after this meeting, prior to the Senior Leadership Team meeting and then the actual HOD meeting.'

I've gone from almost being fired last year due to Miss Simpson's witch hunt against me to AHOD (or technically

ASM) in a matter of months. I'm going for a drink with Rory after school to celebrate.

The pre-meeting with Mrs Jarvis (Deputy Head) was terrifying. Mrs Jarvis is one of those horribly organised people, and so within seconds of walking in, I had an information pack, was signed up to attend four management and leadership training courses, had at least twenty emails, a calendar of planned meetings, a calendar of not-planned-but-will-probably-happen meetings, a calendar of unlikely-but-could-just-happen meetings, and a calendar of definitely-won't-happen-but-it's-best-to-have-a-calendar-just-in-case-for-some-reason-they-do meetings.

'Any questions?' said Mrs Jarvis.

'When am I going to have time to actually teach?'

'Very funny, Mr Spencer,' said Mrs Jarvis laughing.

I wasn't joking and she didn't answer my question. Ominous.

Tuesday 8 January 7.15 p.m.

'What do you think?' said Emily.

'I love it,' I said.

Emily's had a haircut. She's had the same hair for years - long and straight. Her almost black hair has been dyed so it's completely black, and its shoulder length, and she has a fringe. It looks quite sexy actually and I had the sudden urge to take her to the bedroom, but how do you explain to a woman (without getting in large amounts of trouble) that the reason you want to have sex with her is because with the new hair it's like she's someone else, and the idea of shagging someone different is quite a turn-on? In the end, I decided not to open that can of worms and to forgo the sex. Happy wife; happy life.

Thursday 10 January 12.15 p.m.

At school. Eating a chicken and lettuce wrap. Seven days without smoking.

Smoking is all I can think about from the minute I open my eyes until they close again at the end of the day. That and the number of meetings I now have to attend as AHOD/ASM. Today after lessons, I have a pre-meeting with the SLT (Senior Leadership Team), but that is just to discuss what we're actually going to discuss at the actual SLT meeting tomorrow. I thought about asking why we were having a meeting about a meeting, but I didn't want to rub anybody up the wrong way.

4.45 p.m.

Alan Hughes (PE) spent the whole meeting on his iPad, probably sending inappropriate messages to inappropriate girls. I'm starting to wonder whether the increase in salary is going to be worth the extra stress and hours of meetings I'm going to have to endure. In the pre-meeting, Norris Roker (Maths) put forward the idea of a pre-meeting, pre-meeting where we'd discuss topics for the pre-meeting. I laughed, but when I looked around I was the only one. I got a text from Alan Hughes afterwards. Welcome to Hell, is all it said.

I just had a chat with Rory. Miranda is still driving him crazy with baby talk. She wanted to see their GP, but he said they need to have been trying for at least a year before they can do anything. Poor Rory is feeling the pressure. When it's ovulation time he's required to perform as much as possible. Plus, he can't use up any important sperm with mindless wanks, and is banned from smoking, drinking, and basically being human.

8.00 p.m.

Derek rung earlier to tell me his penis is all right. He had it checked by a doctor and it's normal. Hopefully that's the last time I have to talk about my father-in-law's genitalia.

Literally starving. Tonight for dinner Emily made a lovely curry from her new Jamie Oliver cookbook. It was gorgeous, and we had naan bread and chutney and poppadom's, just like from The Spice of Wimbledon. The problem was the portion size.

'Portion size is the key to sustained weight loss, Harry. And the best part is that after a while, once your stomach shrinks, you'll want less too,' Emily said cheerfully.

My stomach had better start shrinking soon because I can't take much more of this.

Saturday 12 January 8.45 a.m.

The day I die is finally here. It's orientation at the gym. Emily's parents are coming over at nine to watch William. I just said my goodbyes. I told William I loved him, but he just looked at me blankly. He didn't know it was the last time he was going to see me alive.

The only good thing about going to the gym is that Emily let me eat some proper food. She made bacon, eggs, beans, and toast. All low fat, grilled and poached, but because we're going to have our first session with the personal trainer (PT), she said we had to eat enough to sustain us. I think I ate enough to sustain us both.

2.00 p.m.

Alive (just). On the sofa. Unable to move.

Any misapprehension I may have had that it wasn't going to be the worst hour of my life was quickly discarded when I met my PT, Tyler. Tyler was tall, blond, and had the body of an East German swimmer. He was wearing a pair of Lycra shorts and a tight vest which showed off every single one of his packs. I always thought six was the pack limit, but I'm sure he had at least eight.

After a brief orientation, Emily and I were strategically separated, and she went off with a man-mountain called Rocky. I laughed because I thought he was joking, but as I soon learnt, people don't joke at the gym.

'What are your workout goals?' said Tyler.

'I want to look half-decent naked,' I said.

Tyler tried not to laugh and then spent about a minute looking me up and down. I literally felt like a piece of meat. A fatty, flabby piece of rotten meat.

'It's going to take a lot of work, Harry. Are you up for it?'

'I think so.'

'Then leave now,' he said pointing to the door. 'Get out!' I was about to call his bluff and leave, but unfortunately he beat me to it. 'I'll ask you again. Are you up for it?'

I knew what he wanted me to say and so I said it.

'I'm ready!' I half-yelled.

'I can't hear you, Harry. Are you ready?'

'I'm ready!' I said a bit louder.

'I still can't hear you. I said, are you ready?'

'I'm ready!' I shouted.

I thought about beating my chest, but it seemed a bit over the top, even for the gym.

'Top man, yeah,' said Tyler and he offered me his knuckles to bump. I bumped them. For shame. 'Right then, let's get down to it.'

And those were the last words I heard before the ringing started in my ears followed by the sweat, the pain, the aching and the humiliation. Tyler ground me down until I was a sweaty, floppy, mess lying on the floor like a wet, limp turd. Then it was time for my rub down (this wasn't mentioned at any point by anyone - the secret rub down). Tyler helped me onto a bench and told me to lie flat on my back with my knees bent. The next minute he was stretching my legs to an almost physically impossible angle, but as I was already in so much pain and to be honest, only partially conscious, I didn't feel a thing.

'See you on Tuesday,' said Tyler helping me off the table.

'Tuesday?'

'You're booked in for another hour on Tuesday night. Top man,' he said. 'High-five?'

'Sure, why not.' I'd already embarrassed myself enough, a high-five to add to the list wasn't going to hurt, but before I was about to high-five he stopped me.

'Forget the high-five, yeah, you're a top man. Big ten for an awesome workout!' he said and then we did it. We performed a big-ten. My humiliation was complete.

I stumbled towards the exit and that's when I saw Emily and Rocky. She was flat on her back and Rocky had her left leg pushed all the way back towards her head with his head basically in her vagina.

'Stretch it out,' Rocky said while Emily moaned and groaned, not unlike the noises she makes in the bedroom. 'Hold it, hold it,' said Rocky.

'Ohhhhhhh Rocky!' Emily squealed.

Outside Emily asked how it was.

'Awful.'

'Rocky said I have the body of a twenty-year-old.'

'Tyler's trying to kill me,' I said, and Emily laughed.

Like I said, the gym isn't the place for jokes, and I wasn't joking. Tyler is definitely trying to kill me, and the worst part is that I'm paying him to do it.

Sunday 13 January 8.30 a.m.

Eating one slice of whole wheat toast and a cup of sugarless tea. Emily is eating cereal that looks like rabbit droppings. William eyeing Emily's breasts. Whole body aches. Desperately in need of a cigarette.

Last night I was going to tell Emily that I couldn't eat half-portions of food because my stomach was getting bigger instead of smaller. I was going to tell her I couldn't keep working out with Tyler because he was almost certainly some sort of voyeur, and I couldn't quit smoking because I was weak and spineless. However, once I had managed to get myself into bed with a lot of groaning, Emily started talking and my plan went out of the window. She told me how much she loved me and how proud she was that I was going to the gym and not smoking.

'And as a reward, I'm going to give you a special treat,' she said with a naughty grin.

I'm not going to lie, I really wanted it to be KFC and a cigarette, but it wasn't. Instead she slipped under the sheets and gave me my first blowjob since William was born last August. It was incredible, but I spent the whole time dreaming about the Colonel's secret blend of eleven herbs and spices. What's wrong with me?

Monday 14 January 6.45 a.m.

No school today because I have management training. I should be excited that I don't have to spend the day in the classroom and instead get to drink coffee, and eat a 'continental style' buffet, while being force-fed government sound bites, but I'm not.

3.45 p.m.

It was worse than I'd imagined. The leadership trainer, Colin Thistle, spent the first thirty minutes telling us that this was going to be different from any training we'd ever had, before he went on to be like every trainer I've ever had. I was in a shabby, cold portacabin with ten other HODs, the lame 'continental style' buffet, and some watery coffee, and it was five hours of PowerPoint, role playing, group exercises and Colin listing off his favourite management sound bites:

1. It's all about moving goalposts (metaphorical goalposts because the one PE teacher got a bit confused)
2. And pushing the envelope
3. And bringing it to the table
4. And taking it to the next level
5. And lots of blue-sky thinking
6. And idea showers
7. Incentivise! Incentivise! Incentivise!
8. There are no problems, just challenges (he obviously hasn't met Alan Gillespie in year nine).
9. If you aren't on board, you're overboard, so you'd better learn to swim (he seemed very pleased with this one)
10. A school is like a pie and you're just a piece of the pie and the pupils are the filling, and the building is the crust, and the headmaster is - he trailed off at this point - I don't think he'd really thought the pie analogy through properly

I have three more training sessions left. I'm dreading them already. As we were heading out of the door, Colin gave us all homework, although in line with current education trends, he explained that we didn't have to do it if we didn't want to, but he'd appreciate it if we did - and therein lies the most accurate management lesson of the day - when you have no power, the only power you have is to beg.

Wednesday 16 January 5.45 a.m.

Emily and William still asleep. In the kitchen. Having a secret cup of coffee with sugar. Pain in side, stomach, back, arms, legs, and head. Raining.

Last night I had a nightmare I was being chased by Derek. He wanted me to look at his penis. I didn't want to, but then my legs wouldn't work and so I was trapped. Derek (who was now a giant), was thrusting his enormous knob at me and then it started shouting at me, but with Tyler's voice. I woke up sweaty and confused.

Last night Tyler was like a man possessed. At one point he stood over me screaming, 'Do it, Harry! For me! For England and St George!' He gave me a fist bump, two high-fives, a big-ten, and one slap on the bum. Emily jogged for a bit, stretched on the mats, did something or other with the big bouncy ball, and then Rocky felt her up on the rub down table. All in all, another disappointing, painful and uncomfortable night at the gym.

6.40 a.m.

Breasts are amazing, aren't they? All of my teenage years were taken up by them - from looking at the underwear section of my parent's Freemans catalogue in my bedroom, to my tentative and embarrassing first attempts at seeing a pair in the flesh. There are millions of websites devoted to them, from celebrity nip-slips to amateur girlfriends' flashing.

And yet.

Watching Emily feeding William is the most natural, beautiful, and non-erotic thing in the world. Right now they're my son's breakfast - tonight they might be something else entirely. I doubt it though. Since William, things in the bedroom have been put on hold. Apart from the surprising blowjob the other night, it's been strictly no-ballroom. The strangest thing is though, I'm not that bothered about it. Harry sans mojo.

Friday 18 January 3.50 p.m.

At school. Chilly. First History department meeting as AHOD/ASM about to take place.

I had a cigarette. Rory was having one and I was nervous about my first meeting as ASM. After the pre-meeting meeting with all of the SLTs, I asked Mr Jones for some advice on how best to handle my first department meeting.

'I could give you lots of strategies, obviously,' said Mr Jones and then he walked off.

8.45 p.m.

On the sofa. Emily watching TV. Eating a carrot and pretending it's a Mars bar.

The meeting went well (ish). I was worried the other teachers might be pissed off I was given the Head of Department role over them. Clive Barker (eldest staff member) congratulated me and even Chris Bartlett (usually annoyed about something) didn't seem too bothered.

'You deserve it,' said Clive.

'Thanks, Clive,' I said even though I knew he probably didn't mean it.

'I would have turned it down anyway. Too old for all the shenanigans. School politics are for the young. Watch out for the French department.'

'Oh, why's that?'

'"Why's that?" he says. Did you hear that Chris? "Why's that?"'

'And you're supposed to be a history teacher,' said Chris and they both laughed, but neither of them told me why I shouldn't trust the French department. The rest of the meeting carried on in much the same vein. Fourth staff member George Fothergill was off sick (again). Apparently, he has (in the words of Clive) the squits or (in the words of Chris) some seriously nasty shit. I had to go through all the pre-meeting targets we've been set, which obviously didn't go down well ('pointless, poxy, unrealistic - we might as well send everyone home now and tell them to work at fucking Tesco,' (Chris)), and then we discussed the upcoming year eight trip to Leeds Castle.

'Remember last year's trip?' said Clive. 'We don't want a repeat performance.'

'I won't let that happen,' I said firmly.

Last year a group of students decided it would be a good idea to swim in the lake around the castle, which wouldn't have been too bad except that one of them (Tony Strang) couldn't swim and almost drowned. Unfortunately, the person who went in to rescue him wasn't a very strong swimmer either and they almost drowned too. A staff member at the castle eventually rescued them both, but they almost drowned too because Tony Strang freaked out and is quite heavy for a child of his age. Eventually, everyone made it back to dry land and no one drowned.

'He "won't let that happen", he says. Did you hear that Chris? He "won't let that happen",' said Clive and they both laughed again.

I had one last cigarette and then I stopped at the garage on the drive home and got some Extra Strong Mints. I also drove past KFC five times debating whether to go in for a sneaky bucket. I think the girl on the drive-thru probably thought I was an escaped mental patient after I drove through twice without buying anything.

'Can I help you?' she said the second time.

'I just want to smell it,' I said salivating like a rabid dog.

'I think you should go,' said the girl.

'Can I look at a bucket? Show me a bucket!' I said taking a whiff of the Colonel's finest, until she threatened to call the police and at that point I decided it was probably best to head home bucketless.

Tomorrow is Saturday. I'm usually excited about the

weekend. The chance for a lie-in, some quality time with William and Emily, and a potter about in the shed. But those were the good old days. Tomorrow we're up at seven for Boot Camp at the gym. Emily also wants to have an official weigh-in. I'm dreading it and I have piles of ASM paperwork to wade through. How did Eddie Collins do this when he was drunk for most of the time?

Saturday 19 January 7.30 p.m.

In bed. Emily in the shower. William lying next to me.

Disaster. I've gained four pounds!

'I don't understand,' I said looking down at the scales.

'I think I do,' said Emily giving me her Death Stare (much worse than the Death Star). 'You've been cheating, haven't you?'

'I haven't, Em, honestly.'

I didn't have the heart to tell her the truth. She was so proud of me, and I liked it. But I also want to eat real food, smoke cigarettes, drink beer, and not be forced to go somewhere called Boot Camp. I hate the gym. I hate high-fives and I hate the scales. I just want to lie down with William and eat cake - let me eat cake!

And in other (possibly worse) news, Emily has invited our new neighbours Mark, Sophie, and Lexus over for afternoon tea tomorrow. They graciously accepted and so Emily is in panic mode. She spent this afternoon cleaning the house and she's off to Waitrose in the morning. She even asked me if I knew where the croquet set was. I told her it was January and not croquet weather. She's making me cut the grass on the off chance it isn't going to be raining or freezing cold. The BBC weatherman (who still looks a bit ropey) has gone out on a limb and predicted intermittent sunshine.

And in another twist, I had a strange phone conversation

with Steve today. Maybe it's the fact that Steve and Fiona have the four kids now (Jane, Joseph, James, and Jasmine - the Js) - or that we have William, but we don't see as much of them as we used to. It isn't that Worcester Park is that far away either, although after spending a week with them last year in Cornwall, my yearly Steve quota was definitely filled.

Don't get me wrong, I like Steve, Fiona and their troop of Js, but they're just a bit much. During university and then after (before they succumbed to the almighty power of parenthood), Steve and Fiona were ordinary, just like us, but since the first J popped out they've become insufferable in their parenthoodness. Steve, who always dabbled with his guitar, suddenly became like a cross between Sir Andrew Lloyd Webber and The Wiggles. Whenever you see him you know a song or a play isn't far behind. Like I said, I love them, they're our closest parent friends, but sometimes it would be nice to see them without the fear of it turning into High School Musical.

'Harry!'

'Steve, how's things?'

'It's funny you should ask,' he said and then didn't say anything else.

'It is?'

'Oh, it is.'

'Steve, as much as I enjoy your cryptic conversations, are you going to tell me what's going on?'

'Can we come by tomorrow afternoon?'

'All of you?'

'The whole clan.'

'We're having the new neighbours over in the afternoon.'

'Even more perfect.'

'Why?'

'You'll see,' said Steve and then he started chuckling. I

heard Fiona in the background and then one or more of the Js started crying. 'See you tomorrow.'

Sunday 20 January 11.30 a.m.

In the shed with William. Emily inside baking. Intermittent sunshine. The BBC weatherman is spot on for once. Listening to Supergrass.

Emily has gone properly mental. William and I have been banished to the shed while she gets ready for the tea party. You would think the Royal Family was coming over. She has the fancy china out and there's bloody bunting everywhere - am I the only person in the world who doesn't like bunting? I'm taking the opportunity to educate William in my musical heritage. Today it's Supergrass and their seminal 1995 album, I Should Coco.

9.30 p.m.

The afternoon tea started well. Mark, Sophie and Lexus came over at two o'clock and we all had tea and little sandwiches. Emily put on some nice music, everyone loved the bunting, and William was on his best baby behaviour.

'He's such a cutie,' said Sophie watching William on his blanket. Sensing the occasion and probably aware he was in his smart clothes; William was at his most adorable. Unlike Lexus, who was being quite a grump.

'Are you thinking of having any more?' said Emily.

'Oh, gosh no,' said Sophie, as if Emily had suggested they pop into town, bring home a tramp and raise it as their own. 'One's enough.' Then she looked at Lexus, who was rolling her eyes and looking as though she was far too cool for a tea party. 'It was hard enough getting my body back after Lexus. I can't go through that again.'

'Do you have any real orange? I don't like squash,' said Lexus.

'Manners,' barked Mark.

'Do you have any proper orange, please?' said Lexus with a fake smile. I can see why they've stopped at one, and Sophie does have an incredible body. I bet she loves Boot Camp.

During a brief pause in proceedings, I asked Mark if he wanted to see my shed. I wanted to get him alone to find out if he was proper bloke friend material. Was the stiff, posh-o routine just for the ladies? Maybe alone he'd relax and start dropping a few Hs and talking about football. I took him out to the shed and we sat down on the new chairs I created from the wooden crates they were chucking away at school.

'Scotch?' I said producing a bottle from underneath the workbench. 'I snuck it in.'

Mark looked at me like I was stark raving bonkers.

'Why on earth did you have to sneak it in?'

'Well, you know, women, right?'

I suddenly got a bit of Dad and Derek deja-vu.

'I have a drinks cabinet in the living room,' said Mark and from that moment on, I knew he wasn't proper bloke friend material. He wasn't impressed by my shed or the Scotch. 'A bit throaty,' he said with a face like I'd given him a glass of bleach. I asked if he wanted a game of darts and he told me he's 'more of a rugby man', and that we should probably head back inside.

The fun really began when Steve, Fiona and the Js turned up. We introduced everyone and for once I was actually happy to see Steve.

'Lexus, after the car?' said Steve.

'No,' said Mark sternly. 'Not after the car.'

'Right, so what does it mean?' said Steve innocently.

For once Mark's sheen of unflappability was broken and he looked, well, flapped.

'It's just a nice word,' said Mark stiffly.

'Oh, right,' said Steve. 'Like blancmange.'

I wanted to kiss him.

Things settled down for a while. The kids all went into the garden and played in the intermittent sunshine. Emily, Sophie and Fiona talked about women's stuff, while Steve, Mark and I stood around sipping our tea like dutiful, middle-class husbands. It got a bit chilly and so we all headed indoors. Inevitably, Steve popped out to his car to get his puppets and guitar and before long was putting on a show. The kids loved it. Even Lexus cracked a smile.

It was just over an hour later when the truth behind Steve's cryptic conversation was finally revealed.

'We have some news,' said Steve standing next to Fiona in our lounge. They both smiled and then said in unison. 'Meet your new neighbours!' Emily and I looked at each other and then at Mark and Sophie. 'Not those new neighbours,' continued Steve. 'These new neighbours. We've bought the house next to you!'

'Ali's old house?' I said.

'That's right,' said Steve. 'After he moved out in October, we spoke to the estate agent. We didn't think we'd be able to afford it, but he wanted a quick sale.'

'But,' I said. What I wanted to say was, 'But you can't move in there, you'll drive me bonkers'. What I actually said was. 'But why didn't you say anything?'

'We thought it would be a nice surprise,' said Steve.

'It's definitely a surprise,' I said.

Last October our Indian neighbours vanished as mysteriously as they'd arrived. I still felt bad for thinking they were terrorists, but when they were suddenly gone for no apparent reason, I felt that maybe my suspicions were slightly vindicated.

'The first thing we're going to do is knock down the fence so we can all play together,' said Steve. I looked at him incredulously. I think I was about to cry. 'I'm just kidding. We can't knock down a whole fence,' said Steve cracking up. Emily laughed along with Fiona. 'We'll just put in a little gate and then we can come and go as we please,' said Steve, but this time he definitely didn't seem to be joking. We might have to move. 'Oh, and before I forget, Harry,' said Steve, 'love the bunting!'

Then, the pièce de résistance, I was about to walk into the kitchen to get some cake when I heard Emily and Mark laughing as though someone had just told the world's greatest joke. I poked my head around the door, and they were stood very close to each other, and Emily definitely had on her flirting face. Mark was being all smooth and then casually touched her arm. I felt like bursting in and shouting, 'Get your hand off my wife's arm you bastard!' but it felt a bit over the top. Instead I walked in casually and said, 'Is there any more cake?' Emily looked at me and she definitely looked a bit guilty, and Mark looked like the snake in the grass he no doubt is.

Thursday 24 January 12.30 p.m.

Rory came into my room this morning looking exhausted. Apparently, Miranda is treating him like a prize stallion.

'Four times last night,' said Rory. 'I tried to explain that I'm not eighteen anymore, but she's having none of it. I'm at breaking point, Harry.'

'Chin up. If you keep this up she's bound to get pregnant and then you won't have sex for years,' I said, and Rory laughed.

'Thanks, and the thing is, I want to have kids, I do, but I'm just not as worried about it as Miranda. I'm sure it will happen in time.'

'Just remember what Bon Jovi said.'

'Lay your hands on me?'

'No Rory.'

'You give love a bad name?'

'No idiot. Keep the faith.'
'Oh, right,' said Rory with a chuckle. 'I will.'

Friday 25 January 6.30 p.m.

Something's happened in the car. Pre-William, I would listen to CDs of my favourite Britpop classics. I'd sometimes rock-out to Pearl Jam or chill-out with Travis. However, post-William, the only thing we seem to get in the car is kid's music. Emily says it's important for his development, which is fair enough, but today I drove all the way to work listening to The Wiggles without even realising it. It wasn't until I found myself humming Fruit Salad during morning assembly that I realised.

I promised myself I wouldn't be one of 'those parents', but the other day I was singing If You're Happy And You Know It, clapping my hands and waving them in the air, and when I turned around, William wasn't even in the car - and I was spotted by a group of kids from school. Something has to change otherwise I'm going to wake up at forty wearing sandals, dungarees (in a non-ironic way), taking my kids to something called 'modern dance', and thinking it's okay to drive a people carrier because they're actually brilliant and the extra space is a blessing when you think about it.

Tuesday 29 January 7.30 p.m.

At home. William asleep. Emily doing Yoga on her new Yoga mat in the lounge. Raining.

We tried William on solid food today. Apparently, you know babies are ready to try 'real' food when they show certain signs. One of the signs is when they watch you eat. Tonight he spent all of dinner time just gawping at me, saliva dripping from his mouth.

'I think he's ready,' said Emily.

Emily had already gone out and bought a whole array of different baby foods. The little fella has a whole shelf of organic, healthy-looking food. He's supposed to start off with baby porridge and so we tried him on some organic Scottish porridge. He couldn't get enough, but I suppose when you've been living on breast milk for the past five and a half months, anything would be pretty tasty.

I can't wait to start him on the posh stuff. He has things like braised aged beef hotpot, free-range chicken and leek pie, and traditional organic trifle. With the way things have been going with my diet, I might have to start eating his food.

Thursday 31 January 11.30 p.m.

'Emily, can I ask you something?'

'Sure.'

'Do you think I'm a good dad?'

'Why are you asking me?'

'Because I was thinking about how hard I'm trying not to be like Steve, who is a great dad, even if he is slightly annoying. But what sort of dad am I?'

'Harry, you're a wonderful father.'

'Am I though? I get annoyed by so many things parents do. I love William to bits, he's the best thing in the world, but sometimes I don't feel very, you know …'

'What?'

'Dad-like.'

Emily looked across at me with that stare. You know the one - the stare when you're being a bit of a plonker.

'Harry, just because you don't carry around a spare pair of bongos in case your main set of bongos break, and you don't know all the words to every Wiggles song, it doesn't mean you're not dad-like.'

'But how am I dad-like?'

'For a start we're having this conversation,' said Emily. 'The fact you're even worried about it means your dad-like. You spend a lot of time in the shed, you moan about the weather, you tell terrible jokes, and you dance as though you've been rogered by a hot stick. It's the way you look at William, hold him, cuddle him, and tell him about bands he's only going to grow up to despise just to annoy you. And you've recently started wearing cardigans. You're a dad, Harry. You aren't like Steve, but then again, most people aren't and that's okay.'

'Thanks, Em.'

'You're welcome.'

'Oh, and FYI, cardigans are back in fashion.'

'Sure they are,' said Emily with a lovely smile. 'Sure they are.'

February

Friday 1 February 6.05 p.m.

'Em, do you think William's head's all right?'

'What do you mean?'

'Don't you think it looks a bit …'

'A bit what?'

'Odd,' I said. 'Look at the shape of it, it's a little uneven.'

Emily and I both had a good look at his head.

'It looks fine to me,' said Emily.

'It isn't fine. It's too long and with that crazy hair he looks a bit weird.'

'Oh, I love his hair,' said Emily. 'It's adorable.'

'He has an old man comb over.'

'But it's so cute.'

'Would it be cute on me?'

'Well, no, obviously.'

'Exactly.'

I'm still convinced he has something wrong with his head. He also has quite short, stumpy legs. I'm worried he's going to be picked on at school because of his strangely shaped head and stumpy legs. 'Weird head stumpy legs Spencer' they'll call him. Children can be so cruel.

9.30 p.m.

Emily's in the shower and I'm lying here trying not to fall asleep. There was a time when I'd be hoping she'd come out of the shower, the lights would go off, she'd slip into bed, and we'd have Friday night sex. Tonight it's the last thing on my mind. I just want something fatty to eat, a cigarette and a good night's sleep. I am officially an old man with no sex drive and a powerful addiction to fried food and fags - every young girl's dream.

Saturday 2 February 4.30 p.m.

In the shed. William in his Thomas the Tank Engine rocker.

Listening to Snow Patrol. Emily inside making dinner.

Next weekend Steve, Fiona and the Js move in. My small piece of England is going to be invaded and my once tranquil garden is going to be filled with the sound of the neighbours from children's entertainment hell. There will be puppet shows, musical acts and I wouldn't be surprised if a circus tent went up. No doubt in time I'll be put to work as a clown.

At today's workout I managed to run two miles without stopping. I was quite proud of myself until I looked across at the old lady next to me who was on mile four - on a steep incline.

6.30 p.m.

Tonight for dinner William had organic lamb shepherd's pie with roasted carrots and broccoli florets followed by strawberry mousse. I had salad followed by nothing. Something is wrong with this.

Sunday 3 February 7.30 p.m.

William asleep. Watching TV with Emily. Starving and busting for a cigarette.

Tonight Emily announced she's going away next weekend with Stella from Kingston-upon-Thames. They're going to a spa in Oxford which means I have William by myself for the whole weekend. Emily tried to make it seem not so bad by telling me that technically, it's just one night, but I'm terrified because it's the first time I'll be alone with him overnight. Already the cogs of panic are beginning to turn and crank out their irrational nuggets of fear. It doesn't matter that they're only an hour away or that Emily will have her phone, and the iPad, and I have the number for the spa, because what if something goes wrong? What if he needs something I can't or don't know how to provide? What if he starts crying and doesn't stop? It sounds crazy, but sometimes William scares the living crap out of me.

Tuesday 5 February 8.00 p.m.

Just home from the gym. Tyler must be on his man-period. He pushed me so hard at one point I thought I was going to have a heart attack. I tried to explain that I might be dying, and he just said, 'No pain, no gain!' Not if I'm dead. It would serve him right if I did die. That would wipe the sheen of youthful arrogance from his square-jawed face.

Thursday 7 February 7.15 a.m.

Eating breakfast. William breastfeeding opposite me. Emily nibbling on toast.

I don't want to sound callous, but since we had William, Emily's periods have been really heavy and so now she has to wear Mega-Pants (big undies and industrial sized sanitary towels). I sympathise, but this morning I walked in on her getting the Mega-Pants on and she wasn't best pleased.

'Is there no privacy in this bloody house?!' she screamed mid-squat, Mega-Pants half on.

'Sorry, sorry, sorry,' I said retreating out of the bathroom and back into the safety of the bedroom.

Emily walked in shortly after.

'I realise that sexually things aren't great between us,' she said sitting down on the bed. 'And seeing me like that doesn't help. With the Mega-Pants.'

'It's fine.'

'But I know since William you don't find me as attractive

and I don't blame you,' she started, and I tried to intervene and tell her I did, but she stopped me. 'And don't try to deny it. I've seen the way you look at me and my horrible stretch marks.'

'Em, honestly, it isn't you,' I tried to say something, but she wasn't listening. She was crying. The thing was, I couldn't tell her the truth because I wasn't sure what the truth was. I was temporarily, and for the first time in my adult life, off sex. I wasn't in the mood, and it wasn't Emily or the Mega-Pants. It was me. It was the metaphorical Mega-Pants in my mind.

'Em, I love you just as you are,' I said putting my arm around her. 'I don't care about the stretch marks or the Mega-Pants. It isn't you, it's …' Could I say me? 'It's everything. The tiredness, work, it's hard. I'm sure all new parents go through this.'

'Maybe we should try and go away for the night,' blubbed Emily.

'Definitely,' I said. 'We'll have to do that.'

'Maybe during half-term.'

'Definitely,' I said. 'And Em, I love the Mega-Pants, they're endearing.'

'Oh, stop it,' she said sniffing up tears and playfully hitting me on the arm.

I gave Emily a kiss, but I'm worried. What's happening to me? To us? Has the spark gone for good? Can I have a sexless life? A sexless marriage? When was the last time we even had sex? We did it that once just before she had William and that was in August - six months ago. Before that, and because of my nearly but not quite affair with Jamie, who knows? A few months before? Could it really have been eight months or longer since we had proper sex? At what point are we just really good friends who happen to live under the same roof and share child-rearing duties?

I just saw our new neighbour Mark returning from his

morning run. He probably runs ten miles before work and then knocks out a thousand sit-ups during lunch. He and Sophie probably shag like bunnies over there; videoing their perfect bodies going at it and then watching it back for tips on how to improve. He's probably doing her right now with his enormous, posh-o, investment banker penis. The bastard!

Friday 8 February 9.15 p.m.

On the sofa. Eating some healthy biscuits Emily made that taste like rubber bands. Tonight for dinner William had organic honey glazed ham with a mushroom and broad bean risotto. I had a dry pork chop on a bed of plain brown rice.

A message on my phone from Mum:

Harry, darling. I'm calling to invite you and Emily to the opening night of my play. It starts next Friday. Can I put you down for two tickets? It's at a small theatre around the corner from our house. Larry Laverne, the director, is very excited about it. He wrote the play himself. It's called, 'A Night with Julie'. I'm Julie. You have to come. I also have some news about your father. He's been made redundant. Voluntary retirement. Call me back. Give William a kiss. Love you. Oh, it's your mother.

I've spent the entire night debating what's worse. The fact that I'm now officially the son of an OAP, or that we have to go and see Mum's play.

Saturday 9 February 10.15 a.m.

It's here. The day life in Wimbledon changes forever. Steve, Fiona and the Js are moving in next door. Their moving van just pulled up outside. Goodbye peace and quiet. Goodbye normal life. Goodbye privacy. Hello annoying songs and twenty-four-seven Steve and his magical array of instruments.

Emily left this morning for her spa weekend in Oxford and so it's just me and William. I have the day planned. This morning I'm taking him to meet Grandad. I've been feeling guilty I haven't brought him to see Grandad's grave yet, and so with the morning to spare, it's time. Then after he takes a nap, we're having another lesson in his musical education. Today it's going to be Oasis. He might be a bit young for Cigarettes and Alcohol, but he needs to listen to Definitely Maybe and (What's The Story) Morning Glory so he knows how good they were before they became a bit crap.

Mark just left for his morning run. Sophie and Lexus left in the Mercedes - both looked quite grumpy. Maybe there's a reason he needs his drinks cabinet in the living room.

2.00 p.m.

William taking his nap. We had a lovely morning with Grandad. William and I went to the grave and we brought a blanket and some snacks. The sun was shining, and I told William all about his great grandad. It was fun and emotional, and I have to admit a few tears were shed, but I think this is just what we needed. Me and my son. The boys. And Grandad too, of course.

4.00 p.m.

I'm worried about William. He woke up coughing and he has a temperature. He was fine before his nap. I've spent the last thirty minutes listening to his breathing, re-checking his temperature and googling every possible site for a prognosis, which has only made it worse because now I'm convinced he has about twenty different life-threatening illnesses. I'm trying not to call Emily because I don't want to worry her. This is why I was so scared about looking after him by myself.

4:15 p.m.

I'm panicking. His breathing seems to be really laboured and his temperature is going up. It's at 104. I'm going to call Emily.

4:20 p.m.

Emily didn't answer her phone. I tried Stella and she didn't answer either. I left messages for them, and another one at the spa. I'm going to take William to hospital. I'm terrified it's something serious and I don't know what else to do.

11:45 p.m.

Home. William tucked up in bed with Emily. I feel sick. I rushed little William to hospital convinced it was something serious - it had to be. I got to A&E, and they took him from me. He suddenly seemed so small and weak.

Emily eventually called me back, by which time I was a mess, but I managed to gabble out what had happened, and she got there as fast as she could. They ran some tests and we waited nervously, but they said it's probably just a virus and gave us antibiotics. The doctor said he should be fine in a few days, but I knew I wouldn't be. It might have been just a virus, but it terrified me. I'm downstairs in the kitchen drinking some Scotch from my private stash in the shed, wishing I had a cigarette and trying to calm the nerves that are still racing like little Pac Men through my brain.

Sunday 10 February 9.15 a.m.

In the shed. Emily and William inside with Steve, Fiona and the Js. Sunny. BBC weatherman looked really rough this morning. Today he predicted 'all sorts of weather'.

Steve, Fiona and the Js popped over for breakfast this morning and I got a sudden glimpse into the future. They're going to be over all the time from now on. I suppose I accept it, roll with it and embrace it, or I stay in the shed. I could probably fit a bed in here if I moved things around a bit.

William was doing much better this morning. I didn't get much sleep worrying about him though. Emily didn't mind that I ruined her weekend, although I don't think she'll be going away again anytime soon. She felt guilty she wasn't there for him, and I felt guilty I couldn't handle it without her - guilt rains down on the house of Spencer.

Off inside to join in with the festivities. Just before I came out to the shed, Steve was about to pop back home and get his didgeridoo.

4.14 p.m.

I just had a cheerful conversation with Dad on the phone.

'I heard about the redundancy,' I said.

'It's fine. It will give me time to focus on my hobbies.'

'You mean golf?'

'And the other ones.'

'Like what?'

'We're thinking about getting a caravan.'

'Oh, really.'

'It depends on your mother. She wants to go on a cruise. Pointless all that sailing about. We could get a decent caravan for the same price and use it year after year.'

'I guess we'll see you on Friday for Mum's play.'

'That bloody thing.'

'What's the matter?'

'It's all she bloody talks about. That and Larry bloody Laverne.'

'The director?'

'The only thing he's trying to direct, Harry, is his penis into your mother.'

'One, eww, that's disgusting (thanks for the mental image), and two, I'm sure that isn't the case.'

'You haven't seen them together. It's a disgrace.'

'Mum would never cheat on you.'

'We'll see about that,' said Dad.

Monday 11 February 4.15 p.m.

At school. Between meetings. Cloudy.

Eddie Collins is back at school. He turned up this morning and said he's feeling better than ever. I asked if he minded me being AHOD, but if anything he's relieved. Eddie said the pressure of the constant meetings pushed him over the edge and definitely played a part in the whole Toys "R" Us incident. He said that going through AA has made him re-evaluate what's important in life. I'm starting to worry that being AHOD/ASM is a death sentence.

Wednesday 13 February 10.15 p.m.

Just back from the pub. Emily and William asleep. Feeling guilty and a bit drunk.

I had a few cigarettes with Rory. He's smoking again because he's in a real quagmire about Miranda and their lack of fertility. Rory needed to talk and so after I went home and put William to bed, I met him in The Alexandra.

'I don't know what to do about it,' said Rory lighting up a cigarette. 'Do you think I should talk to Miranda, or should we just keep fornicating like bunnies?'

'Fornicating like bunnies isn't a bad way to be, is it?'

'I know it sounds like every man's dream - sex on tap, but it's got its downsides. You know sometimes I don't want to do it. I get tired.'

'I know what you mean, I'm thirty-four now, not twenty-one.'

'Right, and women think all they have to do is get naked and we can perform.'

'Like it's that easy,' I said.

'We're not machines. The other night Miranda really wanted to do it and I lied and said I had a headache.'

'That's rough,' I said. 'You know Emily and I haven't had sex in over eight months.'

'Blimey!' said Rory.

'But the funny thing is that I don't really miss it that much. I thought I would, but I don't. I'm starting to get worried. I think I've lost my mojo.'

'I wouldn't mind a bit of a break,' said Rory.

'Maybe we should swap wives?' I said.

'And this is why I wanted to come out for a drink,' said Rory laughing.

'So we can discuss wife swapping?'

'Exactly.'

We sank five pints, went through ten cigarettes, and then had a kebab on the way home. I feel as guilty as hell and tomorrow's Valentine's Day. The day of love, romance, and telling the person you love most how much you love them.

Thursday 14 February 12.15 p.m.

Valentine's Day

Over breakfast this morning Emily said we needed to talk. She thinks we're drifting apart, and we need to have a proper chat about it. I admit that things haven't been great between

Emily and me recently. I mean they're fine. They're average. It isn't like we're on the verge of divorce, but we've definitely lost the spark. The thing is, whereas I'm quite happy to plod along until things pick up (which they inevitably will), Emily needs to talk about it, dissect it, and understand why.

'I'll get William down early and make something special.'

'Maybe we could have our once per month takeaway?' I said hopefully.

'Let me look at the Jamie Oliver cookbook. There's a Thai curry in there I've been dying to try.'

'Can I have real portions though?'

'Harry, it's going to be romantic,' she said, which didn't really placate my worry about starving to death on the most romantic day of the year.

She also snuck a Valentine's card into my lunch, which meant I would have to stop on the way home and get something - I was going to be the cliché bloke at the garage picking up a crappy, but expensive bouquet of petrol-tinged roses. Brilliant.

11.45 p.m.

I got home (minus forgotten petrol roses) and spent an hour with William before I put him to bed. When I came downstairs, Emily had the dinner table set with a lovely looking curry, a bottle of wine and some romantic music. Emily had slipped into something much less comfortable, but infinitely sexier.

'Wow, it looks -you look - wonderful,' I said sitting down.

'Do you like it?' Emily said after we'd had a few bites. I was absolutely ravenous and was scoffing it down in the most unromantic way possible.

'It's like Jamie Oliver popped over and made it himself. It's sensational.'

We reminisced about past Valentine's gone by and how things were so different, which apparently segued perfectly into the main debate of the night. What was happening with our sex life?

'I think it's why I feel so distant from you,' said Emily. 'We barely touch and if we do it just feels awkward.'

'It's tough with William. I'm tired, you're tired. I think we just need to see it out and we'll be fine.'

'You think we just need to see it out? You don't think anything's wrong?'

'I'm sure loads of first-time parents go through the same sort of thing. It's perfectly natural,' I said semi-confidently.

'Then let's make an effort,' said Emily. 'Let's agree to go on at least one date a month and have sex once a week.'

'You don't think that's a bit too clinical?'

'Harry, right now we haven't been on a date since we had William and I can't remember the last time we had sex, can you?'

'There was that time just before we had William.'

'That doesn't count. Before that?'

'A while I suppose. Okay, let's do it.'

'Starting tonight,' said Emily with a mischievous smile.

After we'd tidied dinner away and had dessert, we were off to the bedroom for some much-needed sex, but before we were both naked William started crying. I slipped on a t-shirt and rocked William until he was asleep, which didn't really put me in the most sexual of moods, but when I got back to bed Emily soon had me going again. Emily finally let her sexy lingerie fall to the ground. We were going to have sex and it was going to be amazing - just like the good old days. My mojo was definitely back with a vengeance. But then it happened. The sound that would drench my penis with the coldest of showers and distinguish any flames of passion until they were barely a spark. Through the wall we heard Steve and Fiona going at it.

'What the fuck's that?' said Emily.

Their headboard was banging against our wall like an

outside toilet door in a force ten gale. Then to make matters worse, we heard Fiona (or possibly Steve) reaching climax. 'OMG! OMG! OMG!' Emily and I immediately stopped, the idea of sex out of the window and our romantic evening in tatters. We may never have sex again. Happy Valentine's Day.

Friday 15 February 7.15 a.m.

Having breakfast with William. Emily in the shower. Cloudy outside. The BBC weatherman wasn't on today and in his place was a pretty, young girl. Is it the end for him?

After last night's failed sexathon, Emily and I went to sleep and haven't said a word about it since. I may never get another erection again. Today is the last day of school before half-term and I have my second management training session.

4.45 p.m.

After the 'continental style' buffet and watery coffee, Colin Thistle took us on a journey deep into the mind of an educational manager and then surprised us all with the following statement:

'Being a manager isn't something that can be taught.' All of our hands instantly shot up. 'Ah, questions, yes Mr Flintoff?' he said pointing at Warren Flintoff - the teacher I've labelled as most likely to try and get us all to go out for a drink after we're done just so he can try and shag one of the female teachers (probably Jenny from Twickenham).

'But if it can't be taught, then why are we here?' Warren said eruditely.

'And that is a question with many possible answers,' said Colin. 'So let's blue sky think it, shall we? Let's really move the goalposts on this one. Fifteen minutes to really get the idea showers flowing and then we can bring our ideas to the table. Really push the envelope, yeah, and remember teamwork makes the dream work!'

We sat around in our groups with no idea what we were doing. All we knew is that you couldn't teach management, and we were on a management training course, and we had to really think outside of the box. When it came to presenting our ideas to the group, my little team had nothing, and they had chosen me to explain this.

'So, Mr Spencer, what did you manage to formulate?' said Colin excitedly.

'We decided that actually, you can teach management,' I said.

Colin looked confused for a moment before he started smiling and then gave me a slow handclap.

'Exactly,' he said. 'But only if you believe you can and that's today's lesson. Management is about belief.'

'And blue-sky thinking,' I added.

'Exactly,' said Colin with vigour. 'Gosh, it makes it all worthwhile when you guys really get it.'

When we left, Warren asked us if we fancied going for a pint. We all declined, except Colin, and so Warren and Colin went to the pub together to blue-sky think it all over a few pints. I think Warren would have preferred to move Jenny's goalposts and probably push her envelope a little bit.

6.05 p.m.

Off to see the play Mum's calling, 'The greatest moment of her life'. Obviously I have mixed feelings about this. On the one hand I'm happy for her, but on the other, this means that her performing in a play is greater than having and raising me - her only child.

11.00 p.m.

The play was awful. Mum was, at best, not as terrible as the script or the direction. The play, 'A Night with Julie', was billed as a coming-of-age, post-feminist, post-modern comedy. What it didn't say was that it was a play about a woman (Julie) going through menopause, told from the point of view of her vagina.

Basically, Mum played a giant, talking vagina - the costume was either surprisingly accurate or deeply disturbing, I'm not sure which, and they definitely took it too far when during an orgasm scene Mum shot liquid into the crowd. Apparently, it was meant to be symbolic, but all I saw was fifty disgusted, middle-aged people covered in fake woman-jizz. The best bit was when her husband Frank (a giant talking penis) tried to have sex with her, but she refused and so he chased her around the stage shouting, 'Penis power!' and Mum screamed back, 'You can take away my ability to have children, but you'll never take away my freedom!' The actor in the penis, obviously constrained by the costume, had to hop around the stage and kept falling over and had to be helped up by Mum, which took away from some of the drama. The last time he fell off the stage, he almost landed in the wheelchair section. Nothing ruins a play like a giant penis squashing the disabled audience.

The real drama happened at the end of the night. Dad (who'd had a couple of stiff drinks at the interval) ended up threatening Larry Laverne. Larry Laverne, who I can only describe as something of a Hi-De-Hi, must have spent the last thirty years working the cabaret circuit and was wearing a beret. He called Mum, 'The greatest thing that has ever happened to him'. And then he challenged Dad to a duel!

All in all, a truly terrible night. But at least it's half-term and Emily's parents have agreed to babysit William so we can go on a date.

Tuesday 19 February 4.15 p.m.

Date Night!

I'm excited. It will be our first night out since William was born. Emily is getting all spruced up and looks absolutely gorgeous. I'm in a shirt and tie and William is looking confused.

5.05 p.m.

Derek and Pam are here to babysit William. Things are much better with Derek now I've seen him au naturel. Since What Happened on the Landing, he seems to have mellowed towards me. I guess it took me to see him naked for us to get along. If I'd have known that I would have requested a viewing much earlier in our relationship - perhaps the first time we met.

'Dad, this is Harry. Harry, this is my father.'

'It's a pleasure to meet you, Harry.'

'Just show me your penis. It's going to save us time down the road. Trust me.'

I wonder if I saw Pam naked, would it give us something to talk about? Maybe if we went to a nudist holiday camp we'd be the happiest family in the whole world.

9.15 p.m.

Emily in the shower. Lying in bed waiting. Date night was wonderful. We drank, ate and talked like we haven't in such a long time. It felt like a proper date. I think we were both a bit worried because it's been such a long time, but it really was just like old times.

Emily is having a quick shower and then the inevitable end of date sex. I'm feeling a bit drunk if I'm honest. Emily only had one glass of wine because she's breastfeeding, so I drank the rest of the bottle - and then another one. Here she comes.

10.15 p.m.

Downstairs. Emily asleep. Having a glass of water, a

pick-me-up packet of posh crisps and a pickled onion.

Disaster. We tried to have sex, but I couldn't get it up. This has never happened to me before. Okay, fine, it has happened a couple of times, but never with Emily and the other time I was drunk. And then there was that third time, although I'd already done it once that day, and technically there was a fourth, but I don't think that one really counts as I started admirably but then went flaccid during sex, but as I said at the time - why do we need to keep changing positions so much?

Emily said it was fine. It probably happened to every man - at some point. It's no big deal, she kept saying while I tried desperately to resurrect date night. I begged the little fella to get hard and asked Emily to try the blowjob one last time, but neither Emily nor my penis was having any of it.

'It's all right. I'm too tired now anyway. Let's try again another day,' said Emily.

She went to sleep, but I'm sitting here wondering why I've lost my mojo. Where has it gone? But more importantly, when will it come back?

Wednesday 20 February 9.15 a.m.

I think I'm going through the Manopause. I was researching my recent sexual inadequacies and apparently, after childbirth, men can go through periods of sexual ambivalence. It's all due to lower testosterone production. It usually happens as men get older but can happen after something traumatic - like childbirth. This explains everything.

My parents are coming over this morning. Emily is taking the chance to go out and have a bit of Emily time. I heard rumours of a massage, coffee with Stella in Kingston-upon-Thames, cake, and nails, which all sounds terribly girly and yet I'm jealous.

1.15 p.m.

My parents just left and I'm pulling my hair out. I think I need a massage, coffee, cake and maybe even my nails done. Mum and Dad are a nightmare at the moment. All they do is bicker and argue.

'We would have been here sooner, but someone was on the phone again,' said Dad walking in the front door. 'Hello, son.'

'That's because someone has a blossoming career. Hello darling, where's my little man?' said Mum walking past and giving me a kiss on the cheek.

'If that's a career, then I'm a professional golfer. I'll pop the kettle on, should I?' said Dad from the kitchen.

'You might as well be for all I care. Oh there's my little man. Hello William, let me just wash my hands and I'll give you a big Nanny Spencer hug,' said Mum walking through to the kitchen with Dad. I gave William a comforting smile and he returned one to me.

The rest of the time they were here they argued constantly. Dad kept on making digs about the play and Larry Laverne, and Mum kept jabbing back with stories of my father's apparent new 'old person' lifestyle. Mum wanted to embrace her new-found self, while Dad wanted to crush it beneath one of his driving clubs. It was exhausting.

They got into the Ford, and I could still hear them arguing as they drove off down the street. It's a worrying time. My parents have always argued, but I always felt as though it was mainly light-hearted banter and there was always love underneath it. Now I'm not so sure whether it's light-hearted love or heartless hatred.

Thursday 21 February 10.15 a.m.

In the garden. Emily reading a book. William on his blanket. Sunny.

Emily's annoyed. Last night my on-going battle with Tyler came to an explosive head. He pushed me over the edge on the elliptical machine. I'd been on there for twenty minutes doing the Alpine hill circuit. I was about to pass out and so I pushed the emergency stop button.

'What's the matter?' said Tyler.

'I'm fucked,' I said, bright lights and spots clouding my vision.

'But you weren't done,' said Tyler trying to push the buttons, but I wasn't having it.

'I'm done,' I said sternly.

'You're a quitter, is that right, Harry? A quitter?'

'Yes, I'm a fucking quitter and you know what, Tyler, I don't give a shit,' I said grabbing my towel and getting off the elliptical machine. I started walking back to the changing rooms and by now people were looking at us, including Emily.

'You'll be back,' said Tyler trying to sound authoritative. 'Mark my words. You'll be back!'

But I kept on walking.

'No I fucking won't!' I shouted and then I gave him the finger. I finally realised why people don't joke at the gym. Because it isn't fucking funny.

12.30 p.m.

Emily is still in a huff about the gym. After she put William down for his nap she cornered me in the kitchen. She tried to get me to go back and apologise to Tyler, but I wasn't having any of it. The man is a menace. I don't need some twenty-year-old kid with an eight-pack telling me what to do. Emily tried to argue that Tyler is a trainer and therefore it's his job to push me, but I'm done with him. If anyone is going to kill me, it's going to be me.

2.45 p.m.

Steve has erected a trampoline in their garden. How do I know this? I was in the garden doing a bit of weeding when all of a sudden I heard my name.

'Harry!'

I looked up and couldn't see anything and so I kept on weeding.

'Harry!' I heard and once again I looked up, and nothing.

'Harry!' I heard again, and this is when I saw him. Steve's head popped up over the fence and then down again. Then up again, and down again.

'Trampoline,' said Steve coming up, and then disappearing again.

Any opportunity I had to sunbath nude is now gone. Not that I usually sunbath nude or had any plans to, but it's just nice to have the option.

8.00 p.m.

I'm worried I have prostate cancer. I have to wee a lot and I'm usually forced to get up at least once during the night. I googled it and I have most of the symptoms. I'm going to keep a log of how many times I have to wee and then I'm going to a make an appointment to see Dr Prakish. The Manopause and now prostate cancer. Brilliant.

Friday 22 February 10.15 p.m.

In bed. Emily asleep. Nibbling on something Emily made that contains no gluten, no dairy, no wheat, no sugar and no fat. It tastes just as you'd imagine it to.

Steve and Fiona had sex again tonight. We definitely have

to do something.

We have Boot Camp in the morning, which I'm dreading for two reasons. Firstly, I might bump into Tyler and secondly, it's horrible. When we leave Boot Camp I hear all the other boot-campers talking about how great they feel and how much more energy they have. Yet all I feel is complete and utter agony, followed by annoyance, more pain and finally self-loathing. I'm supposed to be getting fitter, leaner and healthier, but I'm not.

Maybe I'm genetically designed to be a slob. Maybe it's impossible for me to get fitter. Maybe I've evolved. Perhaps I'm the future. The world isn't ready for me yet – not ready for the horrible truth that this is what humanity will become - a race of physically weak, shed-dwellers. I hope I'm not the blueprint for the future or, to quote my wife, we're all going to be deeply unhappy.

Wednesday 27 February 9.30 p.m.

I wouldn't class myself as a big worrier. A medium worrier maybe, but since William was born all I've done is worry. Maybe it's just how parenthood is. 1% enjoyment, 99% worry. I worry about William all the time. There was a kid at my middle school who couldn't say 'cinema'. He pronounced it 'swinema'. And of course, all the mean kids would make him say it as often as possible. What if William says 'swinema' instead of 'cinema'? What if he breaks a leg, or both legs, and we have to push him around in a wheelchair with him saying 'swinema'?

Then there's the now. I wake up most nights and listen to him breathing on the baby monitor, but without fail I decide I can't hear him, and I go in his room to check on him. Sometimes I lie in bed and tell myself to stop being silly and just go to sleep, but I can't. I have to check on him. But even this is okay against the bigger worry of when I can't protect him. When he's at nursery, or primary school, or secondary school or just at the park without me, and I can't be there if he needs me. He's only six and a half months old and already I'm worried about the rest of his life. I just want him to be happy. I just want him to be able to say 'cinema' properly. Is that too much to ask?

March

Saturday 2 March 8.25 a.m.

Emily feeding William. Cloudy with a chance of scattered showers - according to the new BBC weather girl. I went for a wee twice during the night.

I'm going to Yoga. I can't believe it. Not that I have anything against Yoga per se. I just don't think it's for me. A bunch of hippies groaning and moaning, getting all relaxed and spiritual, and downward dogging to the sound of whales and wind-chimes. Maybe I'm wrong, but I don't see how Yoga is really a workout. I often see them when I'm almost throwing up on the treadmill, lying around on their annoying little mats, and then they come out all relaxed and Zen. Hardly the same as the two-mile incline (level 5) on the treadmill, is it? Em's been bugging me to do it for weeks and so we're off to do some Yoga.

11.30 a.m.
Back from Yoga.

We got there and I managed to secure a spot at the back of the room. It was the usual crowd of long-haired, middle-aged men (who no doubt play guitar and talk a lot about the sixties), older women who look as though their marriages might be in trouble, girls with lower-back tattoos, one young bloke who probably thought it would be a good chance to perv at girls, and then came the instructor. Her name was Eleanor, and my first impression was that she was your typical annoying, 'Nothing ever fazes me man because I'm so in tune with the universe man and I only eat organic grass and yeah I write Beat poems and I haven't worn a bra since the seventies' type. That, however, wasn't the thing that made the class unbearable.

As soon as she walked in, the first thing she did was

come and sit right in front of me.

'Today this is going to be the front of the class. Changing perceptions is all part of the Yoga experience,' she said smugly. I was now at the front of the class. Brilliant.

After a brief warm up, Eleanor turned on the 'calming music' which instantly put me on edge. As soon as she stood in front of me I saw it, and I couldn't stop looking at it. She had the most distinguished camel-toe I've ever seen. I spent almost an hour bending, stretching, and trying not to look directly at it.

'What do you think?' said Emily when it was all over.

'Yeah, all right.'

'So you'll come again?'

'Never.'

'Why?'

'Did you see the camel-toe?'

'The what?'

'The camel-toe. Eleanor's camel-toe.'

'You were looking at the instructor's vagina?'

'I didn't want to, Em, but it was like she was shoving it down my throat. You could practically see her clitoris.'

'Sometimes you're so immature,' said Emily and then she huffed and walked away.

That's the last time I go to Yoga. No more downward-facing camel-toe for me.

Wednesday 6 March 7.25 p.m.

I got home from work after more long and pointless meetings to find Emily and Mark talking in the kitchen over a cosy cup of tea.

'Hello,' said Mark looking a bit sheepish. 'We were just having a natter.'

'Hi, honey,' said Emily giving me a kiss.

Emily never calls me "honey".

I looked down at William who was asleep in his rocker.

The lucky little bugger. I had nine wees today. I must make an appointment to see Dr Prakish.

Thursday 7 March 6.25 p.m.

In the lounge with William. Emily having a bath.

Steve popped over earlier.

'Are you excited?' he said.

'Should I be?'

'Oh yes, my friend. You should be very excited.'

'Why?'

'Because of this,' said Steve producing a flier from his back pocket.

'The Alexandra pub quiz, Monday at eight o'clock,' I read. 'So?'

'A pub quiz team!' said Steve. 'It will be our thing.'

'Not happening.'

'Why? It's perfect.'

'Is it?'

'Yes. Come on, Harry. What do you say?'

'I already said no - just then.'

'If I can get someone else onboard will you reconsider?'

I thought about it for a moment and suddenly Mark came to mind. He would definitely say no. A pub quiz with me and Steve on a work night. There was no way he would agree to it.

'Fine, if you can get Mark to join, I'm in.'

'OMG! It's going to be brilliant!' said Steve and off he went to rope Mark in.

I didn't think anything of it until Steve came back with a huge grin.

'He's in,' said Steve. 'Beers for Fears is happening!'

'Beers for Fears?'

'Our team name!'
Oh. My. God.

Friday 8 March 1.45 p.m.

In class. Year ten is having quiet reading time because I can't be bothered to talk. I'm too worried about my possibly cancerous prostate.

6.00 p.m.
I made a decision today and I wanted to talk it over with Emily.
'I've made a big decision,' I said over dinner.
William looked up from his blanket on the floor. He's started trying to roll around now and it's adorable.
'Okay,' said Emily, a note of caution in her voice.
'I've decided to switch from boxer-shorts to boxer-trunks. It's time. I'm not a young man anymore. It's time I grew up and made the switch.'
'So let me get this straight. You own a house, you're married, you have a son, and yet changing your underwear is the sign that you're a man?'
'Exactly,' I said.
'Harry.'
'Yes.'
'You're an idiot.'
'Thanks,' I said and then William rolled over my feet.

Saturday 9 March 8.25 a.m.

Getting ready for the gym. Emily getting ready for Yoga. William rolling everywhere. Raining.

I got an email from best mate Ben. After his wedding last year to Aussie Katie, they've been living back in Sydney.

Ben's been my best friend for as long as I can remember, and I never imagined he'd be living so far away.

G'Day Mate

Hello from sunny Sydney. Sorry it's been a while. The meat pie business is keeping me very busy. We've just bought a house too, which cost an arm and a leg. Property in Sydney is more expensive than London, which means I'm working all the hours I can. Plus, we're expanding and opening new shops in Byron Bay and another in Airlie Beach, which means I'm flying backwards and forwards all the time. I can't remember the last day off I had. At least I get to work with Katie, so we see a lot of each other.

How are things with you? Have you spoken to Emily about coming over this summer? We'd love to have you and it will give me an excuse for taking some time off work and having an actual holiday. I'm working harder and longer than I ever did in London. Missing my old mate and drinking buddy too.

Speak soon.

Benzini X

The poor bugger sounds a bit stressed. I will have to talk to Emily about going over in August, even though I know what she's going to say. 'We can't afford it.' 'It's too expensive.' 'It's too far for William.' And she's right, these are all true, but this is Ben and I quite fancy a trip down under. Time to put on my persuasive hat.

11.45 p.m.

William woke up screaming at ten o'clock. He's teething. The poor little bugger is in agony. Emily rubbed some teething gel on his gums, and I've just got him back to sleep. I'm exhausted. Off to bed.

Sunday 10 March 2.15 a.m.

In the living room with William.

Teething is a serious and exhausting business. I think we've been incredibly lucky with William. I hear a lot of parents complaining about lack of sleep and kids waking up during the night even at a year old, but William has slept through the night since he was two months old. Until now.

4.14 a.m.
Up again. I rubbed some teething gel on his gums and gave him his bottle. Emily still asleep.

6.00 p.m.
Teething day. William was sleeping, eating, or crying. And he wasn't that hungry, so it was mainly sleeping and crying. He wouldn't go down for his nap and so we ended up going for a drive. He cried for such a long time that we ended up in Brighton.

It was a nice day, so we had a walk on the beach, an ice cream, and a bag of chips before we headed back to Wimbledon.

Monday 11 March 8.35 a.m.

At school. Tired. Eating half a Twix. I'm saving the other half for lunch. Cloudy.

I slept in fits and starts last night. William was up again for most of the night. Emily was like a zombie this morning. At least when I left William was asleep.

4.35 p.m.
In an attempt to navigate the new and unsettling world

of the male Manopause, I have decided to take affirmative action. I'm going to get some Viagra. If my testosterone starved body can't get erections by itself, then the little blue pill it is. The trouble is I have no idea how to get some without an embarrassing trip to see Dr Prakish. Luckily, I'm friends with Alan Hughes (PE) and if anyone I know can get some, it's probably Alan.

'Alan, I need your help,' I said in hushed tones.

'Anything,' said Alan.

'Can you get me some—'

'Some what?'

'Drugs?

'Harry, I didn't know you were into that sort of thing.'

'No, not drugs, drugs, I need some … Viagra,' I said in even more hushed tones.'

'Oh,' said Alan with a huge smile on his face. 'And what makes you think I could get you some?'

'Because you're filthy, Welsh, and I know you dabble in all sorts of recreational fun. Can you get me some or not?'

'For you, of course. Just give me a few days.'

'Thanks,' I said, and Alan walked off laughing to himself.

7.35 p.m.

Off to the pub. William asleep. Emily looking a bit frazzled. I gave her a kiss on the cheek, pulled a Cornflake from her hair and she plodded upstairs to bed. I'm off to drink as many beers as I can while answering general knowledge questions with Steve and Mark - or as we're known on the pub quiz circuit, Beers for Fears.

11.45 p.m.

In the kitchen. Emily and William asleep (phew). Eating crisps and drinking a beer.

Quiz night went far better than I'd imagined. It was a bit

stuffy at first, but soon Beers for Fears united in our competitiveness and mutual hatred of team Quizzitch (a group of four IT nerds who actually came dressed as characters from Harry Potter).

We got there and managed to nab the last table and then the quiz began. It took us a while to get into our stride, but once we delegated areas of expertise we were flying.

Steve took Entertainment, encompassing music, musicals, film & TV, and celebrity trivia. Mark took Sports and Geography, while I took History and Literature.

'What character did Una Stubbs play in Worzel Gummidge?' said Brian - the portly and pissed pub quiz host. Brian had obviously confused pub quiz night for pub pissed night.

'Aunt Sally,' whispered Steve and I jotted it down.

'In which Shakespeare play did the character Puck appear?'

Mark and Steve looked at me. I wasn't completely sure, but I went with my gut.

'A Midsummer Night's Dream,' I said.

It was during the early rounds that we first noticed team Quizzitch. Every time they knew an answer they would all shout out phrases from Harry Potter like, 'Furnunculus!' or 'Muffliato!' Then they started getting personal, and looking at other teams and saying things like, 'Must be Mudbloods,' and then they would all laugh. We were sitting next to team Let's Get Quizzical, and we were both tired of Quizzitch before the half-time sausage rolls.

'What's up with them?' said Mark.

'Seems like they have a case of the Potters,' said Steve.

'I'd like to shove a Muggle right up their Hogwarts,' I said, and Mark and Steve laughed, and we vowed, along with our allies Let's Get Quizzical that we had to beat them. Unfortunately, Quizzitch won the quiz with an impressive forty-seven out of fifty and we came in third with forty-four. Team Quizimodo came in second with forty-five.

Tuesday 12 March 4.02 a.m.

Up with William. The poor little fella has another tooth coming in. I need to be up for school in just over two hours. I suspect I won't be getting any more sleep.

12.15 p.m.
So tired. I need an espresso drip.

12.45 p.m.
An email from Mr Jones. I have been called to a meeting after school. Brilliant.

6.00 p.m.
Home. Very tired. William full of the joys of spring. Emily making dinner.

I turned up for the meeting with Mr Jones to find Alan Hughes, Rory, Chris Bartlett and Eddie Collins already there. What was going on? It felt like an intervention.

'Is this an intervention?'

'An intervention? No. God, no,' said Mr Jones. 'This is the year ten trip to Dartmoor committee,' said Mr Jones.

'Excuse me?' I said.

'You're all going on the Dartmoor camping trip in April. Five days of camping, hiking, mountain climbing, canoeing, abseiling and orienteering. It's going to be so much fun!' said Mr Jones.

'I thought it was voluntary?' I said.

'It is, but I thought I'd get my dream team together first. What do you all say?'

'I'm in,' said Alan quickly.

'Me too,' said Rory just as quickly. I suspect a week away from Miranda and her sexual demands is just what Rory needs.

'You can count me in,' said Eddie Collins.

'I suppose so,' said Chris Bartlett. 'I was in the Territorial Army for ten years, so it makes sense.'

'Fabulous,' said Mr Jones. 'Harry?'

'I need to talk to my wife first,' I said. 'New baby and all that.'

'Just let me know by the end of the week,' said Mr Jones.

After the meeting, Mr Jones had me stay behind so he could speak to me about Eddie.

'Eddie's still going through the process, AA and all that, and so we thought it would be good for him to get away. A few days in the fresh air. What do you think?'

'I think it's a great idea,' I said. 'I'm more worried about Alan.'

'Oh, Alan's harmless,' said Mr Jones.

Obviously he doesn't know Alan Hughes very well.

Wednesday 13 March 10.15 p.m.

Nibbling on a piece of Danish blue cheese. Emily and William asleep.

I had the conversation with Emily about Dartmoor. I really thought she'd be against it, but she thinks it's a brilliant idea, and so I guess I'm going. That reminds me. Next week is the school trip to Leeds Castle. I still need to double-check the coach booking, make sure everything is paid for and all the pupils have signed consent forms. This was much more fun when I wasn't Head of Department, AHOD, ASM or whatever else it's called.

Friday 15 March 5.15 p.m.

Alan came by my room and slipped me a small bag with two blue pills inside. He told me to take just one half-an-hour before I wanted to see the effects. Tonight's the night.

7.30 p.m.
I took one small blue pill. Awaiting results.

8.30 p.m.
Nothing. Maybe my testosterone starved body is incapable of erections.

8.45 p.m.
If anything it's smaller.

9.00 p.m.
I took the second pill. Hopefully this does the trick.

9.30 p.m.
The second pill definitely did something. I'm as stiff as a quadruple whisky.

10.45 p.m.
Exhausted.

'What's going on?' said Emily an hour ago. 'Why the big smile?'

> I had dragged her into the bedroom. I dropped my trunks, and the little fella definitely wasn't little. 'Blimey, Harry!'

'Viagra.'

'What?!' said Emily incredulously.

'After the incident the last time we tried, I thought we could do with some insurance. He should be hard for another hour at least.'

'Then I suppose we'd better make good use of it,' said Emily with a smile.

That was the last thing we said. Since then we've done it three times. Although, now I'm exhausted, a bit sore and I still have a raging hard-on. Emily, who stumbled, barely able to walk out of the room unaided, is in the shower. The Viagra was definitely worth it.

Saturday 16 March 12.15 a.m.

I'm getting a bit worried. I still have a huge stiffy and it's getting quite painful.

12.45 a.m.

'I think you need to go to hospital,' said Emily.

'I can't,' I said, my boner still going strong. 'It's embarrassing.'

'It says here,' said Emily looking at her iPad. 'If it lasts for four hours or longer, you should seek immediate medical assistance.'

'But it hasn't been four hours yet. It might go down in a minute.'

'But if it gets to four hours, you need to go to the hospital.'

'Fine.'

1.15 a.m.

Off to the hospital. On my own. With a raging erection.

Sunday 17 March 10.15 a.m.

St Patrick's Day

The day of drinking and debauchery and I'm in bed recovering from a Viagra overdose.

I rushed to hospital (penis still as hard as a rock) which made driving quite a painful experience. Unfortunately, in the rush to get there I drove a little too quickly. I was in a t-shirt and tracksuit bottoms (pulled down to give my boner some room to breathe) when the flashing lights appeared behind me. I couldn't bloody believe it.

'Do you know how fast you were going, sir?' said the policeman.

'I'm really sorry,' I said.

'Forty-five miles an hour in a thirty mile an hour zone.'

'Yeah, I'm really sorry, but I was trying.'

'Sir, what is that?'

'What?'

'That. Sticking out of your trousers?'

'Oh, this,' I said looking down at my penis.

'Is that your —'

'It's my penis, yes.'

'Could you put it away?'

'I really can't.'

'Sir, you need to tuck that thing back in again,' said the policeman, shining his torch and illuminating it.

'Trust me, I wish I could,' I said and then I told him everything; the whole sordid, embarrassing truth.

'You took both pills?'

'I didn't think it was working.'

'We'd better get you to hospital, sir,' said the policeman. 'Follow me.'

He then proceeded to give me an escort to the hospital - flashing lights and all. After I got there and had to suffer the ignominy of walking into a packed A&E with an erection and a policeman in tow, I had to explain to the nurse what had happened.

'Isn't it obvious?' said the policeman. 'Look at it.'

He pointed to my still erect penis.

The nurse looked down at it.

'Viagra?' she said.

'For some reason, he took two,' said the policeman.

'You'd better come with me,' said the nurse.

'Oh, one last thing,' said the policeman. I was expecting his best wishes, maybe a blokey slap on the shoulder, but what I wasn't expecting was, 'Here's your speeding ticket.'

I took the ticket and then went off with the nurse to get my swollen and painful penis looked at. She gave me some drugs and luckily within half-an-hour it had gone down. I didn't get home until gone three in the morning.

'How's your penis?' mumbled Emily when I clambered into bed.

'Sore,' I said.

'The same as my vagina,' she said and then she rolled over and went to sleep.

That's the last time we have chemically enhanced sex.

Monday 18 March 7.10 p.m.

Benzini

Hello mate. Great to hear from you. Sorry it's been so long. Since we had William life has gone from busy to busier.

The headlines from over here are that William is rolling everywhere. I've been made Head of Department, which is both exhausting and annoying. Steve, Fiona and the Js have moved in next door. Steve, me and Mark (new bloke across the street) have started going to the pub quiz at The Alexandra. We're called Beers for Fears. It's fun, but I'm missing my best mate and drinking wingman.

I'm going to talk to Emily about Australia. I really want to come, but I know she'll probably say no. Sounds like you're busy. Make sure you don't work too hard.

Take care
Harry X

Tuesday 19 March 4.10 p.m.

Off to see Dr Prakish. He's going to put his finger up my bottom. Emily called to wish me luck. She offered to come and hold my hand, but that seemed even worse. You need to keep a bit of mystery in a marriage. Yes, I saw William coming out of her vagina, but she doesn't need to see me bending over with Dr Prakish's finger up my bum.

6.15 p.m.

I'm fine. Let me rephrase that. My prostate is fine. I'm still coming to terms with the feeling of another man's finger up my bum. You know when you hear stories of people who lose limbs, and they can still feel them (it's called phantom limb)? That's how I feel about Dr Prakish's finger.

Tomorrow is school trip day and I'm dreading it. My first school trip as Head of Department and nothing can go wrong - which obviously means something will.

Wednesday 20 March 8.15 p.m.

Home. Exhausted. In bed. Emily in the shower. William asleep.

Incredibly nothing went wrong. The day was practically perfect. Okay, we almost lost a couple of kids, the lunches were missing for half an hour, and there were rumours that Nicola Price was offering a quick peek of her breasts on the coach for money. These rumours appeared to be unfounded, although Nigel Simcock and Joey Bradley both somehow lost their five pounds spending money before we arrived at Leeds Castle.

Clive Barker spent the whole day moaning about the French department. Chris Bartlett spent the morning complaining about the coach driver's rather enthusiastic driving, and George Fothergill was off sick again - possibly with Dengue fever. Eddie Collins is like a new man since his Toys "R" Us episode. He's clean-shaven, doesn't reek of alcohol, and actually does his job with a smile. All in all, not a bad school trip. Maybe I can be AHOD/ASM after-all.

Friday 22 March 8.15 a.m.

Last day of school for two weeks. The pub after school.

11.45 p.m.
Home. Emily and William asleep.

Rory is convinced his balls don't work and is getting quite depressed about it. Chris and Clive spent the night complaining and ignoring Gloria Day (French), which meant I ended up talking to her a lot, mainly about the Dordogne and trying not to laugh at her ridiculous HTL (high trouser line).

Saturday 23 March 11.15 a.m.

Sunny. The lovely BBC weather girl is right again. I have a bit of a crush on her. Just back from the gym. Emily and William playing on the blanket. Nibbling on a peach.

I saw Tyler at the gym today. I thought about apologising, but he was too busy terrifying the life out of this quite chubby woman - I've never seen anything wobble so much.

Monday 25 March 10.45 a.m.

Somewhere on the M4. Still in shock. William asleep in the

back. Sunny.

This morning I was woken up by a car horn beeping outside. I was confused at first, but the horn kept going off and so I clambered out of bed and went downstairs. Emily and William were nowhere to be found and the horn was still going off. I opened the front door, ready to give them a piece of my mind, but parked outside our house was an old VW campervan, and inside were Emily and William.

'Surprise!' shouted Emily.

'What, the,' I said walking out in my dressing gown.

'It's ours for the week. Where do you want to go?'

I was completely gobsmacked.

'Fucking hell, Em,' I said jumping inside and giving her a huge kiss.

'Earmuffs,' said Emily covering Williams's ears.

'Sorry.'

'It's ready to go. I already packed our clothes. We can grab breakfast at a service station. Let's get cracking,' said Emily. 'The Spencer's are on holiday!'

2.45 p.m.

Torquay, Devon.

We found a campsite for the night. We parked the VW and we're heading off for a look around town. On the drive down, Emily explained why she'd booked the VW van.

'I had a secret New Year's resolution,' she said.

'Oh, and what's that?'

'To say yes more. I remembered the conversation we had last year about buying that campervan and I was so quick to say no.'

'But you were right, it would have sat on the driveway.'

'I wasn't though. Part of the reason why I love you so much is that you're impulsive and reckless, and yes sometimes it needs controlling, but sometimes it's good.'

'Then thank you,' I said reaching across and squeezing her leg.

'I know a lot has happened in the last year and we've both made mistakes, but I want us to be more positive, and a part of that is saying yes more often. Being more—'

'Impulsive?'

'Yes,' said Emily.

With impulsiveness in the air and driving in the campervan, I thought it would be a good time to ask her about going to see Ben in Sydney. After a brief pause, Emily looked at me with a smile and said yes. With William babbling away in the back, Emily next to me, some good tunes on the radio and sunshine, I don't think I'd ever been happier.

Wednesday 27 March 9.45 a.m.

Newquay, Cornwall. Sunny. Happy days.

We drove through Devon yesterday and now we're in Newquay - the surf capital of England. People were looking at our VW campervan (which we've named Bess after Emily's first dog) as we drove around town. I'm booked in for a surf lesson today. We're off to have breakfast in a minute. Life in the campervan is wonderful and William seems to have discovered talking Welsh on this trip.

'Bwa, naa, fwad,' he said when I woke up this morning.

2.45 p.m.

William and Emily taking a nap. Sitting outside the van and enjoying the sunshine.

The surf lesson was hard, but I did manage to get up a few times. Admittedly, I spent most of the time under the water, but it was still fun. The only part I didn't enjoy was getting the wetsuit off - I felt like an escapologist. I eventually managed to get free of the wetsuit and we had a coffee at Costa. We're staying here tonight and tomorrow night before we make our way back towards London.

Friday 29 March 11.45 a.m.

(A really) Good Friday

I was watching William play in the sand at the beach this morning. He's growing up so quickly. He was rolling around and then he sat up and ate some sand. I'm so proud and so in love with him.

'Fwed, brr, krring,' said William.

'Love you too,' I said.

'Fwack!' said William.

Last night, after William was asleep, Emily and I were sitting outside, drinking wine and looking up at the stars.

'We should do more of this,' said Emily.

'I know. I'm so happy right now.'

'Me too,' said Emily. 'It's a shame we can't really have sex though.'

'What do you mean?'

'It's pretty cramped in there. We can hardly do it with William right there.'

'I promise I'll be quiet,' I said.

'Be gentle, that thing rocks like a bitch,' said Emily and we disappeared inside and had sex for the first time in the campervan - and the first time without the use of drugs for a while. William didn't wake up, although some passing teenagers did cheer as they walked past. I guess I wasn't that gentle, but who cares. My penis works!

Sunday 31 March

Dad turned up on the doorstep tonight.

'I've left your mother,' is all he said before he burst into tears.

April

Monday 1 April 8.45 a.m.

April Fool's Day/Easter Monday

In the kitchen. Dad, Emily and William asleep. Drizzling with rain. Drinking coffee.

Last night, after the initial shock and tears had died down, Dad and I had a long talk about why he ended up on our doorstep.

'What happened?'

'You know your mother,' said Dad.

'But what actually happened? I know her, I know you, and you've been married for years. Something must have happened.'

'It's him.'

'Who?'

'Who do you think? Larry bloody Laverne.'

'Not this again. Do you really think Mum would cheat on you?'

'I don't think so, son. I know so. She told me—'

'What?' I said incredulously. 'She confessed to having an affair?'

'Not in so many words, but it's obvious.'

'Why? What's going on?'

Dad huffed, sighed and took a long swig of his beer.

'It started during rehearsals. Coming home late, constantly talking about what a genius he was, the brilliant play, blah blah blah. After that first night and ever since, they've been spending more and more time together and so I told her, "You're a married woman, you can't be going on like that. It's either him or me".'

'And what did she say?'

'She called me a miserable old sod and then went and saw him. She chose him,' Dad said and then he looked like he was going to start crying again. It was at that point I decided to go to bed. I love Dad, I wanted to be there for him, but he's an awful crier. Not that he cries much, but when he does it's difficult to be around. I left him with a bottle of Scotch.

I can't believe Mum would have an affair. It's Mum. Mums don't have affairs. They don't have sex for that matter. Mums knit and cook and complain about queues at the Post Office. They don't have lurid affairs with beret wearing play directors.

Tuesday 2 April 10.45 a.m.

Emily's gone out for a few hours so I can have a chat with Dad about what he's going to do next. It's my parents. They can't breakup after thirty-something years of marriage because of Larry Laverne. I don't care what happened, Dad needs to go home, stop being a martyr, and start being a husband.

11.30 a.m.

I walked into the living room and Dad was sitting on the floor listening to a Doors CD and reading On the Road by Jack Kerouac - it's like we have an American teenager from the sixties living with us.

'Can we talk?'

'Actually now's a good time because I've been thinking.'

'Fantastic,' I said hoping he'd been thinking about going home and talking to Mum.

'And I know we haven't always, you know, had the deepest conversations, but I want to change. Leaving your mother has made me re-evaluate my life. It's like a light bulb went on in my head. For the first time in years I know what I want. I'm going to start living. Seeing you and Emily go off to Yoga, I thought to myself, I'd like to try Yoga. I want to travel. I want to get out there. I quite want to play the bongos!'

Dad's obviously having some sort of old-life crisis.

'That's nice and I'm all for that, obviously, but what I wanted to talk to you about,' I started, but Dad was on a roll.

'And I know I can't stay here forever, but can I stay for one month and then I promise I'll be out of your hair?'

Dad looked at me with an expression I hadn't ever seen before. It seemed to be love or maybe the early signs of dementia. Of course I was going to let him stay. He's my dad, what other choice did I have? It was probably only going to be for a few days anyway. I'm sure he's overreacting. They'll probably sort things out and he'll be home before we know it.

2.00 p.m.

'What do you mean he's staying for a month?' said Emily.

'He's my dad, Em. What could I say?'

'You could have said, you're a married man, go home and sort this mess out.'

'But he's hurting. If we give him a few days, maybe a week.'

'Or how about you go and see your mum now?'

'I suppose I could.'

'He can't stay for a month. I love your dad, you know I do, and this whole break-up must be hard on you, Harry, but a month is too long and I'm sure he's overreacting. Do you really think your mum could be having an affair with Larry Laverne? He wears a beret, Harry, a beret.'

Off to see Mum.

7.00 p.m.

I turned up and Larry answered the door - still in his annoying beret, flower print shirt (half-unbuttoned), shorts, and a cocktail in his hand with a little umbrella in it.

'Oh, Harry, so lovely. Do come in,' he said as though he

was living there.

'Larry,' I said sternly.

To set the scene, Mum and Dad's house is usually fairly quiet. The TV might be on or sometimes the radio in the kitchen, tuned religiously to Radio 4. Today I walked into a suburban bordello. I might be over-exaggerating a bit, but it wasn't the house I was used to. ABBA was playing loudly in the living room and Mum was dancing around - cocktail in hand – bare feet, wearing a long flowery dress. The air was pungent with incense.

'Harry!' she exclaimed when I walked in. She raced over and gave me a big kiss.

'Can we talk?' I said above the din of Dancing Queen.

'Of course, darling. Larry, Harry and I are going to talk in the kitchen.'

'Righty-oh,' said Larry with a wink.

'What the hell's going on?' I said as soon as we were in the kitchen.

'Cocktail?' said Mum.

'Sorry?'

'Cocktail? Larry does marvellous Martinis.'

'I bet he does, but Mum, seriously, what's going on?'

'What do you mean, darling?'

'What do I mean? Dad turns up on my doorstep telling me he's left you because you're having an affair with Larry Laverne. I come over and it looks like he's moved in.'

'I wouldn't say moved in, exactly.'

'So it's true? You're all loved up with that ... lovey?'

'In a manner of speaking,' said Mum and that's when I felt the rush of blood to my ears and stormed out.

'Harry, come back, have a Martini!' Mum yelled after me, but I just wanted to get out of there and back to Wimbledon.

Friday 5 April 8.45 a.m.

William started talking with a distinctly Asian accent this morning. I'd just got him up and was bringing him downstairs when he said, 'Antwa goziwa yaa!' Since then he's been sounding more and more oriental. Emily said it's probably just a developmental phase. I think it might be to do with the amount of tofu we've been eating.

Monday 8 April 11.45 p.m.

Home. Emily and William asleep. Eating an apple and drinking a glass of water.

The pub quiz was brilliant. Beers for Fears were on fire, and we only finished one point behind Quizzitch. I'm convinced they're cheating. I'm also getting really fed-up with their smug Harry Potter phrases and the way they point their wands at us and yell, 'Stupefy!' In the immortal words of Kevin Keegan, I'd love it if we beat them.

The most interesting part of the night was the conversation I had with Mark when Steve was off on an extended toilet break. I invited him, Sophie and Lexus over again, but I definitely detected something in his voice. He made it clear that he'd like to come over, but that Sophie is always too busy. Something is definitely up.

Tuesday 9 April 8.45 p.m.

I was putting William to bed, and he said, 'Oyasumi nasai otosan.' I looked this up and it means, 'good night father' in Japanese. Is William a genius? I hope not. They always end up depressed and alone.

I ran three miles at the gym without stopping and when I looked in the mirror before my shower, I noticed a difference. I'm starting to look semi all right naked. I'm no David Beckham, but there are subtle signs of improvement.

Thursday 11 April 7.45 p.m.

I got home from work tonight and Dad was particularly cheerful.

'What's up with you?'

'I have a date!' said Dad.

'A what?!'

'A date!'

'With whom?'

'Eleanor, the Yoga instructor.'

'Camel-toe?'

'What?'

'Nothing. I don't understand. How?'

'I went to Yoga this morning. We got talking and have a lot in common.'

'And you don't think it's a bit soon after Mum?'

'It's just a drink, Harry, we aren't moving in together.'

'But—'

'It's okay,' said Dad (annoyingly calmly) and then he went off to get ready.

Mum is dating a cocktail making, beret wearing lothario and now Dad is going for 'just a drink' with a camel-toed, Yoga instructor. Whatever next?

Saturday 13 April 9.15 a.m.

At home with William. Emily at the gym. Dad out with Eleanor (CT). Steve just left. Raining.

Question: What's about six feet tall and looks like a sheep?

Answer: Steve in a sheep costume.

He's trying out a new character. Steve the Sheep. It's for a kid's party he's agreed to do the entertainment for.

'What do you think?' said Steve.

'William, what do you think?' I said.

'Saru mo ki kara ochiru,' said William.

'Was that?'

'Japanese, I think.'

'Well, thank you, William,' said Steve. 'If this goes well I'm thinking of turning it into my job.'

'You're going to quit accounting and become a children's entertainer?'

'I'm pondering it.'

'Nanakorobi yaoki,' said William.

At this rate we're going to need a Wagamama menu to decipher his first words.

I need to go shopping and get some appropriate clothes for my school trip to Dartmoor. I also have to do one of the worst things in the world - I need to get a new mobile phone and so that means going to the mobile phone shop. Apprehensive gulp.

12.15 p.m.

I walked into the mobile phone shop with William and within ten seconds I was verbally assaulted by a spotty, red-haired teenager called Wayne.

'All right, Chief? How can I help you?'

'Just browsing, thanks.'

'Okay, Guvnor, but just to let you know we've got specials on the—'

'It's all right, I'll have a look.'

'No worries, Boss, it's your call,' said Wayne smiling inanely in his best Topman suit. 'Just one more thing.'

'What's that Wayne?'

'Do you want the best deal today?'

'No Wayne, I want an average deal that doesn't involve being hassled by you,' I said finally losing my patience, but then Wayne looked hurt, and I felt bad. 'I'm sorry, Wayne.

I know you're just doing your job.'

Then Wayne pulled the master stroke.

'I know, man. They tell us to say all that. I feel the same as you,' he said all chatty and blokey. 'I'll leave you alone. Sorry, man.'

Wayne was good. He'd used the word 'man' twice. I was powerless.

'Show me what you have,' I said and that was it. I left the shop twenty minutes later with a phone that cost twice as much as I'd intended to pay, and an upgraded plan – locked in for two years. I'd been well and truly Wayned.

2.15 p.m.

Emily's running a 10K next month - with Mark. This means that I have to do it too. Apparently it was his idea, and I shouldn't be annoyed or jealous, but I am. So I told her to sign me up too. Not excited.

Monday 15 April 4.15 p.m.

At school. Sunny. The new BBC weather girl is spot on again. Not only is she easy on the eye, but she knows her weather. I think that's it for the weatherman - wherever he is.

I had a cigarette with Rory. I'm stressed about everything in my life and Rory is still worried about his balls.

'The longer it goes on the more I'm worried my balls are broken.'

'My parents are dating other people,' I said. 'And I'm on a pub quiz team with Steve.'

'I just can't imagine a life where I can't have children.'

'I never thought my parents would break up. I especially didn't imagine Dad would be sleeping at my house and dating a Yoga instructor with a camel-toe.'

'It's just, what, sorry, did you say 'camel-toe'?'

'I've seen Dad's new girlfriend's vagina before he has.'

'That's—'

'Disturbing?'

'Yes.'

'I'm sorry your balls don't work, but you know it only takes one time and boom, you're having a baby.'

'I hope it's soon because every time Miranda gets her period she cries for days.'

'Mum's boyfriend wears a beret.'

'Fine,' said Rory. 'You win.'

Tuesday 16 April 10.15 p.m.

I had a beer with Dad in the shed and asked him how things were going with Eleanor. Apparently, it's going fantastically, which is obviously terrible news for me on many levels. Firstly, he's dating Eleanor who is annoying, has a camel-toe, and is Emily's Yoga instructor. Secondly, he's still married to my mother and I'm hoping this is just a blip. Lastly, I already think Dad is having some sort of old-life crisis and the last thing he needs is to be shacked up with a bloody new-age hippy putting all sorts of weird ideas in his head.

'She mentioned a holiday to Thailand later this year,' said Dad. 'Some sort of Yoga retreat.'

This is exactly what I was worried about. This is how it starts and before long it will be sandals and a ponytail.

Saturday 20 April 11.15 a.m.

A message on my phone from Mum:

Harry, it's me. I know you're confused about all of this. I'm confused. I didn't mean for it to happen, it just sort of did and I don't know what's going to happen next. I'm sorry you came over the other day and Larry was here and I'm sorry your father is there. Is he driving you crazy? He does that, he drives people crazy. Maybe that's why it happened with Larry. I don't know. We're old and life doesn't get any easier at our age. You think it does, but then you get here and realise it's just the same. Take care of your father. I love you. Give William a kiss too. Oh, it's your mother.

11.45 a.m.

Emily thinks I should talk to Mum. We were sitting in the living room at either end of a blanket and William was rolling around between us. Dad was out having brunch with CT. I wanted to talk to Mum, but what would I say? Emily thinks I just need to let her explain. She also wants Dad to move out. I gave Mum a call and I'm meeting her for lunch at Cafe Rouge. French seemed appropriate given her recent behaviour.

3.15 p.m.

Just back from lunch with Mum. Dad still out with CT. William napping. Emily ironing.

'Hello,' said Mum sitting down opposite me. I got there early and was sitting with a beer. I needed something to take the edge off. The truth was I was mad at her. She had cheated on Dad and worse, destroyed the notion that my parents, despite their weird idiosyncrasies and foibles, were happily married. I suppose it's never easy to find out the truth when it's easier to live with the lie.

'Mum,' I said and then we had a stand-off. It must have been the longest I'd ever been with her without her talking. But then she burst into tears, and I fell apart too.

'I'm so sorry. I never meant to hurt anyone, and I don't

know what happened with your father, but Larry came along, and he was paying me attention, and all your dad did was play golf. I didn't mean for this to happen.' She stopped and I put my hand over hers.

'It's okay, Mum, we'll figure it out.'

'But what if it's too late? I've really hurt your father and Larry told me he loved me. What am I going to do?'

Luckily our waitress came along at just the right time, and we ordered our food and more alcohol.

'I guess you need to figure out who you want to spend the rest of your life with,' I said. The words sounded ridiculous even as they were coming out of my mouth. 'Were you and Dad that unhappy?'

'I don't know. It wasn't like we were arguing all the time, but I suppose that's part of the problem. The passion had gone. We barely spoke, we never kissed, and we didn't argue because we didn't care enough. Then along came Larry.'

'And he cared.'

'Exactly.'

'It's funny because since Dad started seeing Eleanor—'

'Wait, Eleanor? Who's Eleanor?'

I'd forgotten she didn't know about CT.

'Dad's dating Emily's Yoga instructor,' I said limply, and Mum started crying again. 'You can't blame him, Mum. You cheated.'

'I know. It's just all so silly.'

I felt bad for Mum. She obviously just wanted to have a bit of fun in the twilight of her life. The funny thing is that with Dad acting the way he was and with Mum seemingly regretting what she'd done, maybe there was hope for them yet. Maybe they'll remember why they got married in the first place.

Sunday 21 April 7.15 p.m.

Home. Packing for Dartmoor. Emily putting William to

sleep. Dad out with CT. Still raining. I fear Devon might be a bit of a mudfest.

This is my last diary entry for a week. Tomorrow I'm off to Dartmoor on the school trip. Five days of camping, hiking, abseiling, canoeing, cooking, trying to get seventy kids to sleep, realising that half the boys are trying to get into the girls' tents during the night, making sure they don't, waking up too early, sharing a tent with Rory and Alan (who has a disgraceful bottom at the best of times), trying to stop the parents who volunteered from drinking and smoking around the kids, and missing Emily and William terribly - I'm sure it's going to be fine.

I'm going to finish packing and then I'm going to make love to my wife like a man who's about to leave for war and might never come back.

8.15 p.m.

Emily has a spot of thrush. I had no sex like a man about to head off to war with the horn.

Saturday 27 April 9.15 a.m.

It's possible that in my absence William has become a Nazi.

'Look at this,' said Emily excitedly. 'I taught William to wave. William, wave at Daddy. Show Daddy how you can wave.'

Then William did what I can only describe as a Nazi salute.

'What the fuck was that?' I said.

'Earmuffs,' said Emily putting her hands over his ears.

'Sorry.'

'That was his wave.'

'That wasn't a wave, Em, it was the Nazi salute.'

'Oh, Harry, don't be silly.'

'William, wave at Mummy,' I said. 'Wave at Mummy.'

William took one look at Emily and then did the Nazi salute again.

'Oh, now you mention it,' said Emily. 'It is a bit …'

'Yeah, our son is a Nazi!'

First Japanese and now this. I'm getting worried.

The trip to Dartmoor turned out to be a lot of fun. Most of the parents stuck to the rules and some were even helpful. Mr Jones did a great job with the food, and we didn't injure, lose or scare any of the pupils off camping for life. Eddie Collins seemed to really enjoy himself and spoke a lot about positive thinking and putting his energy into physical pursuits to help his recovery. He's in training to run the London marathon next year.

The highlight of the week though was when Chris Bartlett got stuck on a cliff. After all of his bragging and stories about being in the Territorial Army, Chris had a panic attack while abseiling and had to be rescued and escorted down the cliff face. He was taken away wrapped in a blanket and was last seen drinking a Minestrone Cup-a-Soup in the back of a Land Rover. All in all, a decent week - although due to a diet of mainly beans, the methane cloud around my bottom remains at threat level critical.

10.45 a.m.

Dad didn't seem very happy this morning and when I asked him if he was all right, he just grunted about needing a game of golf.

Sunday 28 April 9.15 a.m.

Home. Eating a 'healthy' fry-up. William breastfeeding. Emily nibbling on a banana. Cloudy.

Last night Emily and I tried to have sex. We had a bath, lit some candles, and I even gave her a sensual massage before we started to get into some pretty heavy petting. But then it happened. Steve and Fiona were going at it, and it sounded like they were doing some sort of role play. I heard Fiona ask Steve if he had the large package she needed. There was some rustling around and then Steve said in a dodgy French accent, 'You wanted the extra-large baguette, mademoiselle?' Fiona moaned and said she was starving and hadn't had a 'solid stick' for ages. The last thing we heard before we turned the television on was Fiona saying, 'c'est magnifique!'

'You have to talk to him,' said Emily.

'Why do I have to talk to him? Why can't you talk to her?'

'Do you want to ever have sex again?'

'I'll do it tomorrow.'

10.00 a.m.

I popped over and had a chat with Steve.

'What's up, old boy?' said Steve shining his trumpet - this isn't a euphemism, he was actually shining his trumpet.

'Nice trumpet.'

'Oh yes, she's a beauty.'

'You know, I'm sure I heard you playing it last night - in your bedroom.'

'No, no, I don't think so,' said Steve.

'Yes, I definitely heard it through the bedroom wall. Those walls are so thin. I definitely heard you playing your trumpet last night,' I said looking at Steve and hoping for a flicker of recognition. 'In the bedroom.'

'No, like I said, I wasn't playing it last night. This old lady hasn't been played for quite a while, have you, have you?' said Steve, oblivious to what I was saying and talking to the trumpet like it was a dog.

'Steve, we heard you and Fiona having sex last night,' I

said bluntly, and Steve stopped shining his trumpet. 'I'm sorry, but we did, and it isn't the first time.'

'Did you hear everything?'

'Everything.'

'Even the bit where I pretended to be the lost baguette salesman and Fiona was the charming village girl who needed a fresh stick?'

'Unfortunately, yes.'

'Oh,' said Steve.

'And it's nothing to be embarrassed about, but it's sort of hurting our sex life. Every time we try and do it, all we can hear is you and Fiona banging against the wall.'

'Harry, say no more,' said Steve. 'We'll move bedrooms.'

'You don't have to do that. Just move the bed or—'

'I insist. You shouldn't have to hear that and to be honest, I'm a little embarrassed.'

'Why?'

'The role playing, the characters, it's all Fiona, she loves it. I do this one thing where I'm Michael Caine - she makes me do the voice and everything.'

'Do you mind doing the voice?'

'No, not at all, it's a bit of fun and it gets Fiona quite, you know, horny,' said Steve.

'Right, well, thanks.'

'We'll move today,' said Steve. 'It's Sunday and Fiona likes to do …'

'I'll be off then, see you later,' I said, not really interested in what happens on Sundays. I did, however, get an idea what might perk up our sex life.

9.45 p.m.

I got Emily to bed, and we did our usual pre-sex warm-up, but then I brought out my extra-special gift just before kick-off.

'What's that?' said Emily.

'Not what, who. And this one's for you. Put it on and I'll be back in a sec,' I said and dashed into the bathroom before emerging seconds later. 'Mrs Spencer, do you have that report I demanded?' I said very sternly. I was dressed in my 'sexy' boss's outfit. Emily was on the bed in her very sexy office girl costume. Emily giggled. 'This is no laughing matter, Mrs Spencer, do you have the report or not?'

'No, sir,' said Emily.

'Then you'll need to be punished,' I said.

'And what do you have in mind?'

'You'll be taking down my briefs Mrs Spencer,' I said, and it took off after that.

Best sex in ages.

Monday 29 April 12.05 p.m.

No pub quiz tonight because Steve is meeting with an agent. It makes more sense that Steve is a children's entertainer than an accountant. He's far more comfortable singing about numbers than he is putting them in Excel spreadsheets.

4.00 p.m.

Off to the gym for a big run. I need to start training for the 10K next month. Not excited.

8.25 p.m.

Exhausted. I ran almost four miles, but nearly passed out and threw up on the treadmill (luckily I managed to catch most of it in my mouth). Emily ran five miles and only had a faint spattering of sweat. She's going to easily beat me at the 10K. She'll probably run it with Mark. They'll cross the finish line hand-in-hand before they'll go off and make slightly sweaty love while wearing their winner's medals. I'll finish last with the octogenarians, and we'll pool all of our money and go to the nearest cafe for a cup of tea and a slice of cake.

Tuesday 30 April 5.05 p.m.

Today was the third management training session with the effervescent Colin Thistle.

'Today is all about freedom,' said Colin. A few hands went up. 'Yes?'

'What do you mean?' said Mike from Watford.

'Management is often about giving people the freedom to make their own choices, to make their own mistakes, to rise to their own challenges. So today, you get to choose what we do and where we go.'

'We can go anywhere we want?' I said.

'Exactly,' said Colin.

Like his pie analogy, I wasn't entirely sure he'd thought this through.

'Like anywhere?' said Jenny from Twickenham.

'Anywhere,' said Colin. 'But bear in mind that whatever you decide, you must all agree upon it.'

'Pub?' said Warren.

'Oh, yeah, there's a nice one around the corner, they do a lovely full English,' said Frank from Epping Forest.

'Now hang on, does everyone agree?' said Colin nervously. We all nodded and said we did. 'Because we could go anywhere - the world's our oyster, or as I like to say, the world's our Oyster card!' Colin laughed, but no one else did and we all got up and went to the pub.

7.45 p.m.

Dad and I were having a game of darts in the shed when I decided to broach the subject of him moving out, but before I even said the words, Dad had broken down and started blubbing. I poured him a shot of Scotch and asked him what was going on.

'It's Eleanor.'

'Camel-toe?'

'I can't keep up with her, Harry. She's driving me into an early grave with all of her activities and bloody vegan this, and poxy low fat that, tofu bloody cheese, and we're always going to art galleries and the theatre. Not the actual theatre though, but the upstairs of pubs theatre and it's always something existential and weird with robots. And I don't like Yoga. There I said it. I don't like it. I just want to play golf.' Dad took a big gulp of air and I smiled. 'Why are you smiling?'

'Because you're back. I knew you'd hate all of that hippy stuff.'

'I tried, I did, but it isn't me. And it's not like I want to go back to how things were because I don't. I just can't eat another bloody falafel sandwich and she was talking about juggling the other day, son, juggling.'

Dad and I laughed, and it felt good because it felt like I had my dad back - my proper dad, and also because it gave me hope that maybe he and Mum could fix things after all. I told him to take his time moving out and he gave me that look again. I must Google the early signs of Dementia.

May

Wednesday 1 May 6.15 p.m.

Home. Emily next door talking to Fiona. Drinking tea. Tired.

I made a decision today. I decided I wanted to be honest with Emily. After the whole VW campervan surprise, it made me realise just how much Emily is trying to change and improve. It also made me think about how I'm not. We were cleaning up dinner and I sat her down and told her I'd been smoking again and cheating on the diet.

'Oh, Harry, why?' said Emily, the disappointment fitting across her face like a glove.

'I don't know, I'm sorry, Em,' I said, and her face dropped.

'And there was me thinking you'd changed. That old Harry was gone and new Harry, the father, was prepared to change and grow up.' Emily was suddenly super angry. 'And I'm sorry about your Mum and Dad, but that doesn't give you the right to start smoking again. Do you know why I wanted you to stop? Because I want you to be around forever. I want you to see our kids grow up and get married. I don't want you to die of lung cancer,' she said and then broke down in tears. I hugged her and then we had probably the longest conversation we've ever had. Two hours later, I promised her the world.

'I'm going to change, Em,' I said. And it looked like she believed me, but more importantly, I think I believed it myself.

Thursday 2 May 9.15 p.m.

Exhausted. Watching TV with Emily.

With the 10K fast approaching, I made a decision. I was going to go back to the gym and ask Tyler to train me again. It was the only chance I had of finishing the race and not embarrassing myself in front of Emily - and of maybe beating Mark and his biceps.

I got to the gym and Tyler was waiting for me. He had a smug, 'I told you so,' smile on his, 'Look at me, aren't I incredibly fit,' face.

'You're back,' said Tyler.

'I'm really sorry about what happened.'

'The storming out or the finger?'

'I was out of order. I just want to say that I'm really sorry and if it's all right, would you train me again?'

'Of course,' said Tyler with a glint in his eye. 'I'd love to.'

I explained about the 10K and how I had to do well, and Tyler said he could get me ready. Five minutes in and it was obvious he was out for revenge. He wanted to abuse me, teach me a lesson and grind me down into a sloppy, messy pile of pathetic flesh - and he succeeded. An hour of running, jumping, squatting, pushing, pulling, sprinting, crawling, star-jumping, bench-pressing, ball balancing and the final insult, a double big-ten, and my nightmare was complete. I left a broken man, more convinced than ever that I'll never be able to run a 10K let alone compete against Mark. I am doomed.

Friday 3 May 5.15 p.m.

Still at school. Emily and William having dinner with Fiona and the Js. Steve's rehearsing for his children's party tomorrow.

Today's department meeting was its usual mix-and-match disaster. Chris Bartlett spent the whole meeting complaining about the ridiculous pressure of test scores, which I agree with, but Chris takes moaning to a whole new level and now

I'm AHOD/ASM I have to listen to him.

'It takes the whole point out of teaching,' said Chris. 'If we're just here to teach them facts to pass a test and make some Whitehall spin doctor happy, then what's the point? I became a teacher to make a difference, to give kids a well-rounded education, but now it seems all I'm required to do is read from a book.'

'I understand your frustrations,' I said. 'I think we all feel the same.'

'Then let's do something about it!'

'That's the spirit,' said Clive.

'Like what?' I said to Chris. 'We have to teach to the syllabus.'

'Or we could teach them properly. Fuck the syllabus!' said Chris.

'Let's storm the bloody Bastille!' yelled Clive.

'Okay, calm down. Let's get back on topic.'

I've only been AHOD for a few months and already I had a revolution on my hands. The problem is they're right. The other problem is that I'm now the voice of 'Them in Charge'. No matter what I say about positive change, forgetting about test scores and focusing on giving our pupils the education they deserve, all the suits want is the right numbers to put in their little boxes so they can tick us off and say we're doing a good job - whether we are or not. It's all about the stats.

8.15 p.m.

Over dinner, Emily casually dropped into the conversation that we're going to her parents' house tomorrow for dinner and we're staying the night. I'm not happy about this for many reasons, but mainly because she mentioned the possibility of playing Monopoly.

'You do remember what happened the last time your dad and I played?'

'The Monopoly incident, how can I forget?'

To be fair, the Monopoly incident was mainly Derek's fault. He is ridiculously competitive at everything - and especially his favourite board game, Monopoly. We were at their house when the board came out and the girls soon lost out to Derek's ruthlessness. Emily likes to play the rule that if someone buys one of the streets in the set then no one else can buy the others, to keep it fair. Derek laughed at this ridiculously anti-capitalist idea. 'It's the whole point of the game; to crush your opponents,' said Derek slamming his fist down on the table - Mussolini-esque.

Three hours later when I had him by the short and curlies, about to take his last hotel and rather enjoying it, things turned nasty. Long story short, Derek tossed the board up in the air in a fit of rage and everyone blamed me (the dog piece is still missing). That was three years ago, and we haven't played a board game since.

'Maybe I should stay here. Why don't you and William go?' I said hopefully.

'That was years ago. You and Dad get on so much better now and he's calmed down a lot.' Then Emily said the four words that always sent a shiver down my spine: 'It will be fine.' Which translates as - it will be an absolute nightmare.

Saturday 4 May 8.23 a.m.

In the kitchen. William on his blanket. Emily at Yoga. Cloudy with a chance of rain - according to the BBC weather girl (who was looking extra lovely this morning).

Over breakfast William said, 'Ogenki desuka'. Since his recent linguistic explosion, I've started carrying around a Japanese phrasebook. I quickly looked it up and apparently it means, 'how are you?' I looked up a reply and said back,

'Watashi wa genki desu. Arigato. Anatawa?' This means, 'I'm fine, thanks. And you?' William looked at me, his face deadpan, as though he was mulling over his response, but then he burst out laughing. Had he understood me? I tried a few more phrases, but just more laughter. I don't know if he was laughing because he's only eight and a half months old or because I had a terrible Japanese accent. I gave him some more organic Scottish porridge before he started rolling around the kitchen.

11.45 p.m.

On the sofa at Emily's parents' house. Emily, William, Derek, Pam and Emily's ancient grandmother Beatrice Lamb asleep upstairs.

Another gaming disaster. I don't know why they insist we keep playing Monopoly. It always ends in tears. This time it wasn't because of Derek, but because of Emily's ancient grandmother Beatrice. I haven't seen her since last year's 'rape' incident when I thought she was dying and gave her mouth-to-mouth (the right thing to do), but apparently it looked as though I was trying to rape her (the wrong thing to do).

As soon as she saw me she cowered against the wall and called me a rapist. She can't remember to shave her moustache or wash regularly, but she remembers that.

'Grandma, its Harry,' said Emily. 'My husband.'

'The rapist!' screamed Beatrice grabbing hold of the cross around her neck and shoving it towards me as though I were Dracula.

'No, no, no, that was just an accident, remember? He thought you were dying. He was trying to save you.'

Beatrice mumbled something and shuffled off. A few hours later (after William had been accosted by the tissue from Beatrice's sleeve for the umpteenth time and then put to bed) we all sat down to play Monopoly. Two hours later and only Beatrice and I were left, but at just gone ten o'clock

I finally had her on the ropes. She owed me two thousand pounds and we all knew she didn't have it.

'I guess we have a winner!' I said triumphantly, but when I looked around the room all I got back were stares of disapproval - I put my victory dance on hold.

'Could you help me to bed?' said Beatrice to Derek. 'I'm not feeling well.'

Derek helped Beatrice upstairs, shooting me the evil Lamb stare on the way through.

'Proud of yourself?' said Pam when they'd left the room.

'What?' I said confused.

'Making an old woman sad like that,' said Pam.

'Why didn't you let her win?' said Emily.

'I was just playing the game,' I said and then Derek came back downstairs and said he'd never seen her so down and gave me more daggers.

I tried to apologise (though technically I'd done nothing wrong), but Derek and Pam went to bed without saying goodnight and then Emily followed soon after. I had been abandoned. An outcast. A year ago I tried to help Beatrice Lamb because I thought she was dying, and I was accused of rape. This year I beat her at Monopoly, and I'm charged with making her the saddest she's ever been. I give up. Life will be a lot easier when the old dear finally pops her clogs.

Sunday 5 May 7.23 a.m.

'SHE'S DEAD!' Pam shouted down the stairs hysterically.

Derek was washing up in the kitchen and ran upstairs with the bubbles still on his hands like a pair of marshmallow gloves. Emily, who was breastfeeding William, tore him off her nipple, passed him to me and followed Derek. I waited downstairs hoping and praying she wasn't dead. I didn't want her last memory to be losing to me at Monopoly.

'Unsan musho,' said William.

I didn't understand what he said, but I could tell from the look on his face that he knew what he was talking about. The next minute I heard more tears upstairs and I knew that Beatrice Lamb was gone.

Derek was the first one down. I tried to look sorry and asked if there was anything I could do, but he walked past me without a word and stormed off towards the kitchen. Next was Emily.

'Em, I'm so …'

'Not now!' she said giving me the hand.

'But, Em.'

'I said not now!' she yelled before heading off towards the kitchen.

7.00 p.m.

I was in the shed having a game of darts and a beer when there was a knock at the door. I told whoever it was to come in, not sure who to expect because no one had ever knocked before. It was just Steve. He came in, sat down, and I got him a beer. I asked him about the birthday party he'd done and suddenly his face lit up. He said it was magical and I think it was the happiest I'd ever seen him. Then he told me he'd had an epiphany and wanted to be a professional children's entertainer.

'Good for you, mate,' I said. 'Follow your dreams.'

'I will. Once I have the courage to tell Fiona.'

'She isn't behind it?'

'She is. It's just the mortgage and the kids. It's a big risk.'

'But if it's what you really want to do.'

'You're right. I'm going to do it. Steve the Kid Fiddler is going to be a reality!'

'You might want to re-think the name.'

'You don't think children like fiddles?'

'I'm sure they do, it's the fiddling that's the problem.'

Tuesday 7 May 5.30 p.m.

Off for a run with Emily and Mark.

8.45 p.m.

Physically and emotionally drained. We ran seven miles. Well, Emily and Mark ran seven miles. I ran, walked, sat, almost threw up, popped into public toilets for a wee (twice), had a lie down on a bench, ran some more, walked a bit, got stitch, popped into a newsagent for a Lucozade, ran some more, walked quite a lot, and then eventually crawled.

'Where have you been?' said Mark. 'We got back thirty minutes ago?'

'Oh, you know, pacing myself.'

'What for? The over eighties 10K?'

'Oh, stop it, Mark, he's trying,' said Emily idly hitting Mark on his big bicep with the side of her hand. Mark casually put his arm around Emily's shoulder; their sweaty flesh touching, and I felt a shudder of jealousy.

Wednesday 8 May 5.30 p.m.

I got home from work and Dad was pacing up and down the hallway.

'What's the matter?' I said.

'I'm going to break up with Eleanor.'

'Oh, camel-toe removal, it's about time.'

'I just - how do you do it?' said Dad. 'I've never had to do this before, and I don't want to hurt her.'

'Like a plaster Dad. Quick and painless.'

'Right,' said Dad. 'Quick and painless.'

'Good luck,' I said as Dad grabbed his coat and went off to do the deed.

'Where's he going?' said Emily when I walked into the kitchen.

'To break up with Eleanor.'

'Oh, brilliant. Maybe he'll move back home now.'

'Let's see.'

'He needs to move out, Harry.'

'I know. Let's see how it goes tonight and then maybe we can broach the subject.'

Emily just gave a low huff. She's still a bit annoyed about the whole Monopoly/ Beatrice dying incident. For some reason the whole Lamb family seem to think that somehow it's my fault. She was in her nineties and had been on the verge of death for years, I don't see how I pushed her over the edge. A nudge perhaps, but definitely not a push.

8.15 p.m.

Dad got back looking quite sombre.

'How was it?'

'Let's just say she wasn't very Zen about it.'

'All that new-age hippy stuff was all a facade?'

'She threw an acai berry and wheatgrass smoothie at me,' said Dad. 'And then she tai-chi'd me quite hard in the balls.'

'Ouch,' I said. 'At least you did it and now maybe you and Mum—'

'I don't want to talk about it,' said Dad. 'I'm off to bed.'

Emily thinks it's our big chance to get Mum and Dad back together and convinced me to go and see Mum tomorrow.

Thursday 9 May 7.30 p.m.

Home. Eating dinner. Cloudy. William asleep. Emily concocting a plan.

After school I went to see Mum. I was worried that Larry Laverne was going to be there, and I'd have to listen to him going on about the theatre while Mum danced around pissed on Martinis, kissing me far too much. But when I got there it was all quiet. I said 'hello' a few times without reply before eventually Mum said something. I walked through into the kitchen and found her sitting by herself next to a half empty bottle of wine.

'What's going on?' I said giving her a kiss on the cheek and then sitting down opposite her. 'Where's beret boy?'

'Who?'

'Jesus Mum, how many people do you know who wear berets?'

'Oh, Larry, he's at rehearsals for a new play he's working on'.

'And you aren't involved?'

'No,' said Mum shortly.

'Is everything okay? You seem a bit down.'

'I'm fine,' she said. 'I'm just, I don't know, a bit lost. How's your father?'

'The same. He just broke up with Eleanor.'

'Oh, really?' said Mum, the smallest hint of happiness blinking for a second across her face.

'I think he's missing you,' I said. 'Are you missing him?'

'I don't want to talk about it,' said Mum, and then she started asking about William and Emily, but I definitely got the impression she was missing Dad - which leads me onto Emily and her cunning plan. Emily's convinced that my parents are still very much in love and just need a little push to get them back together again. She's also desperate to get Dad out of the house and so she's going to invite Mum over for dinner and tell her that Dad is out. She's not going to tell Dad that Mum's coming over and once here they'll be forced to talk.

'It's risky, Em. What if it all goes to shit?'

'We have to do something, Harry. The other day I walked in on your dad on the loo.'

'That's not so bad.'

'He was naked, Harry.'

'I'll give Mum a call.'

Friday 10 May 10.29 p.m.

Home. Emily and William asleep. The BBC weather girl predicts rain for another week.

Funerals are always difficult. I wasn't particularly close or even friendly with Beatrice Lamb, but it was still very sad - mainly because there were so few people there. We all like to think that when we die the church will be jam-packed. When Grandad died last year it was standing room only. It was symbolic of not only the sort of man he was, but of the life he'd led. His loss felt significant. But today there were less than ten people there - including the vicar and the organist.

The funeral was short and, in some ways, almost meaningless. After it was done we all petered outside and stood under our umbrellas. Even the wake at Emily's parents' house was drab and anti-climactic. The longer it went on, the sadder I got. I was mulling over another devilled egg (was eight too many?) when I saw Emily heading out to the conservatory. I followed her and asked if she was okay.

'Yeah, just a bit blah.'

'It's been a weird day.'

She had forgiven me for my part in the death. We had a talk about it, and she agreed that they all overreacted about the Monopoly.

'It's just so sad, isn't it? I mean she was alive for ninety-six years and this is all she has to show for it,' said Emily.

'To be fair, most of her friends are probably dead. It definitely hit the guest list big time,' I said, and Emily giggled.

'Oh, Harry, stop it,' said Emily and then she looked at me with her serious face.

'What?'

'How many more kids do you want?'

We had talked about this before, a long time ago, pre-William. I'm an only child and so I always knew I wanted at least two. Emily had mentioned four - which had scared the shit out of me, obviously. Just do the maths. Four kids - that's at least twenty-four years with kids at home, assuming we have one every two years, and they all go to university. More likely is that at least one or two will be more than two years apart and knowing my luck two of them won't go to university and will sponge off us for years to come. I'm already thirty-four, so if Emily still wanted four kids, we could forget about having any sort of life post-kids. I'd be about seventy when the last one left home. In fact, the kids would probably just stay in the house and put me in a home.

'One more would be nice. Especially if it's a girl,' I said.

'Yeah, that would be nice. One boy and one girl.' (Phew).

'The perfect little family,' I said, and we both smiled. 'Why are you asking me now?'

'Just with everything today. It makes you think, doesn't it? Life is short.'

'To be fair, she was ninety-six, Em. Not that short.'

'You know what I mean, smart arse. Life is short and I want us to do so much and have adventures and holidays and, I guess what I'm saying is, I want another kid and then that's probably going to be it.'

'Sounds like a brilliant plan,' I said, leaning across and giving her a kiss on the cheek.

'And I want them close together. I don't want to be one of those stay-at-home-for -fifteen-years-raising-kids mums.'

'How close?' I said suddenly not sure where this conversation was going.

'Less than two years,' said Emily with a smile.

I did a quick calculation in my head. William was going to be nine months old soon, so if she wanted to have another one within two years that meant we only had about five months left before we had to start trying.

'You're serious?'

'I've never been more serious about anything in my life,' she said. 'I loved Gran, but she led a really dull life. She never did anything or went anywhere. I don't want to be like that. I want to live.'

'Me too,' I said.

And that was that. We agreed to think about trying 'soon'.

The wake ended as the rest of the day had gone - it slowly stopped, and we all went home. The end of Beatrice Lamb, a stubborn old lady who refused to die until she was ready - or if you believe Derek, who died because I beat her at a game of Monopoly. I'll tell you something, that's the last time I play Monopoly with a member of the Lamb family.

Saturday 11 May 5.45 p.m.

Home. Playing with William. Emily making the dinner table pretty. Dad taking a shower.

Mum's due at seven o'clock. Dad thinks he's just having dinner with us. Mum thinks she's just having dinner with us. Neither of them suspects that they're actually having dinner with each other.

10.00 p.m.

'What's he doing here?' said Mum.

'What's she doing here?' said Dad.

'Surprise!' I said.

Mum and Dad just stood there and looked at each other and then they looked at me and Emily, and then Mum started to cry. Dad stopped looking so annoyed and asked if she was all right and then Emily told them the plan. Luckily, neither of them walked out and instead they looked at each other and smiled.

'I'm game if you are,' said Dad.

'Then I suppose I don't have any choice,' said Mum.

Emily and I served dinner and left them alone to talk. Two hours later, they walked into the lounge together.

'Well?' I said hoping for good news.

'The lasagne was a bit bland,' said Dad.

'Not the bloody food,' I said. 'Your marriage.'

'He's going to move back home and see what happens,' said Mum.

'Yes!' said Emily rather too enthusiastically. 'Sorry, I mean, that's great. I'm so happy for you.'

'Me too,' I said.

'I'll just go and get my things,' said Dad.

That was half-an-hour ago. Dad came downstairs with his sad bag of bachelor possessions, and they got in the car and drove off with Emily and me waving until they were out of sight. My parents on the road to reunion.

Sunday 12 May 8.45 p.m.

'Em.'

'Yes, Harry.'

'Do you think there's any chance William could be speaking Japanese?'

'No.'

'Not even the slightest?'

'Harry, he can't speak English yet, his mother tongue. I think it's safe to say he definitely can't speak Japanese.'

'But I've heard him. He's said things to me that could only be Japanese.'

'I've heard him say all sorts of gobbledygook too, and yes, some of it sounded a bit Asian, but it wasn't Japanese. He's a baby.'

'What if he was Japanese in another life? You hear about weird things happening all the time. People waking up and speaking French or going somewhere they've never been before and knowing where things are.'

'Do you believe in reincarnation?'

'No, of course not, it's ridiculous.'

'Then William doesn't speak Japanese.'

'Fine, but he does do the Nazi salute.'

'That I'll give you. We must teach him to wave properly.'

'Agreed. The other day he did the Nazi salute to the poor old lady behind the till at Waitrose. She looked horrified. I think she may have been Jewish.'

Monday 13 May 4.15 p.m.

Home. Emily making dinner. William reading the 1984 Guinness Book of World Records.

Its pub quiz night and we're more determined than ever to beat team Quizzitch. Steve and Mark are coming over in an hour for a pre-quiz warm-up.

11.55 p.m.

From the moment the quiz started we were on fire. It was like everything aligned perfectly. The right questions came up again and again, the beer was flowing and at the end of the night, we got forty-nine and a half out of fifty (a pub quiz record). We waited with bated breath as Brian read out the final standings.

'And in … hick … second place … hick … this week's runners-up are … hick … Quizzitch, which means the winners are … hick … Beers for … hick … Fears!'

This would have been the perfect moment for dignity in victory. Quizzitch annoyed everyone with their sly Harry

Potter references and their surprisingly canny costumes. This was our chance to show that Beers for Fears were a serious, grown-up and dignified team. It would have been the perfect chance, but instead we chose a slightly different path.

'Hah!' shouted Mark, standing up and pointing at team Quizzitch. 'Shove that up your Dumbledores!'

Then the pièce de résistance. Steve, who is never one to gloat or be confrontational, got up on his chair and unloaded a diatribe of considerable force. It was outstanding. Funny, cutting, filthy and when he sat down the whole room cheered. Quizzitch slumped in their chairs, defeated and demoralised. We were the champions. The untouchables. That was until the pub landlord came over, asked us to leave, and banned us from the pub quiz for life.

Beers for Fears, as one, got up and walked out. The other teams stood up and slow clapped us as we left the pub quiz for the last time. We got nods of approval from teams Quizimodo and Let's Get Quizzical, but we were done.

'That was fun,' said Steve.

'I didn't know you had it in you,' Mark said to Steve.

'Neither did I,' said Steve with a proud giggle.

'You're a wizard, Steve!' I said.

Thursday 16 May 9.15 p.m.

On the sofa. Watching TV with Emily. Knackered. Raining.

I had my last workout with Tyler tonight and he made me run a full 10K. Despite my reluctance to come back and train with Tyler, I must say he's got me in tip-top shape. I might not like him, he might not like me, but I need him and his annoying high-fives and big-tens, and he probably needs my thirty pounds a session.

Friday 17 May 7.15 p.m.

Sick as a dog. I just carb-loaded for the race. I scoffed nearly a whole pound of pasta carbonara. I might throw up. We're about to watch Run Fatboy Run. Emily picked it - is she trying to tell me something?

Saturday 18 May 4.45 a.m.

The Day of the Big Race

What I don't want to happen during the race

I throw up.

I piss myself.

I get beaten by someone old enough to be my parent or worse my grandparent.

I fall over and injure myself in an embarrassing way.

I get an erection.

2.45 p.m.

The race started and Mark, Emily and I set off together. I was actually doing well. We got to mile three still together. I hadn't thrown up, pissed myself or got an erection. However, on mile four I started to flag, and Mark took off. I was just ahead of Emily, but I knew I had no chance of catching Mark and so I decided to run the race with Emily. I thought we could cross the line together, hand-in-hand. It would be romantic.

Emily and I ran together, and we were about half a mile from the finish line. I was breathing heavily, I'd had stitch for the last mile and my knees, calves, and shins were in excruciating pain, but I was going to do it. Then we saw him. Mark was just ahead of us, hobbling along at a slow jog. Emily asked what had happened and apparently he'd tripped and twisted his ankle. Mark put his arm across Emily's shoulder, and she was going to help him over the finish line. We were going to finish together.

I don't know what happened, but suddenly I got a huge burst of adrenalin. I left Emily and Mark and sprinted towards the finish line. I crossed the line, raised my arms in the air and gave myself a mental high-five (MHF). It wasn't until I'd taken in some water and collapsed on the ground that I saw Emily and Mark stood over me.

'What the fuck was that?' said Emily.

'What?'

'The Rocky finish? I thought we were doing it together?'

'I got a bit excited,' I said.

'It's fine, Em,' said Mark playing the injured hero to perfection.

'It's not fine, he's being a knob,' said Emily.

'Sorry,' I said, but Emily was already walking Mark off towards the medical tent and then I threw up a little pasta carbonara in my mouth. Technically, I had beaten Mark, but it seems all I've done is piss off Emily and make Mark look like a bit of a God.

Sunday 19 May 5.45 p.m.

'Fifty thousand pounds!' said Emily.

We were at her parents' house having a roast.

'She was tight with her money,' said Derek. 'She had a lot put away.'

'Fifty thousand pounds!' said Emily again.

'That's right,' said Pam.

'Fucking hell!' said Emily.

'Earmuffs,' I said quickly covering William's ears.

'Sorry,' said Emily.

'She left us enough to buy our second home in Tenerife,' said Derek. 'We're going out in two weeks to buy something.'

Emily looked at me and I looked at her and we both smiled. This was going to change everything. Beatrice Lamb, God bless you.

8.45 p.m.

After we put William to bed, Emily and I talked about the fifty grand. We decided to make Australia the trip of a lifetime and Emily mentioned getting the new kitchen she's dreamed about since we bought the house. I would like a new car. The old VW has been brilliant, but it's time to get something a bit 'jazzier'. We were having a brilliant chat until Emily broke it off because she wanted to go and check on Mark and make sure he was okay after the race.

I don't know why Mark bothers me so much. Yes, he's handsome, successful, tall, good looking and rich, but he's married to Sophie. I suppose it's that he makes me feel insecure because he's the me I wish I was. When I look at him, I don't see how any woman could turn him down. And I trust Emily, of course I do. It's just silly. Mark and Sophie match and Emily and I match. There's absolutely nothing to worry about.

'Sophie's moved out and taken Lexus with her,' said Emily when she got back forty-five minutes later. 'Poor Mark is devastated. I've been consoling him.'

Absolutely nothing to worry about.

Wednesday 22 May 8.45 p.m.

'Push it,' said Emily.

'No, you,' I said.

'Just do it, Harry, for me?'

'Why don't you want to push it- just in case something bad happens?' I said.

'Nothing bad is going to happen. Give me your finger.'

'No way, you do it. I don't want the blame.'

'Fine,' said Emily looking at me with a salacious grin. 'I'm going to bloody do it.'

'I want you to do it.'

'You just want to watch me do it, don't you? Admit it?'

'I do. Go on, Em, do it.'

'Are you sure about this? Once I push it, that's it.'

'I'm sure. I want this. Don't you want it?'

'I really do.'

'Then do it, Em. Push it.'

And then she did. She pushed the button. We waited, our hearts in our mouths, until the page changed and there it was. We'd done it.

Congratulations, your seats have been confirmed. Three travellers. Two adults and one child in lap. London to Sydney.

We're going to Australia to see best mate Ben and Katie in August!

Thursday 23 May

Grandad always went on about the good old days. I loved that about him. The funny thing is though, we don't really know when we're in the good old days. It seems impossible to know at an exact moment that it's something special. You can be happy, you can know that a particular time is important, but you never know if it's the good old days until it's gone.

I was thinking about it because I was sitting watching William having a bath with Emily and I realised how happy and in love I am and how precious these fleeting moments are. If there's one universal truth about having kids, it's that they grow up so fast. There he was in the bath, barely still a baby. He'd be a toddler, a kid and then a teenager before we blinked. Right now it was peekaboo and the tickle-monster game, but before we knew it, it'd be school, girlfriends, and then he'd be calling from university to ask for money.

Saturday 25 May 11.24 a.m.

Home. Eating a bacon sandwich. Emily drinking tea. William looking at a map of the world.

Steve's head popped over the fence this morning while I was mowing the lawn.

'Hello neighbour,' said Steve.

'Hello, mate,' I said. 'What's going on?'

'I come with the promise of food, games, music, costume and some mega news.'

'Is this to do with the Steve the Kid Fiddler?'

'Maybe,' said Steve with a grin. 'Pop over about two o'clock?'

'Okay.'

'See you then,' said Steve excitedly and then his head popped back over the fence.

4.15 p.m.

In the shed. Everyone at Steve and Fiona's.

I just popped back to pick up some extra alcohol.

We got to Steve and Fiona's at two o'clock and the kids went off and started playing. William and the youngest J were rolling and crawling around the garden, while Emily, Fiona, Steve and I sat on deck chairs in the sunshine. After a while, I had to ask what his mega news was, and Steve got all excited and said with a big smile,

'Let me get my guitar.'

Steve popped back into the house and reappeared moments later dressed as a cowboy.

'I knew it. You're gay and this is your coming out song,'

I said.

'I'm not gay,' said Steve. 'I'm a cowboy!'

'And they're never gay.'

'Harry, let the poor man tell us his news,' said Emily.

'Fine, go on Lone Gaynger,' I said, and Steve started playing his guitar and singing.

'So you're probably wondering what this is all about,
I'm in a cowboy costume, but please don't doubt,
You might be thinking I've gone a bit crazy,
I quit my job, but not because I'm lazy,
I'm now in the showbiz game,
Kids parties is where I'll make my name,
Steve the Entertainer is who I am,
And that, my friends, ain't no sham!'

Steve finished and apart from the obvious feelings of shock and, 'why did he have to sing his big news in a cowboy costume?' we were all happy for him.

'Mate, I'm so proud of you,' I said shaking him by the hand. 'Great song and a much better name than the Steve the Kid Fiddler.'

'The Kid Fiddler?' said Emily incredulously.

'It was supposed to be like the Pied Piper …' said Steve.

'But more paedo,' I said.

'I definitely prefer Steve the Entertainer,' said Emily.

'It was my idea,' said Fiona. 'He wanted to go with Touched by Steve.'

'Oh, mate,' I said.

9.15 p.m.

Home. Emily in the shower. William asleep. Slightly pissed.

The rest of the evening at Steve and Fiona's was really fun. We drank, ate, Steve the Entertainer put on a show for the kids, and we sat around until it got too cold to be outside and we moved the party inside. William and the Js played together with a ball, and I had a fantastic time with Steve.

It wasn't that long ago that I thought Steve was a bit annoying, but now we've become really good friends. I don't think it's him that's changed though. It's me. I've grown up and the things that used to annoy me about parents, I've become. I want to talk about William all the time because he's amazing. If he does a banana-shaped poo, I want to tell everyone and if he speaks Japanese fluently (which I'm still convinced he does) then I want to shout it from the rooftops. Obviously we're trying to keep the Nazi salute quiet.

Children change us, or maybe it's our love for them that changes us. They melt us, and all the things that seemed a bit naff and annoying before, we see with new eyes. The eyes of a parent.

Monday 27 May 1.24 p.m.

Hot. The BBC weather girl said we're having a heatwave this week - maybe she'll present the weather in a bikini to celebrate. First day of half-term. Emily over at Mark's.

As soon as William went down for his nap, Emily went straight over to see Mark. He's taken the week off work because he's all distraught about his marriage. I'm meeting Rory later for a drink. He's still distraught about his broken balls. For once it seems I'm not the one in trouble or with potentially serious medical issues.

2.45 p.m.

Emily just got back from Mark's house and she's telling me all about his break-up with Sophie. Apparently, they broke up because of something sexual. She didn't know what exactly, but she's meeting him for coffee tomorrow to find out. What the hell is something sexual? Does Mark have problems in the bedroom? Does Mr Fantastic have a floppy little fella? I can only hope. I'm a bit annoyed that Emily has to see Mark again (he sees more of her than me these day), but I'm probably being a bit of an idiot and I just have to do my best to seem fine with it because it's Emily. She's nice. She's just trying to help him through a difficult time and yes, it would be easier if he looked more like Quasimodo than Prince Charming, but I trust Emily implicitly.

'What's going on tonight?' said Emily.

'Rory and I are going out for a drink. He and Miranda are still trying for a baby.'

'Give him my best, and just so I can prepare myself, are you going to get hammered, stagger home, wake me up in the middle of the night and try and have pissed sex with me?'

'That's the plan.'

'Oh, Harry, you old romantic.'

Tuesday 28 May 12.02 p.m.

Home. Emily having coffee with Mark. William taking a nap. Squirrels frolicking in the garden. Looking at a bacon sandwich - dare I eat it? Hot.

When I was younger (so much younger than today) I could drink a lot. I remember going out at university and drinking ten pints, followed by copious amounts of shots. I could dance until two in the morning and still make it in for morning lectures. Goodness knows how I managed to get my degree.

Even in my twenties, I could still drink with the best of them and function. Drinking and Harry Spencer have always gone together like bacon and eggs. However, after last night, I no longer consider myself a drinker, a partier, a person of youth. It was properly pathetic.

Rory and I started drinking around five o'clock. Our intention had been to get blindingly pissed, get kebabs and fall asleep in a taxi - just like the good old days. However, by nine o'clock and only five pints in, we were both feeling a bit knackered. We didn't even last until closing time before we slunk off home early. Emily was awake when I got back.

'What are you doing back?' she said incredulously.

'Apparently I'm old,' I said.

'Oh,' said Emily. 'I was wondering what that smell was.'

Wednesday 29 May 9.02 p.m.

Camber Sands Caravan Park. Sitting outside and looking up at the stars. William and the Js asleep.

Today was hot and so Emily suggested a day at the beach. She also wanted to invite Steve, Fiona and the Js. It wasn't that long ago that asking them would have brought me out in a nasty rash, but things were different now.

'Sounds good. I'll pop my head over the fence,' I said. I got out the small stepladder from the shed and looked over the fence. Steve was doing his morning, dance like a twat routine. 'Morning.'

'Morning,' said Steve. 'Just doing my Tai Chi. It helps start the day in a positive way.'

'Looks like it. Do you fancy going to the beach?'

'OMG! I think it's time.'

'Time for what?'

'The day I get to share a little secret with you. We've been holding off, but now, Harry, now is the time. Let me get out of my Tai Chi clothes. We'll be over in five.' Then Steve started running off towards the house shouting. 'Fiona, it's time!'

I had absolutely no idea what was going on, but

apparently it was something big. Five minutes later and Steve, Fiona and the Js all came over and stood in our lounge and Steve looked fit to burst.

'Harry, Emily, William,' said Steve. 'You're our best friends. We look at you like family, and as such, it's time we shared something with you. Something exciting.'

'You aren't one of those families that sleep together in the same bed, are you? I watched a show about that the other day, it's very creepy.'

'No,' said Steve. 'It's mega exciting.'

'Are you going to star in your own reality television series?'

'Harry!' said Emily. 'Let him finish.'

'Thank you, Emily,' said Steve and then a big smile spread across his face. 'We own a caravan at Camber Sands!' Steve half-yelled. I have to say, I definitely wasn't expecting that.

'You own a caravan?' said Emily cautiously.

'I'm sorry we haven't shared this with you before, Emily, but honestly, we didn't know if Harry was ready.'

'What?!' I said incredulously.

'People know us there Harry, and you can be a bit—'

'A bit what?' I said.

'It's okay, I understand,' said Emily. 'So does that mean?'

'Come down today and stay the night!' said Steve. 'We'll show you everything!'

The caravan itself was actually quite nice and although it was a bit of a squeeze with the nine of us, we just about managed it. Although I don't think we'll be getting much sleep tonight. We went to the beach, to the pool, the arcade, and all in all we had a great day. Then, to put the cherry on the cake, at just after four o'clock we were playing outside the caravan when William stopped rolling, ambled up onto his knees and started crawling. My little boy is growing up so fast.

One of the advantages of keeping a diary is that you can go back and measure how your life has changed. A year ago my marriage was on the ropes and William was still inside Emily's womb. A year later and I'm at Camber Sands, more in love with Emily than ever and William, now nine and a half months old, is crawling around. It makes me wonder where we'll be in a year, or ten years from now. Even in January, I would never have guessed I'd be at a caravan park with Steve and enjoying myself, but life changes, we change and there's nothing we can do about it.

Steve and I are about to go for a drink at the Caravan Park club. I'm expecting the worst, but then again, maybe I shouldn't.

Thursday 30 May 4.42 p.m.

Home. Sitting in the garden. Emily lying next to me in a bikini. William taking a nap. Listening to the radio. V. hot.

The Camber Sands Caravan Park club wasn't that bad. I mean, it was exactly what I expected, but I had a good time. The club was a bit social clubby, and it had the obligatory bored looking teenagers with their slightly drunk parents, who were sitting tapping their feet to Status Quo. The DJ was encouragingly called, Party Time Pete and it was Friday night when 'The music never stops!' (It closed at eleven o'clock), but we had fun.

We danced with some middle-aged, chubby, northern women and Steve completed the entire Grease Mega Mix on stage (by himself). We played pool, drank cheap beer, entered the raffle, encouraged a fat man to enter the wet t-shirt competition (he came in second) and Steve and I concocted a plan.

'I never thought I'd say this,' I said. 'But I really like it here.'

'It has a magnetic pull. There's just something about a

caravan. The freedom—'

'It's a static caravan.'

'I know, but it feels like you're on the road, doesn't it?'

'Not really.'

'And the people are just the salt of the earth, and the kids love it.'

'What about a boys' weekend?' I said.

'A boys' weekend at the caravan?'

'Yeah, why not? You, me and Party Time Pete. We'll have a blast!'

'And Mark?' said Steve.

'Maybe,' I said while inside I was thinking, definitely not.

'You know what, Harry, that's not such a bad idea,' said Steve.

Friday 31 May 4.42 p.m.

Mum has breast cancer.

June

Saturday 1 June 11.25 a.m.

At Mum and Dad's house.

'I'm fine,' said Mum for the twentieth time since I'd arrived. 'Honestly.'

'Mum, you have cancer,' I said. 'You aren't fine.'

We were sitting in the lounge. Mum and Dad were on the sofa holding hands. They came over last night, both looking incredibly solemn, and I knew my world was about to change. What I didn't know then was that it was about to come crashing down around me. Mum said she had breast cancer and I probably stood for a good minute before the tears came. I was in complete shock. Emily hugged me, and then Mum and Dad hugged me, while Mum tried to convince me it wasn't the end of the world.

'They did a mammogram and I'm going back in a couple of weeks for the results of the biopsy. We'll know more after that,' said Mum.

I came over first thing and we've been sitting around drinking tea ever since. Mum was putting a brave face on it (suddenly the best actress in the world) while Dad looked like me; pale, tired and scared. Terrified the love of his life was going to die.

'I should get lunch,' said Mum standing up. 'What shall we have? Fancy a sandwich, Harry? I have some of that lovely ham from the butcher on the high street. Oh, and there might be a pork pie in the fridge.'

'Mum, stop it, please,' I said, suddenly angry. 'Just stop it.'

'Stop what?'

'Pretending nothing's wrong.'

For the first time since I'd heard the worst news in the world, Mum's face wavered and changed. Her eyes glazed over with tears, but she quickly wiped them away.

'Did you stop to think that this is the only way I can cope? I'm not pretending nothing's wrong, Harry. I'm just trying to get through each day as best I can. You're scared, I know, but feeling sorry for myself isn't going to help. So how about that sandwich?'

'I'd love one,' I said with a guilty smile.

'Greg, sandwich?' Mum said to Dad.

'Please,' said Dad soberly.

Sunday 2 June 9.02 a.m.

Home. Eating breakfast with Emily. William asleep.

The past few days have been a blur. I got home from Mum and Dad's yesterday and held William for the longest time. Then after he went to bed I cuddled Emily on the sofa, my mind frazzled.

Emily ordered from The Spice of Wimbledon because neither of us fancied cooking. Steve popped over and tried to cheer me up with a song, which was nice of him. He did his best with the Queen classic Bohemian Rhapsody on the mellotron and even wore a Native American costume to add a bit of spice, but it didn't do the trick.

Since Mum's news, I've had every possible clichéd phrase thrown at me.

'Until we know all the facts, we need to stay positive' - Mum.

'She's a fighter' - Dad.

'Let's take it one day at a time' - Emily.

The truth is that as soon as I heard the word 'cancer', the only thought that came to mind was death. I wasn't thinking about the facts, how brave she was or taking it one day at a time. The only thing I could think was that my mum was going to die.

2.15 p.m.

Emily out running with Mark. William on the kitchen floor playing with pots and pans. V hot. The BBC weather girl has predicted the heat wave will continue for another week.

I'm not Catholic, but I have a confession:

When I was at secondary school there was a boy in my year called Daniel Broad. He was the captain of the football and cricket teams; handsome, intelligent, charismatic, funny - everyone wanted a piece of him. Even at fifteen, he was the sort of person that made you feel good about yourself. He was the most popular boy in the year and was the obvious choice when it came to picking a Head Boy. I knew him to say hello to and I wanted to be just like him. I tried to copy bits of him, from his clothes and his hairstyle to the way he acted, but looking back now, the thing no one could replicate was his innate Daniel Broad-ness. He had the mysterious X-factor.

I feel almost the same way about Mark. Mark has similar qualities to Daniel and it's why I'm feeling so insecure about Emily spending so much time with him. They jog together, he goes to her for advice, she's always talking about him, and he looks like Colin Firth. I can't help but feel a bit jealous. I wish I didn't, but I do.

5.00 p.m.

Emily is serving up a 'healthy' roast dinner, which means less of the good stuff (roast potatoes and Yorkshire pudding) and more of the not so delicious stuff (vegetables).

'How are things with Mark?' I said.

'He's still in a lot of emotional pain.'

'It must be hard.'

'Sophie is living with her parents in Oxford. Divorce is looking likely.'

'And what exactly was the issue again? The sexual issue?'

'I told him I wouldn't tell anyone. I don't want to betray his confidence.'

Seriously?

'I won't tell anyone, Em.'

'I can't.'

Fuckety fuck.

'I see how it is,' I said.

'And how is it?'

'Oh, never mind,' I said and stormed off.

Actually, I didn't storm off because I was laying the table. I did huff quite loudly though, and I put the knives and forks down with an exceedingly heavy bang. I need to find out the sexual reason why Sophie left. Then it dawned on me. I had to invite Mark to Camber Sands.

Monday 3 June 8.05 a.m.

Benzonimo

Hello mate. I am delighted to inform you that me, Emily and William will definitely be coming over in August and we can't wait. Emily is up for it and so you'd better book at least two weeks off work. The flight is booked and so there's no going back now.

Just to let you know because you've always been close to my family, Mum has breast cancer. She's doing okay. We're still waiting to hear back about the biopsy. Fingers crossed. I'll keep you updated.

Take care
Harrydini x

Wednesday 5 June 7.02 p.m.

I was mugged today. Well, technically I wasn't actually mugged, but I was the victim of an attempted mugging.

As part of my on-going initiative to staying healthy, I've been riding my bicycle to work. On my way home today, I got a puncture and so I was walking the bike when I was approached by two hooded youths. One of them told me to give him my wallet while the other one showed me the sharp edge of a knife and promised he'd fuck me up if I didn't hand it over.

My first thought was that I was going to die because I was trying to get healthy, and how ironic that was. Then I started thinking that I'd never really discussed what kind of funeral I'd like with Emily. Not that I have something particular in mind, but there's definitely certain songs I'd like to have played, maybe a photo montage, and I'm thinking everyone should wear white instead of black. Maybe they could do one of those flash mob things in the church and get it on YouTube. But then something happened. One of the youths looked at me and I recognised him.

'Andrew Burchill?'

'Shit, Mr Spencer, sorry, sir,' said Andrew looking as confused and shocked as me.

'And Alex Bernard?'

'Yeah, sorry, sir,' said Alex.

I had Andrew and Alex for History. They only left school last year and now they were trying to mug me.

'What are you doing?' I said.

'It's our first time,' said Andrew. 'Honest.'

'We wouldn't have fucked you up, sir. This ain't even a real knife, it's from the joke shop,' said Alex and he stabbed himself to prove it.

'Come with me,' I said.

'Don't take us to the police, sir, my dad will go mental,'

said Alex.

'We're not going to the police. We're going to that cafe. I'm going to get you both a cup of tea and you're going to tell me why the hell you're mugging people.'

'Yes, sir,' they both said, and we all trudged off to the cafe.

I sat them down, got us tea, and they explained why they were trying to mug me.

'It's tough, innit, sir,' said Alex. 'With the oconomies and all that, there ain't no jobs.'

'But that doesn't mean you can mug people. You do realise you could go to prison?'

'My cousins in prison,' said Andrew. 'He said it was all right. Got TV and that.'

'So you want to go to prison?' I said.

Andrew and Alex looked at each other and I suddenly thought how young they were.

'Well, no, sir, but what other choice is there?' said Andrew.

'There's every choice in the world,' I said, trying to sound inspiring. I was going to Steve Jobs them. 'You know for a moment there, when you had your fake knife pointed at me and I didn't know you were two ex-pupils, I realised I might die, and do you know what I thought about?'

'How dying isn't really dying at all, but just the beginning?' said Andrew.

'I'm an atheist,' I said.

'You don't believe in God?' said Alex.

'No.'

'Wow, that's mental. We go to church every Sunday,' said Alex.

'I'm Catholic,' said Andrew.

'And yet you tried to mug me. Anyway, the point is, I thought of my family and my legacy. You don't want your legacy to be that you spent time in prison, never had a job, and I assume you want to get married and have kids one day.'

'Been seeing Stella Mansbridge for six months, sir,' said Andrew.

'I've been with Claire Southall for over a year,' said Alex.

'And there you go. Life can be whatever you want. Don't blame other people or the economy.'

'Oconomies,' said Alex.

'Right, oconomies. Don't blame that. Go out and find a job, do anything and work your way up or go back to sixth form. I remember you were good at sport Alex, and you were excellent at English Lit Andrew. Don't throw your life away. Do something.'

Then something incredible happened. Alex started to cry and so did Andrew. They both broke down and told me about things they wouldn't mind doing and how they wished they'd gone to sixth form, but that they were going to try and do something positive, and they wouldn't let me down.

When I left them outside the cafe, they both shook my hand and promised me they'd stop the mugging. As I walked my bike home, I felt a great sense of accomplishment. Maybe I'd helped turn their lives around. Maybe I'd made a difference.

It was only as I started walking that I realised I'd pissed myself a little bit. It must have been because of the fear I felt when they said they were going to fuck me up.

Friday 7 June 7.42 p.m.

Over dinner, Emily announced that William is spending tomorrow night with her parents so we can have a night together.

'Have you warned them about the Nazi salute?' I said.

'Not yet. Do you think I should?'

'Maybe he won't do it.'

'I hope not.'
'So, us, a night in, it sounds exciting.'
'I have plans,' said Emily.
'Sounds even more exciting.'
'Just you wait.'
I can't wait.

Saturday 8 June 4.50 p.m.

Home alone with Emily. Derek and Pam just left with William. The house is strangely quiet.

I had a quick chat with William before he left. He was sitting in his car seat and Derek and Pam were inside talking to Emily.

'Listen buddy,' I said. 'You're going to stay with Grandma and Grandpa for the night. It's going to be fun, but there are two things you can't do. Don't speak Japanese because they won't understand you and don't do the Nazi salute. I realise you don't know what a Nazi salute is, you're only a baby, but it has certain connotations. And be a good boy for Daddy.'

William looked at me and then smiled. 'Goshinpai naku,' he said with a cheeky grin, and then Derek and Pam came out and he was gone, although as they were driving away, I saw him through the window, and he gave me a perfect, wonderful little wave - with no sign of the Nazi salute.

11.10 p.m.

We had a lovely dinner. Emily really pulled out all the stops and made a delicious beef wellington with gravy, mash and minted peas. We drank wine, talked and laughed. It was wonderful, but then Steve turned up. He needed a quick word. Emily let him in, and we had a chat in the lounge while Emily disappeared upstairs.

'Next weekend,' said Steve excitedly.

'What about it?

'The boys' weekend in Camber Sands. You in?'

'Of course. Did you ask Mark?'

'Not yet. I just got the okay from Fiona and came straight over here.'

'I think you should,' I said.

'Right, will do,' said Steve. 'And I was thinking board games, maybe a Risk marathon?'

'Steve, this is a boys' weekend away. We're going to be drinking and having a laugh, not, and I repeat not, playing Risk.'

'Chess?'

'No.'

'The Game of Life?'

'No.'

'Monopoly?'

'Definitely no.'

'Twister?'

'Steve, it's going to be two, possibly three men, together, in a small caravan, do you think Twister is a good idea, really?'

'How about I bring along a selection and we can see—'

'It's a no on the board games. Just go and ask Mark and see what he says.'

'Righto,' said Steve. 'OMG! I'm so excited!'

Emily came downstairs after Steve finally left. She told me to get upstairs and lie naked on the bed if I wanted some dessert. She got out the lotion and started a massage, but then the doorbell went again. I told her to ignore it because it was probably just Steve, but it rang again and again.

'I better get it. Don't go anywhere,' said Emily.

It was Mark and he really needed to talk. I was upstairs for nearly an hour when Emily finally came back to bed.

'He wants a word with you. Something about Camber Sands?' said Emily.

I got dressed and went downstairs.

'Mark,' I said. 'You all right?'

'Yes, of course, you know, difficult times and all that, but Em's been great.'

Em? Since when did he start calling her Em?

'She's a great listener,' I said trying to keep my head in a sexy place, but with every passing moment it just seemed to get further and further away.

'I'm in,' said Mark. 'Camber Sands sounds great. Just what I need at the moment.'

'Fantastic. You, me and Steve.'

'I'm not sure about the board games though, not really a board game fan.'

'There'll be no board games. That's just Steve. Once we get a few beers in him, he'll soon forget about the Risk marathon.'

'Bloody hope so,' said Mark. 'Nothing quite as depressing as three men sitting in a caravan playing Risk for ten hours straight.'

After Mark finally left I went back upstairs to resume dessert with Emily, but within five minutes her phone started buzzing furiously. Emily answered it and it was her mum. William wasn't going to sleep and was talking in a 'funny language'. Emily spent thirty minutes on the phone with them. By the time she came back to bed I was watching a repeat of Sherlock in bed.

'Sorry, do you still want to?' Emily said, but I could tell she wasn't really in the mood anymore.

'I think the moment's gone,' I said.

'Yeah,' said Emily and got in bed next to me, our romantic night alone in tatters. Still, it's like they say - it's the thought that counts.

Sunday 9 June 10.15 p.m.

Derek and Pam dropped off William and Pam said,

'I don't want to alarm you, but William did something strange last night.'

'What?' said Emily looking worried.

'Your father was watching a documentary about the Third Reich and William did ... oh I don't want to say.'

'Was it the Nazi salute?' I said.

'You know?' said Pam incredulously.

'It's how he waves,' said Emily. 'We're trying to wean him off it.'

'That's probably a good idea,' said Pam. 'You just don't expect to see a baby doing that sort of thing.'

I didn't mention the Japanese.

Monday 10 June 6.15 a.m.

I can't sleep. I've been up for the past hour thinking about Mum. William and Emily are still asleep. Today we get the results of the biopsy. Today we know what we're dealing with.

2.15 p.m.

At the pub. It's good news. The tumour hasn't spread beyond the breast, and they've caught it early. The doctor didn't want to give too much away, but he seemed pleased. The sort of cancer she has is called a Ductal Carcinoma, which is the best we could have hoped for, apparently. Mum needs to go in soon for surgery, followed by a course of radiotherapy. Her chances of a full recovery are very high.

Dad cried, Mum cried, and I cried, and then we came to the pub. The doctor went on to talk about the possible side-effects and risks, but my man-tention span kicked in at that point because all I could think was that Mum wasn't going to die. At least not for a while anyway - and knowing her, probably long after me.

It's funny that surgery followed by harsh radiotherapy that will make her sick and weak is suddenly good news. It wasn't that long ago that I was annoyed at her for cheating on Dad, but suddenly she's sick, and my mum, and I love her more than anything in the world.

9.15 p.m.

'Do you want to talk about your mum?' said Emily.

'Oh, no, it's okay, I'm fine.'

'You see, that's what I'm talking about.'

'What?'

'That, I'm fine-ness. You can't be fine because your mum has cancer, Harry. You need to talk about it and not bottle things up.'

'And I will talk about it, honestly, just not yet.'

'I'm here for you, Harry. Don't shut me out. I want to be a part of it.'

'Em, you are a part of it,' I said and gave her a kiss.

I know Emily just wants to help, but just having her here is enough. I know she wants to talk about it because that's what she would need if it was her mum, but I don't want to talk about it. It's easier to keep it inside, let it bubble away on its own where I can control it, rationalise it and protect it. If I start talking about it, if I let all the feelings out, who knows what will happen? It's a risk I'm not prepared to take.

Tuesday 11 June 6.15 p.m.

'Like this,' said Emily showing me the pictures from her magazine. You know the sort of magazine - lots of photos of beautiful houses that cost millions and make us feel bad because we still have the same crappy sofa we bought ten years ago and the peeling wallpaper in the bathroom. 'It's

Ben Fogle's house.'

'That posh, floppy haired fella who rowed across the Atlantic?'

'The gorgeous one, yeah.'

'Is he gorgeous?'

'Definitely, but not as gorgeous as his house. Look at this,' she said shoving the magazine in front of my face. It was gorgeous. It was the sort of house you just want to move into - Sorry Ben, good job on the decor old boy, but this is ours now, sling your hook and run across Africa for charity. 'Why can't our house look like that?'

'It could if we had more money.'

'But we could do things on the cheap. How about the floorboards? We've been meaning to do the floors for ages. We could do it ourselves. I was reading the other day about refinishing wooden floors. It didn't sound that hard.'

'Sure,' I said casually. Too casually apparently.

'What?' said Emily bullishly.

'What?'

'You said "sure" like, "sure, but we aren't actually going to do it".'

'Did I?'

'Yes, Harry, you did.'

'It's just, it's the sort of thing you're always going on about, but never actually do,' I said and straight away wished I hadn't. Her face immediately changed to that look of annoyance - of, 'I'm going to show you, you lazy, worthless piece of shit,' and, 'Why am I married to you and not Ben Fogle?'

'Just because it's something you can't do,' she spat. 'You shouldn't assume it's something I can't. Ben wouldn't do that.'

'Who's Ben?'

'Ben Fogle!' she shouted and stormed out of the room.

Wednesday 12 June 12.15 p.m.

Harry-zat!

I'm so happy! I can't even begin to tell you how excited I am to see you, Em and little Willy. You'd better get yourself ready because it's going to be the holiday of a lifetime!

I'm really sorry about your mum. Make sure you tell her I'm thinking of her. If it's any help, Katie's mum had breast cancer a few years ago and made a full recovery - she even runs marathons now! Miss you guys.

Speak soon you old bastard,
Ben-Nevis x
Ben-der

It is going to be brilliant. Good news about Mum. They caught the cancer early and it hasn't spread and so they're hopeful of a full recovery. She still has to have the surgery and radiotherapy, but it's looking good and apparently they want to go travelling when she's all better!

Take care
Hazza! X

8.45 p.m.

Home. Watching TV. Emily researching wood floors. William asleep.

I got home from work and Mark was over having a cup of tea and some homemade fruit cake. Apparently, it was an old family recipe, passed down through generations of Marks.

'The secret is dates. Would you like a slice, Harry?'

'No thanks,' I said. 'Still watching my weight.'

'And yet amazingly you still haven't lost any,' said Emily sarcastically.

Thursday 13 June 9.35 p.m.

'Sorry I've been in a mood about the floors and everything,' said Emily.

'The Ben Fogle stuff.'

'It isn't about Ben Fogle. It's about what he represents. Anyway, I'm sorry.'

'Why?'

'Because it isn't fair, is it? Just because I want something, it doesn't mean you have to jump to it. I'm not trying to change you. I love you just as you are.'

'But you'd prefer it if I was more like Ben Fogle?'

'And I'm sure you'd prefer it if I looked more like, I don't know …'

'The new BBC weather girl?'

'You like her?'

'She is very attractive and always gets the weather spot on. What's not to like?'

'Then I'll stop trying to change you.'

'But I want to change, Em,' I said. 'I mean, it's hard, but of course I want Ben Fogle's house, who wouldn't? And I know I'm lazy, but it doesn't mean I can't do better.'

'Fair enough.' There was a slightly awkward pause, until Emily said, 'So would it turn you on if I pretended to do the weather before sex?'

'It couldn't hurt.'

I sense an erection coming in from the West.

Saturday 15 June 9.35 a.m.

Packing for Camber Sands. William in the bath with Emily. Sunny.

I have no idea what this weekend is going to be like. I need to find out why Mark and Sophie broke up (something sexual?) and I need to stop Steve from forcing us to play Risk.

10.15 a.m.

William just said his first proper word! I was saying goodbye to him, and he looked at me and said, 'Bye.' He said it clearly and definitely, and without any hint of an Asian accent.

'Did you hear that?' I said to Emily.

'He said bye. Aww, his first proper word.'

'Bye, buddy,' I said. 'Bye.'

'Bye,' he said again.

My little man is growing up so fast.

7.15 p.m.

Camber Sands. Slightly drunk. Warm.

Mark drove and so we got to ride in the Mercedes. It was the smoothest journey I've ever had and unlike our car, it wasn't full of baby things: extra nappies, clothes, food, and general kid detritus. Our car often resembles the inside of a skip with all of William's stuff, and I've seen inside Steve's and it's even worse. It's also been a long time since I've been in a car without listening to The Wiggles. It was just me, Steve and Mark listening to Radio One and enjoying ourselves. I felt, for the first time in a while, a sense of freedom.

Once we got to Camber and settled in, the drinking started. We played cards (as a board game compromise), went to the beach, and now we're getting ready for the night. It's Saturday so it's disco night or as it's called here - Party Pete's Powerhouse!

I had a good chat with Steve this afternoon. His new career is really taking off. He has an agent and already has birthday parties booked all the way through to July. He's even getting ready for his first musical performance - he's playing a thirty-minute set at a shopping centre in Guildford. Steve the Entertainer is off and running. Luckily, the Kid Fiddler and Touched by Steve never got off the ground.

Sunday 16 June 1.45 a.m.

Back at the caravan. Steve is snoring like a trooper and cuddling his pillow. Mark is missing - presumed to be shagging the woman he was snogging at the Powerhouse.

Mark is a sex addict! He's a roaring perv who needs to have sex all the time and it tore his marriage apart. I managed to get this from him just before he went off and started snogging the most attractive woman at the Powerhouse (the competition wasn't that fierce). He told me how he can't help himself and it's like a powerful drug. I felt bad for him, but mostly I was thinking about how he's been spending all his time with Emily and confiding in her about his sexual addiction. It's no wonder Emily didn't want to say anything. I don't know how I feel about it. Obviously he has a problem and needs help, but I don't want him to shag Emily either.

8.15 a.m.

At a service station near Maidstone, Kent.

We were woken up by frantic knocking at the door. Steve was first up and clambering across the caravan. I woke up next. I looked at my watch and it was just past seven o'clock.

'What's going on?' I said.

'I don't know,' said Steve.

Steve opened the door and the banging suddenly turned into Mark who burst into the caravan, still half naked.

'We have to leave. NOW!' said Mark in a panic.

'I don't know what's going on,' said Steve. 'But we can't go anywhere.'

'Steve,' said Mark grabbing him by the shoulder. 'In a minute, a man is going to come to this caravan looking for me and when he does, he's going to kill me, and then he might kill you too. So I suggest we stop talking and start packing.'

We were all packed and in the car in less than four minutes, just as a large, bare-chested, tattooed man came charging towards us with a pair of nun chucks.

'Is that him?' said Steve.

'What gave it away, the nun chucks?' I said.

Mark put the Mercedes into gear and his foot down. We raced through the caravan park, the sight of the crazed, nun chucked maniac, slowly fading in the mirror. It wasn't until we reached the M20 that Mark eventually slowed down and he explained what had happened.

'The woman I ended up with last night,' said Mark. 'That was her husband.'

'She was married?' I said.

'I didn't know,' said Mark. 'She was at the caravan for her friend's hen weekend. I

didn't ask if she was married, but she wasn't wearing a ring and so I assumed she wasn't. I went back to her caravan last night, we did the business, but then this morning her phone starts buzzing, and it was her maniac husband. Apparently, he isn't the trusting sort.'

'I wonder why,' I said.

'So you did a runner?' said Steve.

'I tried, but he was outside and started chasing me. Fortunately, I lost him, but I knew it was only a matter of time before he found out where I was staying.'

'So that means he's still back at the caravan park and he knew where you were staying?' said Steve.

'Right,' said Mark and then it dawned on him. 'I'll pay for any damages.'

'Oh,' said Steve.

'The important thing is that we didn't get nun chucked,' I said.

We're currently having breakfast. It isn't exactly like the film The Hangover, but if you saw us, lined up at the cafe, looking rough, unwashed, and hungover, you might be forgiven for thinking it was.

11.15 a.m.

I got home to find Emily and Derek hard at work refinishing the hardwood floors in the hallway and lounge. William was off with Pam discovering the joys of the Natural History Museum. Derek is one of those annoying men that can do anything. Need a wall built? Ask Derek. Broken oven? Ask Derek. Need some bulkhead fittings for the butt hinges? I have no idea what this is but ask Derek. The man always makes me feel like an incompetent fool and today was no different. As soon as I walked in, he looked at me and said, 'Man's work, Harry, keep out of the way.' I didn't get much better from Emily. 'Move along, Spencer, hard work in progress. Something you know nothing about.' I retreated to the bedroom.

9.45 p.m.

I confronted Emily about Mark being a sex addict and she tried to brush it off as though it wasn't a big deal. As though my wife spending all of her time with a handsome sex addict is perfectly natural and I have absolutely no reason to be jealous or insecure about it. Apparently, he just needs someone, and Emily wants to help, although when I asked how exactly she planned on helping him, she called me a facetious knob.

Monday 17 June 9.35 p.m.

Emily and Derek finished the wood floors today. I got home from work, and they were just clearing up and I made the mistake of asking if I could help.

'Oh, now he wants to help,' said Derek.

'You can put the kettle on,' said Emily.

William was out with Pam and so I was demoted to chief tea maker, grease monkey and work experience boy. The good news is that the floors look brilliant. I think even Ben Fogle would be proud.

Tuesday 18 June 4.35 p.m.

I spoke with Dad today. They've scheduled Mum's operation for Tuesday July 16th. I asked how Mum was doing and Dad tossed me the usual bones. She's scared but strong. You know your mother. Then he announced that when she's all better they're going interrailing around Europe. Ladies and gentlemen, my parents - the backpackers!

Thursday 20 June 4.35 p.m.

I had my last management training session with Colin Thistle today.

'I want us to really move floors,' said Colin enthusiastically while rain hammered against the portacabin's roof. 'It's our last session together and I really want us to, you know, brainstorm the big ideas.'

'And what are we doing today?' said Irish Joyce from Raynes Park.

'Ah,' said Colin. 'This is the good bit. I thought it would

be fun to give you guys the ropes!' This was ominous for poor Colin. The last time he gave us some freedom, we spent the day in the pub.

'What do you mean?' said Warren.

'I mean exactly what I said. You guys are the leaders. This is management training and so I'm going to let you guys manage. Let's see what you're made of. Time for some big balls!' said Colin, sitting back confidently in his chair.

After an hour of relative silence while people checked their phones, ate the 'continental style' buffet, drank the watery coffee and gossiped about EastEnders, Colin had reached breaking point.

'What's wrong with you people?' he shouted. 'You're supposed to be management!'

'And you're supposed to be training us,' said Warren.

'I am training you. This is a very effective method of training from Denmark called self-training.'

'It's a bit of a cop-out though, isn't it?' said Warren. 'Imagine if I went into my classroom and said to the kids, right, today you're teaching yourself. It would be chaos.'

'But they're kids, Warren. You're grown-ups. I did this same thing last week at a bank in the city and they were fantastic. They really took it—'

'To the next level?' I said.

'Exactly,' said Colin.

'So you don't usually train teachers?' said Jenny from Twickenham.

'I do all sorts, Jenny. Corporate usually.'

'Well there's your problem right there,' said Warren. 'We're teachers. We wouldn't survive two seconds in the corporate world. We're different animals, Colin. You give a suit the chance to shout at someone and they'll bite your hand off. Give a teacher the same opportunity and they'll more than likely find a good reason not to shout at them. Our lives are constantly being shaped by politicians with no idea what we do and what our pupils actually need. We're at the mercy of the suits, and so the last thing we need is someone else shouting at us and telling us what to do.'

'Oh,' said Colin. 'Is that how you all feel?'

We all nodded, and the rest of the day turned into a bit of a therapy session. Colin was in tears at one point and then he really did take it to the next level.

'I'm gay!' announced Colin. 'There, I said it. I've been having some doubts and I haven't even told my parents yet, but hearing your stories today, you've inspired me. I'm gay and proud!' said Colin standing up and we all started clapping.

The outcome of the management training course was that we learnt nothing about management or leadership, but Colin leapt from the closet and is now a proud homosexual.

6.25 p.m.

William is crawling around the house saying, 'Bye,' to everything and everyone that will listen. I'm trying to get him to say other words too.

'Say "Daddy", William. Say "Daddy".'

'Bye,' said William.

'William, say "Mummy". "Mummy".'

'Bye. Bye. Bye.'

'Say "bye", William, say "bye".'

Silence.

Friday 21 June 12.45 p.m.

Miss Patagonia is sick and so apparently, I have to teach sex education this afternoon. I'm dreading it.

4.15 p.m.

Sex education was going fine until it came to the Q&A portion. I purposely left only ten minutes for questions just in case my worst fears came true.

I asked if there were any questions and literally every hand in the room shot up.

Here's a selection:

It says in the toilets that Mark Packham has knob rot, sir. Is it catching?

Is it true the G-Spot is up the bum?

Can you get pregnant swallowing semen?

Answer: No Claire, you cannot.

If you can't get pregnant, why won't my girlfriend swallow my spunk?

Answer: I don't know Sean.

Is semen supposed to taste like gone off fish fingers?

Answer: I don't know Claire, probably not.

Why do vaginas taste manky?

Answer: I don't know Sean.

Sir, please tell Sean he's dumped.

Answer: That isn't a sex education question, Claire, although I think you and Sean have some talking to do after the lesson. Any further questions on sex education?

It says on the toilet door that you're gay, sir. Is that true?

Answer: No, I'm not gay. I'm married.

It also says in the toilets that you're married to a man.

Answer: I'm not married to a man.

How many times have you had sex, sir because I've done it at least eight times?

Answer: That's none of your business.

Luckily the bell went, and I got out of there before my entire sexual history was dissected. That's the last time I do sex education - especially when I'm not currently getting any and apparently my pupils are. Although by the heated discussion Claire and Sean had in the corridor afterwards, I don't think he will be for a while.

Saturday 22 June 4.35 p.m.

I went to see Mum today. Dad was out and so we got the chance to have a proper chat.

'How are you feeling?'

'Can't complain,' said Mum.

'I don't want the Mum answer, I want the real one. How are you?'

'I'm, you know, as good as can be expected.'

'That's what you're giving me? "As good as can be expected"? I know we're English Mum, but for once can you please just tell me how you're actually feeling?'

'I'm fucking scared, is that what you want me to say?' said Mum, who never swears.

'Thank you,' I said with a smile and Mum's eyes glazed over with tears.

'You want me to be scared?'

'Of course I do. It's terrifying. I'm scared. Dads scared. I'd be pretty pissed off if the only one not scared was you,' I said and Mum sort of laughed and then sniffed.

'I suppose you're right. But you know something?'

'What?'

'A part of me is sort of glad it happened.'

'What?' I said incredulously.

'Before the cancer your father and I were heading towards retirement with sadness and boredom. Then, of course, there was Larry, and your father moving out, but now we're back together and it's like we're twenty-one again. We're talking and having sex.'

'That's enough details.'

'Oh, stop being such a prude. We're going to go travelling when I'm all better and I'm excited, Harry. Maybe it took something this big for us both to see life in a different way and yes it's scary, I'm terrified, but we're finally living Harry and we're happy.'

'Then I'm glad too.'

'It doesn't mean I'm not scared shitless about the operation though.'

'Dad and I will be there for you every step of the way,' I said, and I gave her a long hug, before Dad got back and made us all lunch.

It sounds crazy, but Mum's right. I'm not glad she's got breast cancer and that she still has to go through radiotherapy, but I feel close to both my parents in a way I haven't ever felt before and I like it. I like that we're actually talking and that whatever happens, whatever the outcome, I know we're a better family because of it.

Friday 28 June 3.35 p.m.

At school. We just had our pre-meeting meeting about the upcoming exams in July. We're about to have the actual meeting and I'm dreading it. Norris Roker (Maths) is the timekeeper and Rokers loves a good meeting. The timekeeper's job is to keep the meeting moving forward. Unfortunately, I think this might go down in the Guinness Book of World Records as one of the longest meetings in history.

6.00 p.m.

That was brutal. Rokers was on top form. Even by his standards that was a particularly long and dull meeting. Even the teachers who usually quite like to go on a bit started moaning and groaning and Mr Hecklesford (Science) dozed off and had to be woken up. Off home.

6.45 p.m.

Seething. I was about to pull into our driveway when I saw Sophie walk out of Mark's house. I haven't seen her since she left Mark back in May. She looked across and smiled and so I got off my bicycle and walked over.

'Hello,' I said. 'How are you?'

'Not great, Harry. I had to come and see Mark.'

'Oh, things not going to work out?'

'I assume he hasn't told you everything.'

'I heard a rumour, but nothing more,' I said playing it cool. Maybe she was going to give me all the juicy details that I'm sure Emily already knows but seems unwilling to share.

'Affairs and one night stands galore,' she said. 'The man is a pervert, Harry. I wouldn't trust him around Emily if I were you. He can't keep his penis in his pants.'

'You don't think he'd try anything on with Emily though, do you?' I said, and Sophie suddenly looked a bit awkward, and she stiffened up. 'What?'

'You don't know, do you?' she said.

'Know what?'

'I shouldn't be the one to tell you, Harry. Ask Emily.'

Sophie said goodbye and I was left speechless. I'm waiting for William to go to bed and then I'm going to talk to Emily.

8.35 p.m.

'What happened with Mark?' I said when Emily came downstairs after putting William to bed.

'Excuse me?'

'I saw Sophie outside earlier and she said I should ask you about Mark. She made it seem like something happened between you.'

'I told you, Harry, nothing happened. Will you drop it, please,' said Emily walking off towards the kitchen with William's stinky nappy.

'I guess I'll go and ask Mark then,' I said grabbing my jacket.

'What? Seriously, Harry, it was nothing.'

'So something did happen?'

'It was nothing,' said Emily looking a bit flushed. 'It was right after Sophie had moved out and he was feeling a bit vulnerable. I gave him a hug and he obviously got the wrong end of the stick and tried to kiss me—'

'What?! He kissed you?'

'A peck on the lips. I stopped it right away.'

'Then why didn't you tell me?'

'Because I was afraid you'd react like this.'

'Like what?'

'Shouting and ranting about it.'

'But he tried to seduce you, Em, even Sophie knew about it. Hang on, why does she even know about it?'

'Because she walked in on us.'

'And if she hadn't?'

'Harry,' said Emily, but that's when it happened.

I lost it.

9.45 p.m.

In the shed. Drinking Scotch. Possibly with a broken hand. Emily in bed.

I raced across to Mark's house and rang the doorbell again and again. Emily wasn't far behind me, telling me to calm down, come home and stop being so bloody melodramatic. I didn't care though. I was tired of Mark. I was tired of being fine with her spending all her spare time with a sex addict. I was tired of feeling inferior and being afraid. I wasn't afraid anymore.

Mark opened the door and as soon as he did, I swung. I've never actually hit someone before. I've seen it on TV, and it doesn't look that hard. You swing and hit them in the face, they go down and you shout a pithy remark. This was the vision I had in my head.

I swung, but for some reason I closed my eyes and instead of making contact with Mark's face, I missed him completely and made a very good connection with the door frame.

'Fuck!' I screamed.

'What's going on?' said Mark.

'You bloody idiot,' said Emily.

'You filthy pervert, you stay away from my … ow … that really fucking hurt … I think I've broken my hand … wife!' I yelled.

'Listen, Harry,' said Mark.

'No, you listen, Mark. I don't care that you've got a disease, if indeed being a pervert is a disease. I don't care that your wife left you but stay the fuck away from mine!'

'For fuck's sake, Harry,' said Emily behind me. 'What's the matter with you? I can speak for myself.'

'Stay out of this, Em. This has got nothing to do with you,' I said.

'Oh, really?' said Emily. 'This has nothing to do with me?'

I turned and looked at Emily and she looked really angry.

'No. This is between me and him,' I said jabbing a finger at Mark. 'The perv.'

'Now steady on,' said Mark.

'Harry, remember your New Year's resolution?'

'Yeah, so?'

'Not to do anything really fucking stupid?' said Emily. 'Well congratulations, you've just broken that. I'm going home and don't think about joining me in the bedroom.'

And then she stormed off home.

'How's the hand?" said Mark.

'And you can fuck off!' I said and went after Emily.

Saturday 29 June 8.35 a.m.

Grandad died a year ago today. We're going to the church to lay flowers on his grave. Things are still strained with Emily, and she's gone to see Stella in Kingston-upon-

Thames. I'm trying not to think about it. Today's all about Grandad.

3.45 p.m.

What an emotional day. Mum and Dad met us at the church, along with Audrey, Grandad's wife. I feel so sorry for her. They were only married for a matter of weeks when he died. I haven't seen much of her since his death, but it's difficult going back to the home and I didn't really know her that well. The only thing we had in common was Grandad.

Mum brought a picnic and so we sat on a blanket and told stories about Grandad. The sun was shining, and it was a really nice day. Not a day goes by when I don't think about him. He made me smile and laugh more than anyone I've ever known. It was nice to have William there as well and to see Mum and Dad playing with him.

Sunday 30 June 10.45 a.m.

Home alone. Emily and William at her parents' house. Drinking. Smoking. Listening to the Robbie Williams song Angels on repeat. Cloudy.

'Can we talk?' said Emily this morning.

We were having breakfast and William was still asleep. I knew this conversation was coming. I'm of the disposition that if there's a problem, the best way to deal with it is to leave it alone until eventually it sorts itself out. It may sound like the lazy approach and maybe it is, but it works. Emily, on the other hand, thinks that the only way to deal with a situation is to talk the crap out of it until A: It's sorted out or B: Talking about it has made you so emotionally drained you'll agree to anything, just so you don't have to keep talking about it.

This was different though. Emily didn't want a chat; a debate where we'd agree to disagree on certain things and find common ground where we could. This wasn't going to end with an apology, a kiss, a cuddle, and then in a few days be forgotten. I could see it on her face. This was bad.

'Sure,' I said looking at Emily. My wife. The woman I loved more than anything. The woman I kept pissing off because I have this amazing ability to push self-destruct when things are going well.

'William and I are going to stay with Mum and Dad for a few days,' said Emily. 'They just got back from Tenerife, and I think we could do with a few days apart.'

'No,' I said without even thinking.

'Sorry?'

'I said no, Em. You don't get to leave when things aren't going well. You don't get to take William away because you're pissed off with me.'

'I'm more than pissed off, Harry. You don't even realise, do you?'

'Realise what?'

'What you did with Mark. It was embarrassing, it was childish and immature. You obviously don't trust me - you don't think much of our marriage, and you sure as hell don't think much of me.'

'Wait a minute, Em. You and Mark did kiss. I had every reason to be pissed off.'

'No, Harry, you had every right to be annoyed, but you didn't have the right to do what you did. Mark was hurting, he made a mistake, he didn't deserve you going over there and trying to punch his lights out.'

'And that didn't exactly go to plan, did it?'

'I just feel that when it comes down to it you always let me down. No matter how far I think you've come, when I think I'm working with Harry 2.0 or Harry bloody Vista, when the shit hits the fan, you revert back to factory settings. Harry 97.'

'I prefer Harry classic.'

'It's not a fucking joke! I'm tired of it.'

'Or maybe you're just looking for an easy way out so you can be with him?' I said and that changed everything. Her face went quickly through the gears of emotions; shock, horror, anger, resentment, incredulousness, realisation and then finally loathing. She looked at me and then said she was going to pack their things.

I gave William a long cuddle and kiss goodbye before I strapped him into his car seat. He waved and said bye and I came back into the house and cried because for the first time, I imagined a future where Emily and I weren't together. When I only saw fleeting glimpses of William's life between Happy Meals on Saturday afternoons with all the other part-time dads. He'd grow up and get a new dad and before long he wouldn't want to see me because he'd be too busy with his own life, and I wouldn't know him. My own son.

4.45 p.m.

Maybe Emily's right. Maybe I can't change. Maybe I'm always destined to let her down. Maybe we just aren't meant to be together. Maybe she's meant to be with someone like Mark. He's a proper grown-up, with a well-paid job, with a Mercedes, with his Colin Firth-ness and running before work and his posh accent. I hate Mark. I hate myself. I love Emily.

5.55 p.m.

Is this a bad idea? Probably, but I'm going to do it anyway. I don't care anymore.

6.05 p.m.

I just threw a stone through Mark's Mercedes windscreen. The alarm went off straight away and I heard Mark's front door, but I was already running back across the road. I slammed my front door, turned the lights off, and I'm sitting in the lounge in the dark. That will teach him to mess with my wife. I think I'm a bit drunk.

July

Monday 1 July 7.45 a.m.

Home alone. Emily and William at her parents in Buckinghamshire. Gloomy and wet.

Mark came over last night, banging on the door and shouting that he knew I was there and that he just wanted to talk. I hid in the kitchen and then spent the rest of the night drinking and smoking heavily. Emily's right, when the shit hits the fan, I always revert back to Harry '97 and it isn't classic, it's just a bit shit.

Off to school. Thank goodness there's only three weeks left. I'm not sure I can be Head of Department again. I don't want to end up like Eddie Collins, face down in a pool of my own vomit outside Toys 'R' Us.

6.15 p.m.

I just tried to call Emily, but all I got was Derek.

'Is she there?'

'You know she is, Harry, but she doesn't want to speak to you.'

'But Derek, I need to talk to her, it's important.'

'And when she's ready, she'll call you. I don't know what you've done this time, but she's really upset. Maybe just stay away.'

'Oh, you'd like that wouldn't you?' I said losing my temper.

'Excuse me?'

'You'd like it if I stayed away forever, wouldn't you, Derek? You've never liked me, admit it?' Derek seemed a bit shocked. I was shocked myself, but the sullen silence didn't last very long. The old Derek quickly reared its ugly head.

'Listen to me you snivelling little shit,' said Derek. 'All I want is for Emily to be happy, taken care of and treated properly. If you can't do that and it's obvious you have problems, then I'm more than happy to do it myself until she finds a man who can. Do I make myself clear?'

'Crystal,' I said limply, and Derek hung up.

I fear I might be out of the family circle.

Once again, I find myself alone. I miss Emily and William. I miss hearing his little voice, watching him crawl around the house trying to break into cupboards, and I miss holding him. Off to the shed to drink, smoke and eat something fried and fatty. It's ironic that when things were going well, I just wanted unhealthy snacks, cigarettes and alcohol, but now I've fucked everything up, I'd give it all up in an instant to have Emily and William back.

Wednesday 3 July 8.45 p.m.

Home (still alone). Cloudy. Emily and William in Bucks. Drinking.

Mark came over again tonight and as much as I didn't want to talk to him, I couldn't keep ignoring him forever. I did keep the chain on the door though just in case he wanted to punch me. Despite despising him and his public-school face, I had the feeling that in a straight, old fashioned, school playground fight, I wouldn't stand a chance.

'Open the bloody door, Harry. I just want to talk,' said Mark all buddy buddy. I didn't trust him though. He was probably trying to lure me in and then once inside he was going to beat the crap out of me with his old school cricket bat.

'Sorry, I can't,' I said. 'What do you want?'

'I know it was you who smashed my car windscreen, Harry, admit it.'

'Admit you want to fuck my wife first!' I yelled back.

'Fine. I want to fuck Emily, happy?'

'No!' I yelled again. 'You can't fuck my wife.'

'I don't care. I'm going to fuck her and there's nothing you can do about it. That's right, Harry. Why do you think she's been spending so much time with me?'

'Because she's nice and she was trying to help you.'

'Or maybe because she wants to fuck me too. Come on, Harry, look at you and look at me. Who do you think she's going to choose? I like her, Harry, a lot, and I know she likes me too.'

'You'd better keep your hands off her.'

'I'm seeing her on Friday. We have a date,' said Mark.

'Touch Emily and I'll …'

'You'll what?' said Mark and the truth was, I didn't know. Drink myself into oblivion? Cry? Listen to a James Blunt album? 'Yeah, that's what I thought.'

Then Mark left, and I immediately called Emily to warn her about him, but all I got was Pam and she wouldn't let me talk to Emily. I told Pam to tell Emily that Mark was a snake in the grass, and he wanted to break us up. Pam asked if Mark was the dashing Mr Darcy who'd popped by in his Mercedes to check that she was okay. I said it was him and that he isn't Mr Darcy, but Dirty Den. Pam said she wouldn't chuck him out of bed. Fantastic.

Thursday 4 July 8.05 a.m.

American Independence Day. Sunny. History exams in the main hall start on Monday. I'm supposed to be overseeing them as my role of AHOD/ASM continues to cause me great swathes of pain in the very darkest chasms of my bottom.

I dread school at the moment. As AHOD I have my usual pre-meeting meetings, my actual meetings and now I have meetings about the exams, pre-meetings about the exams, meetings about the looming end of year, pre-meetings about the end of year school dance and then the actual meetings about the end of school dance/excuse for pupils who are leaving to harass us and tell us what they really think about us/excuse for teachers to tell the pupils who are leaving what they really think of them/excuse for pupils who are leaving to try and sneak in alcohol and think they've won because Alan Parry will sneak in a bottle of his mum's vodka and then they'll end the night throwing up in the toilets.

Call me a curmudgeonly old bugger, but I hate the end of year school dance. We didn't have them in my day, and we were perfectly fine. You finished school and then you left, we didn't need a dance to pretend that school actually meant something. Bloody Americans once again spoiling what should have been the end of something. Why can't things just end anymore? Why do we have to celebrate everything? Why do we have to watch as a hundred sixteen-year-olds get dressed up, so the girls suddenly look about twenty-one and a bit shaggable and the boys look like they raided their dad's wardrobe blindfolded? I'll be forced to spend the evening pretending I care whether they're drinking alcohol or not (I don't), while Alan Hughes tells me which girls he'll probably shag in a few years' time. Depressing doesn't do it justice.

12.35 p.m.

I have a supply teacher taking my classes this afternoon because I have too many meetings to attend. First up I have the pre-meeting for exams, then the pre-meeting for the end of year dance, then the actual end of year dance meeting, followed by the actual exam meeting. Then I have my usual HOD meeting and finally I have a meeting with Mr Jones about a new departmental stability continuity and flexibility management training program (DSCFMTP). I have no idea what this is, but it sounds monumentally shit. Off to smoke ten cigarettes very quickly.

6.15 p.m.

Finally home. I grabbed a KFC bucket, a six pack of beer, and twenty cigarettes on the way home. I'm going to sit in the lounge, in my underwear, watch television, eat my bucket, smoke my cigarettes, drink my beer, and I don't care who knows about it.

8.30 p.m.

Disaster. I had just settled into the lounge with my bucket, my cigarettes, and my beer when all of a sudden Emily came waltzing in. Obviously it didn't look good.

'What the fuck's going on?' said Emily looking down at me incredulously.

'Oh, Em,' I said getting up. I was standing in just my underwear, a greasy face from the chicken and a cigarette on the go. 'It isn't what it looks like,' I said, even though quite clearly it was exactly what it looked like.

'What's wrong with you?' said Emily and then she left, slamming the door behind her. I tried to quickly put on some clothes and follow her outside, but by the time I got out there she was pulling away in the car. Then I noticed Mark looking across at me with a smile. The bastard.

Friday 5 July 4.15 p.m.

At home. Still very much alone. Emily seeing Mark tonight. Can I just sit around and wait for my marriage to fall apart?

4.25 p.m.

No. I'm going to do something. I don't know what exactly. Off to do something.

5.15 p.m.

Sitting in Steve's people carrier. He's letting me borrow

it so I can go off and save my marriage from the evil that is Mark. Steve asked if I wanted to borrow a disguise. I asked what for and he said, just in case. I said I didn't understand how sitting in his car with a fake moustache, glasses and a wig was going to help. He offered me his Steve the Sheep costume instead. I declined. Fingers crossed. Deep breaths.

10.25 p.m.

Fuck. Fuckety, fuckety, fuck. I am doomed. Whatever I do it always seems to blow up in my stupid face and I end up looking like a mental, immature, emotionally redundant fuckwit - Emily's words, not mine.

I sped to Buckinghamshire to intercept Emily's date with Mark. I pulled up opposite her parents' house, just as Mark and Emily were walking out. Then suddenly Derek and Pam walked out too, and Pam was carrying William. I haven't seen the little fella all week and so I was a bit emotional, but then Derek and Mark were laughing, and Derek was shaking his hand and patting him on the back like they were old chums.

I hadn't intended to follow them, but I didn't want to cause a scene in front of William and so I waited until Mark and Emily (who was looking gorgeous in a blue dress - a new dress?) got into the Mercedes and drove away. I popped the people carrier into gear and followed them.

They were having dinner at a fancy, upmarket French place (typical Mark - the bastard). I waited until they were inside and then parked the van. I didn't know what I was going to do. I was now technically a stalker. Maybe it would be best to just sit tight and see what went down before I did anything. The last thing I needed was Emily to think I was more of an idiot loser than she already did. Plus, I've watched enough American cop shows to know how these things work. The element of surprise is crucial.

I skulked around outside while they were seated, ordered food and a bottle of wine. They were talking, laughing and seemingly having a brilliant time. It looked like a date. It was hard to watch, mainly because I was trying to peek through the window and people kept getting in my way, but also because it was Emily - my wife. Could she really leave me for Mark? Then something happened. Mark reached across and held her hand. Mark was holding her hand. I'd had enough. I ran inside, pushing past waiters and other customers until I was at their table.

'Harry!' said Emily incredulously.

'Get your hands off my wife, you pervert!' I shouted at Mark.

He was still holding her hand. I looked down and Emily quickly pulled her hand away.

'Now look here,' said Mark standing up in front of me, all Colin Firth-esque. 'I don't know what you think's going on here.'

I don't know what came over me (raging jealousy, probably) but I swung and this time I hit him. I hit Mark square on the nose, and he went down like a sack of spuds, blood streaming from his nose. There was an ooh and an argh from the watching crowd, but the only person I was looking at was Emily. She looked really angry.

'Harry, I can't believe you!' she screamed kneeling down to make sure Mark was all right. 'You're such a mental, immature, emotionally redundant fuckwit sometimes.'

Mark was prostrate on the floor, while waiters were trying to help him up, and then I felt a hand on my shoulder. I turned around and saw Mr Jones - my Head Teacher.

'Come with me, Harry,' said Mr Jones.

'Oh, right,' I whimpered.

I looked down at Mark one last time. Emily was mopping up the blood with a napkin and then Mark looked at me and smiled. A horrible, smug bastard looking smile. I had done exactly what he wanted me to do. I was a knob and Mark was still a God. Brilliant.

I went with Mr Jones, and he took me to a pub across

the road and bought me a pint. We sat down, and he asked me what was going on.

'I'm sorry,' I said. 'I'm having some marriage problems.'

'I hope it's nothing to do with your new role at school, Harry. I know it can be difficult. Look at what happened to Eddie.'

'No, it isn't that. I just think I'm a bit of an idiot sometimes.'

'Ah, yes, I know the feeling myself.'

'Oh, yeah.'

'I was divorced the beginning of last year. It was why I ended up moving to Wimbledon. I had to get away.'

'Sorry to hear that.'

'It's fine, we're better off apart. I loved her, Harry, but we just ended up making each other bloody miserable if I'm honest. She's with someone new and I'm enjoying life in London. I'm dating a photographer from Bethnal Green - she's in her forties, Harry and very sexual. Sometimes it's just better to move on.'

'You think I should move on?' I said, feeling a lump slide down my throat.

'If you think it's for the best. If you really think you'll both be better off apart, then maybe, but if there's a chance it can work you have to give it a bash.' I nodded back. 'I'd better get back to the restaurant. I left my sister in there alone. She's the reason I'm here, but lucky I was, eh?'

'Definitely,' I said. 'And thank you.'

'Just remember, teaching's only a job, an important one, but still just a job.'

Mr Jones left, and I finished my pint before I drove back to Wimbledon alone. I have a lot of thinking to do. Could my marriage really be over? Will Mark bang Emily? Why did Mr Jones tell me he's dating a nymphomaniac from Bethnal Green? As always, there are more questions than answers.

Saturday 6 July 9.05 a.m.

I was woken up by the front door this morning. It was just after eight o'clock and I was barely awake after not going to bed until nearly three o'clock. I was up all night trying to understand where everything had gone wrong and if Emily and I still had a shot at saving our marriage.

'Tea or coffee?' said Emily poking her head around the bedroom door.

I was incredulous. She was the last person I expected to see in the bedroom this

early in the morning. I would have bet on anyone except Emily. My parents, Rory, Steve, Ben Fogle even, but definitely not Emily.

'Coffee please,' I said tentatively.

'Right,' said Emily and then she disappeared downstairs.

I quickly put on some clothes and followed her downstairs and into the kitchen. I didn't know what she wanted, what she was going to say, but I knew this was important. I knew that despite it being so bloody early and that I was tired, a little hungover and had the bedhead from hell, I knew this conversation could define the rest of my life.

'I didn't expect to see you so soon,' I said when Emily passed me my coffee.

'Nor did I,' said Emily. 'But, as it turns out, you were right about Mark. He was just trying to shag me.'

'I fucking knew it!' I said a bit too eagerly.

'You still shouldn't have followed us to the restaurant and punched him though.'

'I know, sorry about that.'

'It's okay, he probably deserved it.'

'So where does that leave us?' I asked hopefully.

'That's why I'm here,' said Emily.

Then she talked. For a long time. She told me how

disappointed she was in me. How after everything that's happened and being a father, she expected so much more from me. How for the first time she had wondered whether our marriage was going to last. How she didn't understand why I couldn't seem to grow up. She said a lot (mainly bad) and then she finished with this:

'But I agreed to marry you, Harry, for better or worse, for richer or poorer and I meant it. I'm going to give us one last shot. I mean it. I can't keep going through this every six months. This is it. You're in the last chance saloon.'

'I won't let you down,' I said.

'You'd better not. Oh, and we're going to see Deirdre St Cloud for marriage therapy. We start next week.'

'Now hang on a minute,' I said, but it was too late.

'I have to go and pick up William,' said Emily. 'See you when I get back.'

I had one last chance and the fate of my marriage depended on the nutter that was Deirdre St Cloud. The same therapist we went to last year after my almost but not quite affair with Jamie, and who nearly ended my marriage. Now it was up to her to put it back together again. It's like entrusting a suicide bomber to rebuild the building they had blown up.

Sunday 7 July 3.05 p.m.

Sunny. In the shed. Squirrels frolicking in the garden. Emily making a roast. William napping.

Today has been brilliant. Things with Emily are still a bit weird. She's back, but it's obvious she's still in a bit of a mood about Mark. No sign of him today. I spent the morning with William, which was fantastic after being apart all week. Steve popped over with the Js and we played in the garden. A lovely morning and now a roast to follow. I hope Emily has forgotten about the diet and makes lots of lovely roast potatoes and maybe even Yorkshire puddings. I wait with hope. Tidying the shed.

4.45 p.m.

We had roast beef, Yorkshire puddings and roast potatoes. It was gorgeous. William tried some mashed-up potatoes, carrots and had a little bit of gravy. He loved it, but then he wanted to try some of my English mustard. I told him it was spicy, but he kept pointing at it and so I gave him the smallest amount. You should have seen his face. Emily and I laughed while William continued to squirm and try to rub his tongue clean. It was so nice to be smiling and laughing with my family. I'm not going to mess this up again.

Monday 8 July 4.05 p.m.

We had exams today. Everything went well. I spent the morning facilitating. No sign of any cheating, although I did spot Gary Satchel looking around with a confused expression for a moment. I went over and asked him if everything was all right. He said he needed to go to the toilet and so I had to escort him to the loo - never a fun job, especially as Gary needed to do a particularly bad poo. It made William's poos seem relatively tame. I had to cover my nose while I waited outside his cubicle. He skulked out and told me he was just nervous. Gary Satchel's nerves smell like hell. Being trapped in the toilet with him was tantamount to chemical warfare. I may need to contact NATO.

Tuesday 9 July 4.45 p.m.

Second day of exams and high drama this morning. Just as the kids were sitting down the fire alarm went off. Some of the pupils cheered and some huffed and complained, but we all had to go and stand outside on the playground. Samantha Chesterton (an unfortunate name for a teenage girl with large breasts) and Phil Cox both told me they thought the distraction would harm their chances of doing well on the exam. I politely told them that it wasn't the fire alarm that would hinder them, but the four years of messing about, not paying attention in class, and the fact neither of them probably did any revision.

While we were milling around, I did have the chance to talk to a few of my better pupils. I was stood around with Claire Sutherland, Pippa Fielding and Jack Rudge, three of my best students who will no doubt go on to university and do great things. They're a good bunch of kids and it gives me hope for William. Sometimes when I see the children from broken homes, the kids who I know don't give a toss about school and who spend their free time vandalising playgrounds, I worry about the future and the life William is going to have. Then when I talk to kids like Claire, Pippa and Jack, who are respectful, bright, intelligent and funny, I know there's hope for William. Then, of course, he might end up like Gary Satchel - he of the dirty bottom.

5.00 p.m.

Rory popped by my classroom when I was tidying up at the end of the day. He looked a lot happier than I've seen him recently.

'How are you?' I said.

'Never better,' said Rory.

'Oh, and why's that?'

'Just things with Miranda, they've improved.'

'And what does that mean?'

'We've reached an agreement about the amount of sex

we've been having.'

'She's stopped treating you as a walking sperm bank then?'

'She's calmed down about the whole thing. We're finally on the same page. It will happen when it happens and if it doesn't, we will cross that bridge when we come to it.'

'So the Bon Jovi quote worked then? She's keeping the faith?'

'Something like that, but we're happy and my penis isn't red raw.'

'I'm happy for you, mate.'

'Thanks, and how about you?'

This was a good question. The truth was my life was as complicated as always. I wasn't sure how things were going to end with Emily, although I did know we were going to see Deirdre St Cloud. Mum was going to have surgery next week and I definitely didn't want to be HOD next year and end up like Eddie Collins.

'Never better,' I said. 'Although I'm already dreading the staff against pupil's football match at the end of the year. I couldn't walk for a week after the last one.'

'I thought you were getting in shape. Didn't Emily make you join the gym? And you ran that 10K.'

'Yeah, but they're nothing compared to running around a football pitch for an hour against eleven sixteen-year-olds with four years of pent-up aggression.'

'You're not wrong there,' said Rory. 'Chopper Benson already said he's going to break my legs and I don't think he was joking.'

9.35 p.m.

Emily in bed. William in bed. Me in the lounge.

Even though she's back, things with Emily definitely aren't back to normal. We're kissing (barely) and cuddling (awkwardly), but everything else seems like it's off the table. Emily wants us to work through everything with Deirdre St Cloud first before she tackles my tackle. I don't trust Deirdre, she's a menace, but it seems that if I ever want to have sex again (I do) then I have to put my penis in the hands of that woman, not literally obviously, that's disgusting.

Thursday 11 July 8.45 p.m.

Home. Frustrated. Eating a block of cheese. Emily watching a repeat of Fresh Meat in bed. Cloudy. William asleep.

Tonight was an absolute disaster from start to finish. Deirdre St Cloud was just as I remembered her. Late thirties/early forties and she looked as though she'd spent the last twenty years playing the role of 'Hippy' at a Woodstock museum. At any moment, I half expected her to put on a Jefferson Airplane record, light up a joint, get naked, and start making daisy chains. She wanted to talk about our deepest, darkest fears, and our relationship from an open and honest place where love could filter out all of the impurities and really cleanse us. Obviously, it didn't go well.

Deirdre: Harry, yeah, it's good to see you back, yeah. So let's talk about your penis.

Me: Sorry?

Deirdre: Isn't that why we're here again?

Me: No, I didn't do anything.

Emily: You did something.

Me: But my penis didn't.

Deirdre: It did, Harry, yeah. It's all about the penis.

Emily: She's right, Harry. It is all about your penis.

Me: But it was Emily who kissed somebody else. I didn't do anything.

Deirdre: This isn't about blame, yeah, Harry, this is an

open and honest discussion about the reasons why you and Emily keep coming back and needing my support, yeah. So, Harry, tell me what happened.

Me: Mark moved in across the street from us and started having marriage problems because he's a sex addict. Emily became his confidant, his shoulder to cry on and then he kissed her. They kissed, but she didn't tell me about it and so when I found out I was a little bit pissed off.'

Emily: He marched over there and punched him.

Me: Correction. I tried to punch him, but instead I punched his door frame.

Deirdre: And why do you think that was, Harry? Why did you punch the door frame and not Mark?

Me: Because I closed my eyes.

Deirdre: Or maybe it was because you didn't really want to hit him, yeah?

Me: No, I wanted to hit him.

Deirdre: Let's focus back on your penis, Harry, yeah. Do you think your penis wanted to punch Mark?

Me: Excuse me?

Emily: I think what she means is, was your motivation sexual jealousy? Did Mark threaten you sexually?

Deirdre: Exactly. Did Mark's penis threaten yours? Was it bigger?

Me: I don't know.

Deirdre: It doesn't matter, yeah. But I think it was.

Me: Why?

Deirdre: What do you think, Emily? Was it bigger?

Me: She never saw it. How would she know -?

Emily: I would say yes.

Me: Why would you say that?

Emily: I don't know, but yours is fairly average and I don't know, Mark seems like the sort of man who might have a larger penis.

Me: Why are we even talking about hypothetical penis

sizes?

Deirdre: Exactly, Harry. Let's explore that, yeah, but first, Emily let's discuss Harry. What sort of lover is he?

Emily: Good.

Me: Just good?

Emily: Definitely a tryer.

Me: What does that mean?

Deirdre: I think we all know what that means, yeah, but it doesn't matter, yeah, Harry, let's focus on the positives.

Me: Which are?

Deirdre: That we're all here trying to make this work, yeah. Now, Emily, would you say that Harry has issues with the size and girth of his penis.

Emily: Definitely. Not that I mind. It's all good. But I think Harry thinks about it.

Deirdre: Do you think about it, Harry?

Me: No, I mean, I didn't until now.

Deirdre: Maybe we should have a look at it. Get everything out in the open, spiritually and literally.

Me: You want me to get my penis out?

Deirdre: If you're comfortable with that, yeah.

Me: No, I'm not comfortable with that.

Emily: It's okay, Harry, I don't mind.

It went downhill from there. I refused to show Deirdre my penis, which is apparently because of my own fears of failure and my passive-aggressive attitude to women. Deirdre St Cloud is a fucking nutter. Emily and I didn't say much on the way home. We have to go again in a couple of weeks. I'm already dreading it.

Friday 12 July 7.45 p.m.

A 'For Sale' sign went up across the road today. Mark's house is officially on the market. There's been no sign of him since the restaurant incident. It seems I have frightened him off. Little old me scared off big old banker Mark or as

Deirdre St Cloud would no doubt say, my penis scared off his penis. My little David scared the crap out of his Goliath. For the record, my penis is of perfectly normal length and girth. It doesn't worry me at all.

In worse news, Emily has started reading a book called The Pile of Stuff at the Bottom of the Stairs. Apparently, it's a hilarious slice of modern life, but the bit that makes me nervous is that the wife starts keeping a star chart behind her husband's back to decide whether he's worth keeping around or not. I fear I may be on the star chart system soon. Am I worth keeping around?

Saturday 13 July 3.45 p.m.

We all went to see Mum and Dad today. She has her operation on Tuesday and so Dad invited us all over for a barbecue. Emily and I put our 'officially happy' facade on, despite things still being a bit frosty - especially after the session with Deirdre St Cloud. William was talking up a storm and crawling everywhere. It was wonderful to see Mum playing with him. She's so alive and happy around William, you wouldn't even know she has breast cancer. I had to hold back the tears when we left. I gave Mum a big hug and told her I'd see her on Tuesday. I've taken the day off school.

Monday 15 July 8.05 a.m.

St Swithin's Day

Sunny (Phew - forty more days of sun according to the old St Swithin's legend). BBC weather girl predicting a glorious week. At school. Eating a banana.

The last week of school before the summer holiday. There's already a party atmosphere in the halls and corridors. The pupils are laughing and joking, the teachers are dressing down slightly (except old Norris Roker who is still in his starched shirts and stiff seventies ties) and the whole school has that air of summer. I love the last week of school. It almost makes up for the rest of the year.

Tuesday 16 July 7.45 a.m.

The day of Mum's surgery.

Her operation is scheduled for three o'clock. I've been with Emily and William all morning, which has been a lovely treat and far better than teaching year eight. Cuddles and playtime with William, or fart noises and constantly telling thirty-four kids to please just shut up. I'm off to Mum and Dad's and then the hospital.

8.45 p.m.

Back at Mum and Dad's. Mum asleep. Having a drink with Dad.

The operation went well, and Mum was soon home again. It felt strange that she had fairly major surgery and yet she wasn't staying overnight. Mum was tired though and went off to bed as soon as we got back, while I loitered around talking to Dad.

'I was thinking about Dad today,' said Dad. 'I wish he was still here.'

'Me too,' I said. 'Grandad always had a way of making everything seem better.'

'He did. He made the world fun and exciting. It's ironic, really, but growing up I always resented him for that.'

'For being fun and exciting?'

'Yes, because I didn't always know how to be fun and exciting. I wanted to be more like him. Fearless, outspoken, the life and soul of every party, but when you grow up with that man, it's hard to get noticed.'

'I guess I never thought about it like that,' I said. 'To me he was always just fun Grandad.'

'While I've always been just Dad,' said Dad and then he smiled. 'It's okay Harry, I think I'm finally starting to see the light. Seeing your mum in there today, it really kicked me in the balls. I'm almost sixty, Harry and it's taken me this long, but fuck it, when your mother's all better we're going to live.'

'Good for you,' I said. 'And what's the plan?'

Dad looked at me and I saw that look again (love or Dementia?) and he smiled.

'I'm going to ask your mother to marry me again,' he said. 'We can renew our vows, have a big party and then we're going to go on a bloody big adventure.'

I didn't know what to say. It was my dad. I wasn't used to this happy-go-lucky, vivacious, adventure junky who wanted to get married again and travel the world. My father was the monosyllabic golfer who never discussed anything deeper than a puddle, but I loved this new Über-Dad.

'I think that's brilliant,' I said.

The thing was though, as much as I wanted to jump on Dad's bandwagon of bliss, a part of me couldn't help thinking; but what if Mum isn't okay? What if she doesn't make it?

Thursday 18 July 6.45 a.m.

At home. Having breakfast with Emily and William. Emily eating organic Dorset Muesli. William eating organic Scottish porridge with organic strawberries and organic blueberries. I'm eating my traditional sports day breakfast of four Shredded Wheat.

Today is sports day at school and for some reason I'm once again competing in the staff against pupil's football match. Two thirty-minute halves of sheer agony, excruciating pain, while realising that any footballing skills I may have once had have long since left my body. Livewire, young sixteen-year-old boys with energy to burn and far more skill than me will spend an hour tormenting me until I end up broken and lying on the field in agony. I can't wait.

3.05 p.m.

In my room. In pain. Can't move. Half time oranges didn't work. Magic spray didn't work. I am doomed.

The match ended 17-2 to the pupils and to be fair, they could have scored more. The only reason we didn't lose by more is because Alan Hughes (PE) is mental. He ran around kicking pupils while the rest of us huffed and puffed like the old men we are. Luckily, we had Rory who is quite useful, and he scored both our goals.

I started the game at right-back before I moved to centre midfield and then to the wing. I had one decent dribble in the first five minutes and then spent the next fifty minutes trying to recover. I was hacked down by Chopper Benson and after that I generally played in what I like to call the 'floating role' (I stood around a lot). An hour of football and I'm broken. Never again. I'm too old, too unfit and I'm a father now. I need to keep my strength up for William.

Friday 19 July 12.45 p.m.

The last day of school. After today it's the summer holidays and then we go to Australia. I am very excited. I get to see best mate Ben and it will be my first time down under. I'd be more excited if things with Emily were better. We have to go back to Deirdre St Cloud next week. I hope it goes better than the first session and she doesn't ask to see my penis again.

4.45 p.m.

I said goodbye to my pupils and then I had a meeting with Mr Jones.

'Harry, please come in. Sit down,' said Mr Jones. 'How are you?'

'Okay,' I said. 'We're seeing a marriage counsellor.'

'Good for you. Nothing wrong with that. I tried it with my ex-wife Anna. We gave it a shot and maybe it helped.'

'But you still got divorced.'

'We did but I think our problems were deep rooted, Harry. I'm sure you and Emily will be able to sort things out. Keep talking, keep the lines of communication open and express your love every single day.'

'Thanks,' I said feeling a bit uncomfortable talking about my marriage with Mr Jones.

'So the AHOD position, how did it go this year?'

'Honestly?'

'It's the only answer I'm looking for, Harry. An honest one.'

'I'm not sure I'm cut out for it. All the meetings, the endless meetings, the training, the pressure, dealing with Chris and Clive. With a young baby and Emily, I ...'

'Say no more, Harry,' said Mr Jones. 'I understand. I'm already thinking about next year and I have you just teaching again. You need to focus on other things and besides, I have someone else in mind.'

'Who?'

'Chris Bartlett.'

'But I thought he was too stuck in his ways.'

'Well, as it turns out, he approached me about the job and wants to take it on. He's prepared to embrace it, do all the courses and you know, he isn't married, he doesn't have kids. He might be a bit of a whinger at times, but maybe that's what the job demands.'

'I think you're right,' I said. 'Just watch out though, he's a bit of a revolutionary. He likes to upset the apple cart.'

'That's okay. I'm firmly in charge of the apple cart, Harry. See you tonight?'

'Unfortunately, yes,' I said, and we shook hands. I'm no longer AHOD/ASM. Thank fuck for that. Although working under Chris Bartlett next year is going to be interesting. Tonight is the end of year school dance. Not excited.

11.55 p.m.

Another school dance over with and this year was the worst one yet. The school dance is always a bit of a nightmare and every year I always feel just a little bit older and out of touch. When I first started teaching, I knew most of the songs, but this year I hardly knew any and at one point I found myself yelling at a pupil, 'When I was your age, we had proper music.' The pupil looked at me as if I was about ninety and said, 'When was that sir? The Sixties?' The sad part is I didn't know if he was being serious or not.

I spent most of the night stood with Rory and Alan Hughes making sure no one was doing anything inappropriate on the dance floor. It's ironic that they gave this job to us, but at least Rory and I were vaguely trying. Alan spent the night perving over the girls and telling us which ones he'd like to bang. When Rory tried to explain that the girls were only sixteen, Alan retorted, 'If there's grass on the pitch, play ball!' He really is a disgusting man.

This year the list of inappropriate behaviour has grown to include holding hands, 'necking' – which was described to us as, 'When one of them puts their head too near the other one's ear.' When I politely pointed out that they might just be trying to hear each other over the music (it is far too loud), I was told that necking could only lead to far worse displays of affection and possibly petting, or worse, heavy petting. 'Or even sexual intercourse,' I added jokingly, but no one laughed and instead Norris Roker (Maths, Head of the Dance Committee, possible party Nazi) wrote something down in his note pad. Dancing in a 'sexual manner' is banned (apparently this is called twerking), as is jumping, waving your arms in the air like you just don't care, getting down on your knees and/or legs, breakdancing, doing 'the robot', flash mob style dancing (I don't think Rokers really knew what this was, but decided to ban it just in case), doing Gangnam Style (I did agree with this one) and basically anything else that involved having fun.

Obviously alcohol was banned, and Rokers instigated spot searches on the door for drugs. A lot of the pupils complained to me that they were being treated like kids. I didn't want them to think I had anything to do with the suppression or the Roker Regime (as it's now been named) and so I agreed with them and let them do a bit of necking. I even let some breakdancing go. I drew the line at Sean McIntyre poking his finger through his flies and pretending his penis was poking out. All in all, a pretty awful night.

A few of the riskier pupils somehow managed to get some alcohol past Rokers' 'stop and search' station. They ended up getting a bit tiddly and one of them told me he loved me. I think at the moment I'm still just about on the side of the pupils. I don't ever want to get like old Rokers. The man kills fun faster than the EU.

Monday 22 July 9.45 p.m.

I had a chat with Mum on the phone tonight.

'How are you doing?'

'Oh, you know,' said Mum.

'Actually I don't. I've never had an operation to remove

a lump from my breast.'

'Oh, Harry,' said Mum with a slight giggle. 'I was sore but I'm fine now.'

'Thank you, and when do you start the radiotherapy?'

'In two weeks,' she said. 'And before you say anything, yes I'm really worried about it. I'm going to get sick, lose weight, have no energy and I might lose some of my hair. It's going to be awful.'

'But then you're going to get better.'

'I hope so,' said Mum.

Wednesday 24 July 7.45 p.m.

William is now cruising. This started happening yesterday. One minute he was crawling and then the next he was up and pulling himself around the lounge. It's crazy with kids because you blink and they're suddenly not these adorable little babies anymore, but devil children whose only mission, it seems, is to get into every drawer, cupboard, or place where they shouldn't be and cause the greatest amount of destruction.

When William started crawling we baby-proofed the house as best we could, but now he's cruising - which is like the baby equivalent of that sport where people run around cities, jumping from one building to the next and doing somersaults down steps. I just looked it up and it's called Parkour - it's crazy. William is doing baby Parkour and spends his time navigating from the kitchen (to make a mess) and then back to the lounge (to make a mess). This morning he cruised into the kitchen and spent thirty minutes turning the place upside down. How I long for the days when he would just lie on me and go to sleep. I suppose at least he doesn't do the Nazi salute anymore.

Thursday 25 July 9.45 p.m.

Tonight we had our second session with Deirdre St Cloud, and it was even worse than the first one. She didn't ask to see my penis, but I feel further away from Emily than ever. I don't know how we reached this point. Tonight Deirdre St Cloud took us from talking to arguing and then to silence. She claims her methods are about stripping us down until all that's left is love. I just hope that when we're both stripped down there's enough love left to save our marriage.

Sunday 28 July 11.45 a.m.

Rory rang and wants to meet in The Alexandra for a drink. As soon as William goes down I'm off to meet him. I wonder what he wants to talk about.

3.45 p.m.
Rory and Miranda are pregnant! Rory is over the moon. Apparently, as soon as they stopped trying to get pregnant, they got pregnant. I'm so happy for Rory. Maybe if Emily and I stop trying to fix our marriage, it will get fixed. I'm going to suggest this.

4.45 p.m.
Emily said no. We have to keep trying.

Tuesday 30 July 11.45 p.m.

In the kitchen. I can't sleep. Emily and William in bed. Eating a bowl of organic Dorset Muesli.

I had a long talk with Emily tonight. I wanted to get

everything out in the open and fixed before we head off to Australia. We leave in seven days and at the moment we're in a very strange place. We aren't fighting exactly, but something isn't right.

'How did we get here?' I said. 'After last year, I really thought we were over all the weirdness and stupid fights.'

'Me too,' said Emily.

'Then let's just move on, forget about everything, put it behind us, and move forward,' I said hopefully.

'I wish it was that easy. The problem is that I'm not really angry about something particular or something you can say sorry for.'

'Then what is it?'

Emily went on to explain what the problem is. She doesn't understand 'us' anymore. She doesn't get why I repeatedly let her down time and time again and then she's wondering if maybe it's her. Does she expect too much of me? Is that the problem or am I the problem? She still loves me but wonders whether she loves 'us'. She used 'us' a lot as though she were talking about a secret undercover military base. She even used air quotes a couple of times. Basically, after an hour, it all came down to one thing.

'I want us to work, Harry, of course I do. I love you. Sometimes though I feel like we're a jigsaw puzzle and we have all the pieces, but I never got a look at the final picture before we started. I don't know what we're supposed to be making.'

I wasn't entirely sure what she meant, but she cried for a bit afterwards and I told her it was going to be all right. Fingers crossed.

Wednesday 31 July 5.45 p.m.

At some point every parent in the world goes through the same traumatic experience. The moment when you find your baby standing, unaided and wobbling at the top of the stairs. I guess people who live in bungalows have different problems, but for us two-story-house-people, the stairs are a constant source of danger.

William was upstairs with Emily folding clothes. I was downstairs. I walked past the stairs and that's when I saw him. William. Stood looking down the stairs with an expression that said (to me at least), 'I can do this'.

'William, don't move!' I screamed.

He looked at me and smiled.

'What's going on?' said Emily appearing behind William. 'Oh, fuck, William, stop!'

Emily reached for William, he smiled at me and then it happened. He took a step forward – and began falling. I leapt up the stairs to grab him, Emily ran down, and William seemed to be whooping with joy.

Luckily, William rolled fairly harmlessly towards me, and I managed to catch him. William thought it was the best game ever and wanted to do it again, while Emily and I have been shaking with fear ever since.

'Stair gate?' said Emily.

'Definitely,' I said.

I spent an hour walking around the house trying to pre-empt any other dangerous areas, but the truth is, no matter how much we plan, William seems to have a kamikaze attitude towards his own personal safety.

I moved all the bleach and other cleaning products to higher shelves, all the cupboards have baby-proof locks, and the stair gates are on. The only problem is that I can't open any of the cupboards and going up and down the stairs is like an episode of the Krypton Factor.

August

Monday 5 August 10.45 a.m.

Bank Holiday

I spoke to Mum on the phone this morning. I wanted to wish her luck. Today she starts her radiotherapy at the hospital. Three weeks of hell and then we find out if the cancer is gone.

'How are you doing?'

'Oh, you know, scared witless. They're going to pump my body full of radiation. I'll get sick, throw up constantly, lose weight and be in all sorts of pain. I'll have no energy or appetite, and after three weeks of that, I still might not be cured.'

'But on the bright side, when you are cured, you and Dad are going travelling!'

'It's the only thing keeping me going, Harry. Your father has been wonderful.'

'I'm sorry we're leaving for Sydney,' I said. 'I really wanted to be here for you.'

'I'm glad you're going away. You don't need to see me all sick and pathetic.'

'I'll call though, make sure you're okay.'

'Harry, go to Australia, have the time of your life and don't worry about me, I'll be fine.'

'Love you, Mum.'

'Love you too.'

1.00 p.m.

Packing. Tomorrow we leave for Australia. Twenty-three hours on a plane. Luckily, Emily has devised a brilliant packing plan. She's going to pack everything for her and William. All I have to do is pack for me. This is excellent because I don't have to worry about forgetting anything (which I definitely would have). Emily is organised and brilliant. I, on the other hand (and despite only having to pack my clothes and toiletries) am disorganised and whatever the opposite of brilliant is. There's a lot to think about and I have to leave room to bring back souvenirs. I also have to pop to WH Smith's and get a book to read.

3.45 p.m.

I just got back from WH Smith's, and I was delighted to see Andrew Burchill (one of the boys who tried to mug me) working there. It seems my little pep talk actually worked. He went from trying to 'fuck me up' to ringing me up. I bought a book by Mike Gayle, Wish You Were Here. It's a book about a holiday and so I thought I'd read it on holiday.

5.15 p.m.

Packing done. I proudly told Emily that I was done in record time and I'm fairly sure I didn't forget anything.

'Great, I'm so happy you're all packed,' said Emily. 'I just have to pack for me, William and everything else we'll need. Oh, and do you know where your passport is?'

'Oh, shit, no.'

'Then lucky for you, I do.'

I have a feeling she's annoyed, but it was her suggestion. Once again I'm in trouble when I thought I was doing exactly what she wanted. Still, tomorrow we leave for Sydney, and I get to have a pint (schooner?) with Ben. It will be the longest flight of my life, but what I'm really worried about is William. What if he cries for twenty-three hours straight? We'll be those people on the plane. The people everyone tries to ignore. The outcasts. We'll be ushered to the back of plane with all the other parents where we'll be forced to huddle together like refugees while our babies cry in unison.

Tuesday 6 August 4.35 p.m.

At home. Waiting to leave. A huge pile of bags by the front door, although apparently making the joke, 'I thought we were only going for a fortnight', isn't very funny. Taxi on the way. Next stop Heathrow and then Dubai and then Sydney.

5.45 p.m.

The taxi driver made the mistake of saying, 'Jesus, you emigrating?' when he saw the bags. Emily glared at him and made him give her back the change (£1.27). He glared back at us, but he should be experienced enough to know you don't piss off parents before a long-haul flight.

The strange thing is that today is Tuesday, but we arrive in Sydney on Thursday morning. Technically we lose Wednesday. A whole day gone. Fingers crossed for the flight.

Dubai. An un-Godly hour.

Here's a breakdown of the first seven hours of our journey:

Boarding. Trying to find room in the overhead bins for our carry-on. The fat American family next to us are taking up most of it. Some argy-bargy ensues. We eventually get seated with William on our lap and carry-on safely stowed away.

Hour one. After take-off William starts crying. He continues for the next hour. Glares of annoyance from nearby fat Americans. Emily walks William around the plane, rocks him and feeds him. He's still crying.

Hour two. Emily gives William to me. I walk him around the plane and rock him. He's still crying.

30 minutes spent looking for his dummy. Apparently I was last seen with it.

10 minutes of finger pointing and blaming before we find the dummy on the floor. We give it a quick clean and pop it in his mouth. He's still crying.

30 minutes later the fat American mum leans across and says in her annoying fat American accent that she's trying to sleep and could we make the baby stop crying. Emily tells Fat American Mum to, 'Fuck right off or she will make her cry by shoving the dummy up her fat American arse!' I'm equally impressed and scared by this.

10 minutes later the stewardess asks us to come with her to the back of the plane. They've had a complaint that we've been threatening other people on the plane. Emily explains that it's impossible to stop a baby crying whether fat Americans complain or not.

5 minutes later the stewardess has William sound asleep. She's obviously some sort of baby whisperer. We both give her a big hug. Emily starts crying. William is asleep.

Hour four. I've watched a film, read some of my book, and I'm trying to get some sleep.

Hour five. I can't get comfortable. I eventually nod off and then I'm woken up by an irate Emily who claims I elbowed her in the face. I give up trying to sleep. Fat Americans are all snoring very loudly.

Hour seven. We arrive in Dubai. The fat Americans give us dirty looks as they get off. Emily glares at them and I 'accidently' trip up the fat American son. I believe he was called Duane and he definitely looked like he deserved to be tripped up.

Thursday 8 August 6.35 p.m.

In Glebe, Sydney. At Ben and Katie's house. Warm. Exhausted. William asleep. Emily and Katie drinking wine and talking in the lounge. Ben taking a shower and then he's taking me to his local pub for a schooner or two.

The flight from Dubai to Sydney wasn't too bad. William did cry, but only for thirty minutes and after that he mostly slept. Emily and I managed to sleep a bit, watch films, and enjoy the complimentary drinks and we didn't threaten any more fat, obnoxious Americans.

We arrived at Sydney, Kingsford Smith airport and Ben and Katie were there to get us (with an inappropriately large sign with our names on). It was hugs and kisses all round, before we all jumped in their car (lucky it was big) and Ben drove us back to his place.

Glebe is super cool. It has a lot of funky old buildings with cafes and pubs all over the place. It's very bohemian and also only a short drive or bus journey into Sydney CBD (Central Business District). Today we're having a recovery day and then tomorrow we're going on a tour of Sydney. Tired but excited.

Friday 9 August 4.35 a.m.

Jet lagged. Despite not going to bed until nearly eleven o'clock, I was wide awake at four o'clock this morning. Everyone else in the house is still asleep and so it's just me, sitting in the kitchen alone, drinking a cup of coffee while I listen to the early morning sounds of Sydney. The birds are much louder and more varied here than back in London.

Last night was brilliant. I went to The Excelsior Hotel with Ben for a few drinks.

'You sounded a bit stressed in your emails,' I said taking a sip of my beer (VB - Victoria Bitter). 'Everything all right?'

Ben looked exactly the same (tall, blond hair, blue eyes, good looking), but I noticed a change in him. The old Ben was fun-loving, easy-going and adventurous. This Ben looked a bit knackered, stressed and burnt out.

'I guess things haven't gone exactly how I thought they

would. I don't know, I'm fine, just working too hard, not taking enough time to enjoy life.'

'And isn't that what it's all about?'

'You know it is'

'It's what you always told me. Don't stress, Harry. Life is short, enjoy it. Travel, laugh, love. You used to sound like a walking sound bite for student travel, but now you sound more like me.'

'Shoot me now,' said Ben.

'Cheers. So what's the answer?'

'I guess I need to do some thinking. And what about you, Harry? How are you?'

'Where do I start?'

I told him everything. I told him about going to the gym, Tyler, quitting smoking, the whole Mark and Emily thing, and how we're back seeing Deirdre St Cloud again. I told him that my marriage is on the rocks.

'Fuck, mate, I thought after last year with the whole Jamie business, you two would be okay. I mean if you can get through that.'

'I guess it didn't properly go away and having William has been a strain on us. I'm really hoping this trip is going to turn things around.'

Then Ben went on to tell me what he had planned for us. He had managed to pack in a full week in Sydney and then a week up north in Queensland for a 'proper' holiday. I got the feeling that Ben needed one as much as Emily and I did.

It's funny, I've known Ben since I was a little kid and we've been through so much together, but we've always been different. Ben has always been the relaxed one, the one who wanted to travel and didn't ever want to settle down and be 'boring' (his words not mine), while I was always looking for that bit of security. I wanted to settle down and yes having William terrified me (still does), but I love him unconditionally and I love being a father. My life has followed the same tried and tested path as most others, while Ben has always marched to his own beat. Yet we find ourselves in a similar predicament. Both of us need to find a new way to be happy.

Ben and I reminisced about the 'good old days', talked about Grandad, his brother Adam, my mum and dad, and sitting in that pub 10,000 miles from Wimbledon, I felt more at home than I had for a long time.

9.35 a.m.

Katie made us a slap-up breakfast to get the day started. Katie is looking even more stunning than I remember from last year. Tall, slim, with a bit of the Heidi Klum about her. She has that blonde German/Scandinavian thing going on. She's also lovely and a perfect match for Ben. Despite our chat in the pub last night, they seem to be very happy together and spend a lot of time kissing and cuddling, which is great for them, but it reminds me how little time I spend kissing and cuddling Emily.

We're off to look around Sydney CBD today. I'm super excited to see the Harbour Bridge and the Opera House. William is surprisingly happy this morning. I can't believe he's almost one. My little baby boy is going to be a whole year old. It's also our wedding anniversary next week - seven years of wedded bliss. I have to think of something special to do. Something that will remind Emily why she started dating me in the first place, and I'm not talking about getting her really drunk on white wine spritzers and putting my hand up her top - although that did work the night we met.

8.45 p.m.

Exhausted. We saw the Harbour Bridge (v impressive), the Opera House (v.v. impressive), walked the beautiful botanical gardens, had lunch at a place called The Rocks, went to Ben and Katie's family pie shop and had a proper Aussie meat pie (delicious), we went to Darling Harbour, and in the afternoon, we took the ferry to Manly and had dinner. I'm in love with Sydney. I can see why Ben wanted to live here. It's beautiful.

William had a great day and is getting closer and closer to walking by himself. He's fast asleep now. Emily and I are still a bit jetlagged and I'm off to bed soon. Tomorrow we're going to Katie's parents' house for a barbecue. They live somewhere called Watsons Bay.

Saturday 10 August 7.35 a.m.

Ben and Kates's. Up early again. Emily and William still asleep. Katie out jogging. Ben having a shower.

Katie asked if I wanted to go for a jog with her. I thought about it, and I wouldn't have minded, but I didn't want to embarrass myself in front of her. She runs marathons and I barely finished a 10K. I had a chat with Ben over coffee this morning. I asked him what he's going to do about his situation with work. He still doesn't know, but he knows he needs to do something. We're off to Katie's parents' this afternoon for a good, old fashioned Aussie barbecue. Apparently, we really are going to chuck some shrimp on the barbie, crack open a few tinnies, and we might even listen to a bit of Men at Work.

10.45 p.m.

Just back from Katie's parents' house. Karl and Sheila were lovely. Karl was a proper Aussie and used the full range of Australian slang: Arvo, beaut, got in a blue (argument), chook (chicken), bonzer, deadset, drongo, fisho (fishmonger), garbo (rubbish man), milko (milkman) and he used the word 'bastard' a lot (Harry, you bastard, pass me another coldie from the bloody esky you bastard). Sheila was lovely too. They made us a proper barbie and we left seven hours after we arrived; full, drunk, and very happy. I bet no one ever leaves their house without being full and drunk - and being called bastard A LOT.

Sunday 11 August 9.35 a.m.

The weather is beautiful once again and so we're off to do the Coogee to Bondi walk, followed by an afternoon on the beach. The walk is about 6Ks and we're going to bring William in the Baby Bjorn.

8.35 p.m.

Another incredible day in Sydney. The Coogee to Bondi walk was beautiful. You walk along the coast from one amazing beach to the next. We stopped off along the way and got a drink at one beach, before we continued on to Bondi. The whole walk took about three hours because we had William, and we were taking our time.

After fish and chips for lunch, the afternoon was spent at the world-famous Bondi Beach. William had a blast and spent ages in the sand (mainly eating it). A brilliant day had by all. Tomorrow is our wedding anniversary. William is asleep and we're about to open another bottle of wine and sit out on the porch. Very happy days indeed.

Monday 12 August 2.35 p.m.

Wedding Anniversary

Ben and Katie are watching William so Emily and I can go out for our anniversary. In an attempt to put the spark back into our marriage, I have organised quite a night out. I mean, how often are we going to have our wedding anniversary in Sydney?

We're going for dinner at the Opera Bar, which is amazingly enough at the Opera House and Emily doesn't know it yet. Then we're going to do the twilight Harbour Bridge climb. I have to admit that I'm a bit scared (a healthy fear of heights), but we can't come all this way and not do it - right? Then we're going to spend the night at a hotel in Circular Quay. It promises to be a wonderful night of great food, adrenalin and excitement, followed by romance and hopefully sex. What a way to celebrate seven years of marriage – and all possible due to Beatrice Lamb (God rest her soul) and her thrifty life.

11.45 p.m.
At our hotel.

Seven years of marriage and one night to remember - for all the wrong reasons. Here are the high (and low) lights:

3.30 - We leave William with Ben and Katie. William is fine. Emily is worried.

4.00 - We arrive at Circular Quay to have dinner.

4.05 - Emily calls to make sure William is okay. He's fine.

4.20 - At the Opera Bar. It's beautiful and the views of the bridge we're going to be climbing are stunning. Emily still doesn't know.

4.45 - I have to explain to Emily that she can't drink any alcohol. She asks why and I say she will find out soon enough. Emily is suspicious but agrees.

5.00 - Dinner is superb. Emily still wary of upcoming events.

5.30 - We have a great dinner and things are going v. well. We're talking, holding hands and we're in Sydney. It seems like we're getting back to normal. Emily is even laughing at my jokes.

6.15 - We have a walk around Circular Quay and I finally tell Emily what we're doing. 'We're going to climb that,' I say pointing at the bridge. Emily gets very excited, but then she suddenly looks at me. 'Are you sure you're going to be all right, Harry? You remember that time we went up the Eiffel Tower?' The Eiffel Tower incident was years before. I got a bit nervous up there and threw up a little bit (a lot, actually), but I was sure I was going to be fine. This was exactly the sort of thing I needed to do to conquer my fear of heights. Emily calls Ben and Katie to check on William. He's fine.

6.45 - We get to the Harbour Bridge climb. It takes an hour to have the briefing, get kitted up and then we're off. Very excited.

7.45 - We start the climb.

7.50 - Very nervous.

8.00 - Shitting myself.

8.20 - Someone asks if I'm okay.

8.25 - I don't want to die on this bridge.

8.35 - The person in charge asks Emily what's going on. 'He won't move,' says Emily. I'm lying down on the bridge, holding on for dear life.

8.45 - 'Don't fucking touch me!' is my response when the instructor tries to help move me.

8.47 - The instructor calls for backup.

8.55 - Backup arrives.

8.56 - 'Don't fucking touch me!' is my response to the backup.

9.25 - I'm finally escorted off the bridge. 'That's never happened before,' says the instructor when he passes me over to Emily. 'That's because you've never had Harry before,' says Emily.

10.15 - At the hotel having a lie down. Emily drinking wine while I try not to throw up.

11.45 - Emily passes out after finishing the whole bottle of wine alone. I get my second wind and I'm wide awake. The night was a disaster. No sex and Emily is married to the only person ever to fail the Sydney Harbour Bridge climb and be escorted down. Happy anniversary Harry.

Tuesday 13 August 10.35 a.m.

We got back from our disastrous anniversary night out to this:

'Watch this,' said Ben, who then pushed play on his CD player. William was standing up, holding onto the sofa and suddenly Gangnam Style was playing, and William was thrusting his groin around, laughing and moving his feet like a baby possessed. 'He loves Gangnam style! Go Willy! Go Willy!'

Brilliant. Just fucking brilliant.

'Oh, we should try the Macarena!' said Katie.

All my work trying to educate William with proper music, and he likes Gangnam Style. Disappointed.

12.45 p.m.

This afternoon we're relaxing ahead of our flight up north tomorrow. Katie is out shopping, and Ben and I are heading to the pub for a couple of hours.

5.45 p.m.

I had a good chat with Ben in the pub over a few VBs.

'I love Emily, but sometimes I feel like I'm banging my head against the wall.'

'I know what you mean,' said Ben. 'I adore Katie, but there are times when I just don't get her logic. It's like I'm being tested, but I don't know what the questions are, what the scoring criteria is, and I'm sure she's cheating.'

'Emily is definitely cheating,' I said, and we both laughed. 'I miss this.'

'I know. Me too. I love it here, but I haven't found a Harry yet.'

'That's because I'm unique.'

'I know, seriously, who has to be escorted down from the Harbour Bridge climb? Old people do that.'

'In my defence,' I started, but then stopped because, well, there wasn't one.

'In your defence, you're a pussy.'

'Yes, I think so,' I said. 'Another round?'

'I'll get these,' said Ben and off he went.

While he was gone, a group of young backpackers came in and sat opposite us. There were five of them, two were English and the other three were a mixed bag of Europeans. I watched them for a moment, and it made me envious. They were young, on a gap year, free, probably single, and miles from home, and enjoying the world. Meanwhile, I was approaching middle age with a great degree of fear and uncertainty, not on a gap year, not free or single and although I was miles from home, I was hardly enjoying the world. We'd be back in Wimbledon before I knew it.

'Why can't we be like them?' I said when Ben sat down with two beers.

'Young, free and single?'

'Uncomplicated,' I said.

'We were once. Well, I was. I'm not sure you ever really were.'

'And maybe that's the problem. You lived. You did all of these amazing things, went

to incredible places all over the world, but what have I done? Maybe it's why Emily is so miserable with me. Maybe it's me. Maybe I'm a miserable person.'

'I wouldn't say that,' said Ben. 'And I don't think Emily is miserable. She's confused.'

'I'm confused.'

'Me too,' said Ben.

'Do you think there's ever going to be a time in our life when we aren't confused?'

'I don't know,' said Ben. 'I do know this though. Confusing is at least interesting. If we didn't have wives and problems, we'd just be two blokes sitting in the pub wondering why our lives were so boring, and then we'd go out, and probably try and pull one of those backpacker girls.

We'd fail, get depressed, get really drunk, and then we'd fall asleep on the bus going home with a kebab on our lap. I know where I want to be, confused or not.'

'I'm with you. Although I wouldn't mind being one of them for a night,' I said, and Ben smiled. 'What?'

'Just wait until we go up north and you'll see,' said Ben.

Wednesday 14 August 8.00 a.m.

Emily and Katie out jogging together. Having breakfast with Ben and William - the boys.

We're flying to Cairns in Northern Queensland today. It's only three hours away, which after the mammoth slog here feels like nothing. It's a lot warmer up there. They also have more spiders and snakes - something I'm not that excited about. Next stop, Cairns.

6.45 p.m.

Blimey. It is a lot hotter up here. It's technically winter, so I can't imagine how hot it gets during the summer. The flight up was good. Having Ben and Katie really helped as we took it in turns to watch and play with William. We checked into our lovely apartment and we're about to have a dip in the pool before dinner.

Thursday 15 August 11.10 a.m.

By the pool. Drinking. Eating. Relaxing. Trying not to get burnt (factor 70). We didn't do much today. We popped into town and had a look around. We had lunch and lazed around by the pool. The Spencer's (plus Ben and Katie) are officially on holiday. Off out to have dinner before an early night. Tomorrow's going to be a busy day.

4.45 p.m.

I just had the scariest experience of my life while sitting on the toilet. I literally shit myself. When you come to Australia people will tell you to always check your shoes before you put them on and look underneath the toilet bowl before sitting down, and these are very useful tips. What no one will tell you though is what to do if you're sitting on the toilet, trying to have a quiet poo when all of a sudden a giant spider the size of your fist appears on the wall next to you. I'd like to say I handled it calmly. I'd like to say that I showed a certain degree of maturity and decorum. I didn't though. I screamed. Like a baby. Ben, Katie and Emily came running and luckily I left the door unlocked and they all came steaming in.

'What's the matter?' said Ben.

By this point I was frozen in fear and my earlier scream was the last noise I was going to make. I pointed at the wall and mouthed, 'spider.' Ben, Katie and Emily all looked and saw the giant spider and Emily had the correct reaction. She screamed and ran out. Ben and Katie, on the other hand, just smiled casually.

'It's just a huntsman, they're harmless,' said Katie. 'No worries.' (No worries?!)

'He's more afraid of you than you are of him,' said Ben (unhelpfully).

'I don't fucking think so,' I said. 'Sorry guys, I need to get up and leave the toilet.'

And so I did (mid-poo). Ben and Katie took care of the spider, while I cowered in the living room, terrified I was about to be attacked and eaten by a giant man-eating spider.

Friday 16 August 7.05 a.m.

We're off to see the Great Barrier Reef today. We're going

out on a boat to the outer reef and then we have the chance to snorkel or scuba dive. I snorkelled once in Turkey but spent most of the time inhaling water and almost drowning. I'm looking forward to doing a bit better, although after the Harbour Bridge experience, I'll just be happy if I survive.

10.05 p.m.

What a day. The Great Barrier Reef was extraordinary. It was beautiful beyond anything I could have imagined. It was gloriously sunny, and it felt like we were the only people left in the world. The boat took us to the edge of the reef, so we were literally miles from land, and we were the only ones out there. It was the perfect setting and the perfect day, but what made it special was what happened with Emily. Ben and Katie were inside the boat with William (who was having a blast and loved his mini life jacket), while Emily and I went snorkelling together.

A little backstory. Emily is afraid of fish. Not fish and chips fish, she likes that, but actual fish. Proper fish that swim about in the ocean. It's irrational and strange, but for her the thought of hundreds of fish swimming around her is terrifying. So her going into the ocean surrounded by fish, is like me, well, climbing the Sydney Harbour Bridge. We were sitting on a little ledge and about to pop into the water when Emily looked at me.

'I can't do it,' she said. 'There's fish everywhere!'

'Em, it's the Great Barrier Reef. You can't come all this way and not go in. It would be like, I don't know …'

'Going to Sydney and not climbing the Harbour Bridge?'

'Exactly.'

'But you didn't, Harry, you got about twenty feet up it and refused to go any further.'

'But that was different.'

'Why?'

'Because I could have died. This is just fish. They aren't going to kill you.'

'A shark might.'

'Well, yes, but that's very unlikely. Look, Em, if you must know, I really regret the whole Harbour Bridge climb. I wish I'd done it, I do, and I know you'll regret this if you don't do it.'

'And you'll stay with me the whole time?'

'Em, I'll always stay with you the whole time,' I said, and she smiled at me. A proper smile. There wasn't a hint of anything but love. It wasn't laced with traces of annoyance, doubt or regret. Just love.

'Love you,' she said.

'You too,' I said, and we dived in.

We snorkelled the Great Barrier Reef together. It was definitely a bucket list moment but looking back now all I can remember seeing is that smile.

Saturday 17 August 5.36 p.m.

Ben took a gap year after university and travelled all over the world. He went from Asia to Australia and South America, and he said it was one of the best years of his life. Of all the things he did on that trip, and all the incredible places he went, one of the first stories I heard when he got back was the night he danced in his undies for money.

It was at a backpacker bar in Cairns called The Woolshed. Apparently, it's a typical backpacker haunt, but their biggest claim to fame is the dance-for-drinks promo. Basically, they have boys and girls strip down to their underwear and dance on tables for the chance to win free drinks. Obviously for cheap backpackers, the chance to earn free drinks is too much to turn down, and so it's a popular event. Ben actually won and had free drinks all night after that. It's a story I've heard many times, so when Ben said over breakfast,

'Harry, fancy the Woolshed tonight?' I knew exactly

what he meant.

'Is that all right, Em?' I said carefully as things were going well with us and after 'the smile' I didn't want to jeopardise anything.

'If the boys need their silly walk down memory lane, we can have a girls and William night in,' said Katie.

'It's fine,' said Emily to me. 'You boys have fun.'

Ben winked at me. Now I knew what he meant back in Sydney when I wanted to be a carefree gap-yearer for one night only. This is exactly what he had in mind.

'Don't wait up, girls,' said Ben.

Sunday 18 August 10.36 a.m.

As soon as I opened my eyes, I knew it was bad. The thumping in my head was already near Last Night of the Proms level and my stomach felt like it had been attacked from the inside by something heinous and deadly. I could barely muster a word as my lips seemed to be stuck together. I looked around the room and at least I was at the apartment. What the hell had happened last night?

After five minutes of trying to remember, I slowly got up and made my way into the living area where Ben, Katie, Emily and William were all up and full of the joys of spring. They did a rousing slow clap for me as I made my way towards them.

'Oh dear,' said Ben. 'Look what the cat dragged in.'

'What happened?' I said. 'Am I dead?'

'Just look on the fridge,' said Emily with a snigger.

'What?' I said walking over to the fridge. 'Fuck!'

'Earmuffs,' said Emily covering William's ears.

'Why? How? I don't remember that,' I said.

'That's why I took a photo,' said Ben. On the fridge was a photo of me, in just my underwear (although not my underwear actually, but a pair of racy and tight Y-fronts - how?) dancing on top of a table in a pub (The Woolshed?).

It looks like I'm having the time of my life. 'You won,' said Ben. 'We drank for free all night after that.'

I turned and looked at Emily. 'I'm so proud of you, Harry,' she said with a smile.

It was then I felt the sickness suddenly rise up inside of me and I rushed off to the toilet and let it all out. Apparently, I had a backpacker story to tell now too. I just couldn't remember a single moment of it.

'And don't worry,' said Ben when I returned and flopped down on the sofa. 'I have lots more photos on my phone.'

Brilliant.

Monday 19 August 8.05 a.m.

Eating brekkie at the apartment with Ben. The girls and William having an early morning swim in the pool. I'm feeling much better than yesterday, although after seeing all the photos of my night out with Ben, my embarrassment and feelings of shame are at an all-time high. I won't go into detail, but suffice to say, the racy Y-fronts weren't the worst part of the night for me.

It's our last day in Cairns and so we're off to the rainforest. We're getting picked up at nine o'clock and we're off to Daintree Rainforest, Cape Tribulation and Mossman Gorge. It's going to be a fabulous last day here. I'm just having a quick bite to eat with Ben before we get ready to leave.

'Any thoughts on the job situation?' I said to Ben.

'Yes,' said Ben taking a sip of his coffee. 'Being off with you guys and enjoying myself, I can't go back to the eighty hours a week I was doing before. If I keep doing that I'm going to be miserable and when we do have kids, I want to see them.'

'So what's the big plan?'

'I have to talk it over with Katie and her parents yet, but I'm definitely going to stop running the shops. I can't keep doing it, mate. It's driving me into an early grave.'

'So what are you going to do?'

'Isn't that the million-dollar question?'

'Apparently.'

'I don't know, but I do know this, I'm done working so hard. I came here to live, to have a better quality of life. I love Katie and I want to have kids, the whole nine yards, but I'm not going to be one of those dads. The ones who are never around.'

'I know what you mean. Having William has really changed things. I didn't really think about not seeing him when I was at work, but I miss him so much. I'm always rushing home to spend a bit more time with him.'

'Exactly,' said Ben. 'Maybe I'll be a stay-at-home dad.'

'From international traveller and adrenaline junkie to stay at home daddy,' I said. 'Although you know you need to have a baby first.'

'We've been trying,' said Ben with a smile. 'Katie doesn't want anyone to know, she thinks it's bad luck so mum's the word, eh?'

'Oh, mate, I'm really chuffed for you.'

'It's early days. I'm not getting any younger though and I don't want to be an old dad. Time to do the business,' said Ben and I gave him a hearty pat on the back. Then Emily, Katie and William came walking in. Literally. William was walking!

'Look what happened,' said Emily. 'He just did it.'

'Come here, mate,' I said to William. He took one look at me and started walking towards me. He wobbled and fell over but got up and tried again until eventually he reached me, falling into my arms. I gave him a huge hug. My little boy is walking.

10.45 p.m.

Home. Exhausted. Another incredible day. The rainforests and beaches were beautiful. We saw the most fabulous places, had a tour of the rainforest, saw bugs and giant spiders (terrifying), and had lunch on the beach. A truly great last day in Cairns, although the highlight of the day was seeing William's smiling face as he walked around by himself. Having a few glasses of wine tonight with Katie, Ben and Emily.

Tuesday 20 August

We fly back to Sydney today and then only one day left before we start the gruelling twenty-odd hour journey home. I'm dreading it already. William is walking everywhere. Emily and I are definitely getting back to normal and no more photos of me in racy Y-fronts have emerged as yet. Time to fly back to Sydney. Tomorrow is William's birthday.

Wednesday 21 August 9.10 a.m.

William's First Birthday

Last day of our holiday and Ben and Katie are having a barbecue at their house to say goodbye and to celebrate William's first birthday. Katie's parents are coming over too, so I expect to be called a bastard A LOT. We're having breakfast and then we're going to the beach before the barbecue this afternoon.

2.45 p.m.

Emily keeps bursting into tears and saying, 'I can't

believe my little man is one already.'

I keep comforting her and then almost crying myself. I can't believe my little man is one already.

3.15 p.m.

'Harry, you pommie bastard, where's the bloody little ripper? Hear the bastard's walking. Get me a bloody cold one from the esky, you bastard. Traffic on the way here was a bastard. Almost got in a blue with another bloke in a bloody Ute. Bastard chucked a yewy and almost hit my bloody car - the bastard. Looked like he didn't have a brass-razoo and you know me Ben, I'll always give someone a fair go, but he was a real no-hoper. I brought over a slab of bloody beer Ben, where'd you want it? And Sheila's got the snags and the prezzie for the little bastard.'

8.15 p.m.

What an afternoon. William had a brilliant birthday. He got some presents, which he generally didn't care much about, although he did enjoy the wrapping paper a lot, and he loved his chocolate cupcake. He smashed it into his face as fast as he could. By the time he'd finished it, he had more chocolate on his face than in his mouth. Then we settled in, started drinking, eating and enjoying ourselves. William was put to bed an hour ago, and so now it's just the adults. Feeling a little bit drunk already. Karl is steaming and calling everyone a bastard. Sheila is pretty pissed too and keeps kissing me on the lips. Emily is still crying about William being all grown up and not a baby anymore. I'm just enjoying being with my best mate again and wishing we didn't have to go home tomorrow.

11.45 p.m.

Very drunk. Emily very drunk. Ben and Katie very drunk. Sheila and Karl passed out, although even Karl's snores sound like he's saying bastard. I'm really going to miss Ben and Katie. Emily just threw up. I blame the jelly shots.

Thursday 22 August 10.04 a.m.

We fly home today. Very sad face. The flight leaves at three o'clock and we don't get into London until seven o'clock on Friday morning. Twenty-three something hours plus a stopover in Dubai. Not excited about it. Hungover. We said goodbye to Karl and Sheila this morning. Karl looked like hell, but he still managed to get in a few bastards. We gave them big hugs and they've invited us to stay with them whenever we come over next. We're just having an early lunch and then it's off to the airport. Extremely sad face.

1.15 p.m.
A long and tearful goodbye to Katie and Ben at the airport. I can't believe our holiday is already over. I had a good chat with Ben this morning and he's promised to keep me up to date with any pregnancy news. The world is definitely getting smaller and I'm so over the moon that Ben and Katie are happy in Sydney. I do wish it wasn't so far away though.

Friday 23 August 12.15 p.m.

Finally home. Exhausted. Just. Want. To. Go. To. Bed. Goodnight.

Saturday 24 August 11.15 a.m.

We literally did nothing yesterday. We didn't really sleep on the plane and so by the time we got back home we were just exhausted. We put William down and then Emily and I fell into bed. Off to see Mum today.

6.15 p.m.

When I got there, Mum was in bed. She was tucked under the duvet. Her face was pale, and the effects of the radiotherapy were obvious. She didn't look good. She must have lost at least a stone in weight. She was tired and her skin was pallid - it was as if the life had literally been sucked out of her.

'Harry,' she said when I walked in. 'Finally.'

'Sorry Mum.' I walked over and sat down on a chair next to the bed. I felt the bubble of tears begin to erupt, but I managed to keep them down.

'How was the holiday?'

'It was brilliant, Mum, but more importantly, how are you?'

'About as good as I look,' said Mum.

'You look terrible,' I said, and she smiled.

'I've missed you, Harry. You know, going through this, it really makes you appreciate things a lot more.'

'How so?'

'Being healthy. Getting up in the morning and going for a walk, being able to do whatever you want, whenever you want. I know it sounds clichéd and I think your dad's getting annoyed because I keep saying it, but it takes almost losing something to realise just how much you want it.'

The second she said that I thought back to last year and my almost fling with Jamie and to the night I punched Mark in the restaurant. Moments when I thought I'd lost Emily.

'I know what you mean, and it isn't cliché.'

'Tell that to your father.'

'You know Dad.'

'I thought I did. For years and years, I thought I knew your father, but now he's different. It's miraculous. In that short time we were apart, he's grown so much and suddenly he wants to do things and share his feelings.'

'So you're saying that Larry Laverne and Camel-toe, I mean Eleanor, saved your marriage?'

'I think they made us appreciate what we had. So, Camel-toe?'

'She had the biggest camel-toe I've ever seen,' I said, and Mum laughed.

'Your dad never mentioned the camel-toe.'

'Would you?' I said.

'What are we laughing at?' said Dad walking in.

'Oh, nothing,' said Mum looking at me.

When I left, Mum was falling asleep. She looked sick and it scared me, but seeing her and Dad together, I knew that whatever happened she was going to be all right. We were all going to be all right.

Friday 30 August 9.45 a.m.

Today's the day. Mum goes to the hospital to find out if she's cancer free.

6.55 p.m.

We sat around a depressing looking waiting room. Of course, we were late going in and the doctor (who I'm sure was just doing his job) spent ages talking about the results when all we wanted to hear was,

'Mrs Spencer, I'm pleased to say you're 100% cancer free.'

I've never cried so quickly and with such joy before. They did scans and there's no sign of any cancer in either breast. He reminded her that it will take a month, perhaps longer, before she's back to normal after the radiotherapy. She has to go back every six months for screenings, just in case, but we were free to leave. Free to resume life again. Back to normal. Well, whatever the new normal was going to be.

When we got back to the house, Mum sat down in the lounge while I made us all a nice cup of tea. While the kettle was boiling, I saw Dad sneak out to the shed and so I followed him. I walked in and Dad was sitting in his chair, crying his heart out. I immediately walked over and put my arm around him.

'She's all right, Dad, the cancer's gone.'

'I know, son. It's just, when you think you might lose someone, it's so overwhelming. I've been keeping so much in for your mother's sake. I just needed a moment.'

'I know,' I said. 'I feel the same way. I couldn't imagine losing Mum.'

'She's the love of my life, Harry. If I'd lost her I'd have fallen apart. All the plans we made would have been for nothing. I think I would have died too.'

'Then it's a good job she's going to be all right then.'

'Yeah,' said Dad wiping more tears from his eyes.

'I'll finish the tea, come in when you're ready,' I said and gave him a pat on the shoulder. I went back in and made Mum tea, and then Dad came in a few minutes later. Finally, and for the first time in a very long time, we were one, big, happy family, the gloomy cloud of cancer finally gone.

September

Sunday 1 September 11.30 a.m.

Home. Raining. Sitting in the shed. Eating pickled onions. Listening to David Gray. Emily and William visiting her parents.

I think I'm suffering from severe-post-holiday-stress-disorder (SPHSD) and on top of that school starts on Monday. I have two days without pupils, but now Chris Bartlett is the new HOD, I have a feeling they aren't going to be the easiest two days of my life. He's already sent me five emails and I'm afraid to open them. Emily and I also have our third appointment with Deirdre St Cloud this week (dreading it) and to top it all off, I gained seven pounds in Australia (ugh).

Now William's walking, life has completely changed. If we leave him alone for a moment he's gone. We seriously need eyes in the back of our heads. The other day I caught him trying to climb into the airing cupboard. He's also talking up a storm. He says so many words now: Jamma (Grandma), Gancake (Pancake), Eenis (Penis), Igga Igga (Peppa Pig – his favourite TV show) and my personal favourite, Icky Artian (Ricky Martin – Emily's favourite singer). The other day William came waddling into the lounge shouting, 'Icky Artian, Icky Artian,' did a little dance and then fell over. Every time William hears Livin' la Vida Loca, and no matter where he is or what he's doing, he will start dancing. Despite my best efforts to educate him with 'proper music', William loves his slice of Latin pop. Today it's Ricky Martin, tomorrow it'll be Gloria Estefan and The Miami Sound Machine, and then where does it end? Shakira? Enrique Iglesias? La Bamba?

2.45 p.m.

Steve popped by the shed and was even more excitable than usual.

'What's up with you?'

He had a huge grin.

'Harry, sit down.'

'I am sitting down.'

'Then, I don't know, clench or something.'

'Clenched.'

'You are not going to believe what's happened. You know I have an agent?'

'Yes.'

'His name's Perry Pembroke, he's a legend in the light-entertainment world. He used to work with Sue Pollard. Anyway, he called me on Friday, and he's got me an interview at.' Steve said leaving a suitably long pause and then doing the drum roll noise. 'The BBC!'

'OMG!' I said. 'Why didn't you come over sooner?'

'We've been at Camber. They want me to audition for a part on a new children's show. I'll be an all-round entertainer.'

'You are an all-round entertainer.'

'I know!'

'I'm really happy for you, mate.'

'I'm just so … I can't believe it. Where are Emily and William? I have to tell them?'

'Oh, they're at her parents',' I said.

'Everything all right?'

'Yeah, yeah, they just wanted to see William. It's been a while with Australia.'

'And there's me blabbing on and I haven't even asked about Australia. And how's Ben?'

'Ben's good and Australia was incredible. But listen, this is huge. You could be on TV!'

'Let's not count our chickens. It's only an interview.'

'Still, Steve the Entertainer on TV.'

'OMG!' said Steve excitedly.

'Lucky thing you changed your name. I don't think the Kid Fiddler or Touched by Steve would have made it on to

CBeebies, not in the current social climate.'

'Probably not. I'd better get off. I have to start practising the routine. The interview's on Friday. I have to dust off my bagpipes.'

'Is that a euphemism?'

'No, I literally have to dust off my bagpipes. They've been in the loft for months,' said Steve and then he was gone.

I should probably go to the gym and work off the extra holiday poundage, but then again, I could pop to The Alexandra instead. It's Sunday and they do a lovely roast.

Monday 2 September 4.30 p.m.

Home. Knackered. Raining. The BBC weather girl has had her hair cut and looks more gorgeous than ever. Emily making dinner. William listening to Icky Artian and sort of gyrating.

Day one at school was awful. Chris Bartlett is really laying down the law. The man who last year wanted to storm the bloody Bastille and start a revolution, is suddenly the voice of authority. I'm starting to think that maybe I should have kept the role of HOD. Chris is instigating more meetings, more accountability, and said that, 'The wasted years of liberal, wishy-washy, namby-pamby school politics was over, and a new hard-line regime was taking its place.' Eddie thinks he's just trying to frighten us. I hope so. I'm not sure I'll survive a hard-line regime. Seven weeks until half-term.

Wednesday 4 September 5.30 p.m.

Ben and Katie's Wedding Anniversary (eCard sent)

Tonight was our third session with Deirdre St Cloud. Since

Australia things have been better with me and Emily. We aren't back to normal, and sex is still off the table (at least I think it is), and there's still an awkwardness between us, but it's definitely better than it was. Emily thinks Deirdre St Cloud is the answer. I think Deirdre St Cloud is a nutter. I hope Emily's right.

8.15 p.m.

Deirdre: So, Harry, yeah, how's things with Emily?

Me: Okay. Good. Really good. Brilliant actually.

Deirdre: Emily, respond, yeah.

Emily: Things are still difficult.

Me: Oh.

Deirdre: And why do you say that?

Then Emily went on to talk about us and hearing her it sounded like she was talking about a completely different couple. It definitely wasn't us. I thought we were on the mend. I thought after Australia and 'the smile' that we were going to be okay. Emily painted a very different picture. She said that she was tired of putting a plaster over our relationship and that it needed a permanent fix, so more blood didn't seep out when she wasn't expecting it. Deirdre sagely nodded at this and looked at me for a response.

Me: Definitely Deirdre.

Deirdre: Definitely what, Harry?

Me: The plaster thing. Totally agree. We need to fix things properly.

Deirdre: That's great, yeah, Harry. Emily, what do you think has to happen? What's the permanent fix, yeah?

Emily: I don't know, but I feel like we need to fall in love again. Re-discover the magic.

Deirdre: Harry, yeah, what do you think about that?

Me: Definitely.

Deirdre: That's fantastic because I've devised a little strategy that we can do, yeah. It's something I want you to take away and next week we can talk about the outcome. This is cutting edge, shit, yeah. They're doing this in Denmark, Harry, yeah. Denmark.

Then Deirdre went on to explain what she wants us to do. Basically, for the next seven days we can't speak or touch one another. The logic is that we're used to being around each other, but not touching or talking is supposed to trigger some sort of animalistic lust and hunger for contact. The downside is that if it doesn't work and it triggers nothing then you know things are beyond repair. It's also really big in Denmark, which is apparently a huge deal.

10.45 p.m.

We got back from our session, and I almost asked Emily if she wanted a cup of tea, but then I remembered we couldn't talk. So far it's been a bit of a nightmare. I can't believe we can't talk for another week. I don't know how we're going to sleep together and not touch. Deirdre St Cloud is either a genius or a complete imbecile. Only time will tell which one. In the end I just made her a cup of tea, but she didn't say thank you, obviously.

Thursday 5 September 11.30 p.m.

Home. Emily and William asleep. Nibbling on a piece of cheese I spotted at the back of the fridge (Wensleydale?). Spitting with rain.

After another awful day at school (Chris Bartlett is living up to his promise of a hard-line regime), I went to the pub with Rory. I gave him my copy of The Blokes Survival Kit for Being a Dad. It's time I passed on the incredibly erudite knowledge from the book that claims to take you on a magical journey deep into the mind of the first-time father, with a foreword by Gary Lineker, although I'm fairly sure it's not the actual Gary Lineker.

'What's this?' said Rory.

'This is the man's Bible to surviving pregnancy.'

'Really?'

'No, it's awful and tells you nothing about the real challenges of becoming a father.'

'So why are you giving it to me?'

'Because strangely enough, and whether this is the genius of the book or not I don't know, it's so bad and so out of touch that it will make you feel like you can be a decent father.'

'Sounds brilliant.'

'You'll love it. How is Miranda by the way?'

'Violently sick, bad tempered, tired, and she blames me for everything.'

'That sounds about right.'

'Just tell me it gets better.'

'It gets better.'

'Are you saying that because I asked you to, or does it actually get better?'

'It actually gets better,' I said. 'But then it gets worse again.'

'Oh, and on that bombshell, another pint?'

'Definitely.'

I wanted to stay at the pub for as long as I could, so I didn't have to go home and not talk to Emily. I'm not sure this Danish method is going to work. Maybe the Danes should stick with bacon.

Friday 6 September 5.30 p.m.

In the shed. Windy. Eating a forbidden onion bhaji from The Spice of Wimbledon. I stopped by on my cycle home from work. I just needed a little bhaji - what's so wrong with that?

'How did it go?' said Steve.

He'd come straight over to the shed when I'd got back from work - the onion bhaji concealed within my rucksack like black market goods during the war.

'I was there all day, Harry,' said Steve. 'It was rigorous, but it went well.'

'Do you think you got it? Am I going to be watching you on TV?'

'I have no idea. I doubt it. There were some wonderful people there. I'm competing against Wacky Wayne, Tricky Tony, The Amazing Andrew and Bobo Jangles, he was on Britain's Got Talent, Harry, so you know what I'm talking about.'

'Yeah, right,' I said even though I had no idea who any of them were. 'But you stand a chance?'

'We'll see. I have to go back next week. Fingers crossed.'

Saturday 7 September 7.30 a.m.

Home. Off to the gym in a minute for my first post-Australia workout. Sunny. Dad's birthday today and we're all going over there later (including Derek and Pam).

10.30 a.m.

Home. Exhausted. Why does it take an absolute age to get in shape, but such a short time to lose it? Before the 10K I was doing well and felt good, but then a few slack months and a holiday and suddenly I'm back at the start again, coughing my guts up and almost passing out. I ran less than a mile. Not good. Emily, on the other hand, jogged effortlessly for nearly five miles and didn't look tired at all. I couldn't talk to her about it of course.

This not talking is driving me around the bend and later we have to go over to my parents' house and so I'll have to tell them what's going on. It will be nice to see Mum up and about, although I'm dreading seeing Derek because the last time we spoke I shouted at him on the phone. He'll probably give me the scary Lamb stare.

9.30 p.m.

Something strange is going on. A week with Derek, Pam, Mum and Dad in Tenerife? Am I back in the family circle? Is it a trick to lure me there so he can get rid of me for good? Will I end up on Crimewatch? Let me start at the beginning.

We got to Mum and Dad's at about two o'clock. Mum was looking much better than the last time I saw her. She wasn't back to her old self, but she'd gained some weight and had some colour back in her cheeks. As soon as we arrived, I took my parents to one side and had the chat about Emily and me. I didn't want them finding out from Derek or wondering why we were acting like complete strangers.

'Emily and I are seeing a marriage counsellor,' I said to Mum and Dad in the kitchen.

'Oh my Christ!' said Mum. 'I knew something was wrong. Didn't I say something was wrong, Greg? What's the matter? Did you cheat on her? Tell me you didn't cheat on her? I couldn't stand it if my little boy did that. Did something happen in Australia? Is it someone at work? Did she cheat on you? Are you okay financially because we'd be happy to help?'

'Mum,' I said. 'I'm glad you're getting back to your old self, I am, but it's nothing like that. We're just having a few issues, it's nothing bad. We're going to be fine.'

'Are you sure?' said Dad.

'Yes, we're fine, although at the moment we can't talk to each other or touch. It's

something our therapist wanted to try. So don't be freaked out if you don't see Emily and me talking today.'

'Is it something sexual?' said Mum. 'Because your father

and I have been experimenting with a bit of the, you know, Karma Sutra,' said Mum in very hushed tones.

'As brilliant as it is to imagine you and Dad experimenting with ancient Indian sexual practices, it isn't that. We're fine,' I said again. 'I just wanted you to know.'

'If you need anything,' said Dad.

'Anything,' said Mum.

'Don't worry, you'll be the last people I ask,' I said with a wry smile.

Then Derek and Pam turned up. Pam and I had our usual in-depth conversation. I asked how she was, asked about her knitting and her brother Sam, and then she wandered off towards the small buffet on the dining table. Derek was eating a Scotch egg when I went over to talk to him. I thought it was best to get it out there, apologise for shouting at him, and hope he'd forgive and forget. Unlikely as that was.

'Derek, I just want to say how sorry I am,' I said.

'What for?'

'For shouting at you on the phone. The truth is I was having a rough time and I'd been drinking. I'd never shout at you like that otherwise.'

Derek looked at me and then he did something super weird and a bit creepy. He smiled. He grinned at me. It was as if for a moment he seemed genuinely human.

'Harry, all forgotten. Don't worry about it.'

'Oh, right,' I said incredulously. 'So we're good?'

'Definitely. We all do things we regret from time to time. I'm no stranger to the old apology myself,' said Derek with the same creepy smile. 'Pam and I have an announcement to make, so let's go into the living room.'

Derek and Pam called everyone into the lounge for their big news. Derek was definitely acting a big oddly (drugs? dementia? brain tumour?). I really wanted to ask Emily what the fuck was going on, but obviously I couldn't. After a minute and once we were all together, Derek and Pam said in unison,

'We're inviting you all to our new place in Tenerife!'

'And don't worry, Harry, it will be during half-term. What do you say?' said Derek.

I didn't know what to say. I was gobsmacked. What was going on?

'And we're paying for everything,' said Pam. 'It's our treat.'

'You can count us in,' said Dad.

'Harry?' said Derek. 'You in?'

I looked at Emily and she smiled. Was that contact? Either way, it was obvious what she wanted to do, and it wasn't like I had anything against spending a week in Tenerife, even if it was with my potentially dangerous and now weirdly friendly father-in-law.

'Yes,' I said. 'Can't wait.'

'That's settled then,' said Derek. 'A good old-fashioned family holiday!'

I'm very nervous. Why is Derek being so nice? Why are we all going to Tenerife? Did Emily know about this? Why do I feel like I'm being setup? I really need to talk to Emily.

We had a cake for Dad's birthday, and he opened his presents (socks from us and slippers from Derek and Pam), and then we had a few drinks before we went home. However, just before we all left, Dad invited us all to a party at their house at the end of September.

'We're inviting everyone,' said Dad. 'It's a cancer free party for the bravest wife a man could wish for.'

10.15 p.m.

I slipped a note across the bed tonight. It just said, 'Why is your dad being so weird and what's really up with the Tenerife trip?' Emily replied quickly with her own note. 'This is communication. We have to stick to the rules.' Bugger.

Wednesday 11 September 8.30 p.m.

Home. Wet and windy. Watching TV with Emily on the sofa. William asleep.

William is sick. The poor little bugger has a cold. It's so sad when kids aren't well. His poor nose is all stuffed up and he can't sleep. Every few hours we have to suction his nose with the little baby suction thing, which he hates and fights like hell to avoid. He just went back to sleep again. It's also difficult when you can't speak to your wife about it. We go back to Deirdre tomorrow. I don't know what we're expected to feel, but all I feel is annoyance. Maybe my animalistic sense is just pissed off.

11.55 p.m.

Up rocking William. He's asleep in my arms. Every time I try and move him back to his bed he wakes up, starts crying, talks in delirious tongues, and so I have to keep rocking him. I'm probably going to fall asleep in this chair.

Thursday 12 September 7.30 a.m.

Emily came in and woke us up this morning. I'd fallen asleep with William, and I was going to be late for work. Emily couldn't talk or touch me, so she poked me with an umbrella. This is getting ridiculous.

12.30 p.m.

I rushed into work and made it just in time. Chris Bartlett spotted me, pointed at his watch, and then made a note in his annoying little note pad. This is what happens when sad little men get positions of power.

4.45 p.m.

Tonight is our session with Deirdre St Cloud. I finally

get to talk to Emily. I wonder what she's going to say. I wonder what I'm going to say. Who knows what Deirdre is going to say? No doubt it will be utter drivel.

9.30 p.m.

Home. In relationship limbo. Dark and cloudy. As usual I left the session with Deirdre St Cloud with more questions than answers.

Deirdre: Harry, Emily, welcome back, yeah. Harry, have you and Emily spoken or touched this week?

Me: Does being poked by an umbrella count?

Deirdre: I don't think so, yeah. And how did you find it?

Me: Infuriating.

Deirdre: Emily?

Emily: Interesting.

Deirdre: So let's start with you, Harry, yeah. What did you find infuriating about it?

Me: I didn't see the point and I couldn't talk to or touch my wife. I know we're here so obviously we have issues, but I don't see how not talking about it and not touching is going to help, do you? We need to talk, don't you think, Em?

Emily: For once I agree with Harry. I understand the reasoning behind it, Deirdre, I do, but it does feel a bit like a wasted week.

Deirdre: What if I was to say that this past week was supposed to feel like that, yeah? It's designed to give you both a break from all the communication, so you realise, yeah, that actually, you need to talk, yeah, to touch, yeah. This was the whole point. Now you know you have to talk, yeah, so let's talk. Let's start with you, Harry, what do you want to say to Emily and really open up, yeah? Let it all flood out, yeah. It's been a week, let all the tension and frustration and thoughts just fall out of you, yeah. Go!

I didn't know what I was supposed to say. It's one of the

many problems with therapy. Sometimes I think I know what they want me to say and at other times I don't, and then I get confused and end up not even knowing what I want to say.

Me: What's going on with your dad, Em? He was really weird the other day.

Emily: Excuse me?

Deirdre: After a week that's what you wanted to say?

Me: I've just been thinking about it a lot. He usually hates me, but he was really nice and even shook my hand and gave me a pat on the back when we left. I was wondering if something's happened. Is he dying?

Emily: No, Harry, Dad isn't dying.

Me: Then what is it? Brain tumour?

Emily: If you must know he's on medication for his blood pressure. He was getting too irate and so the doctor prescribed some medication to help with his mood swings and high blood pressure. Happy?

Me: As long as he stays on them.

Emily: You see what I'm dealing with here, Deirdre? It's hopeless.

Deirdre: Emily, what did you want to say to Harry, yeah?

Emily spoke in great detail about all the things she'd been thinking about during the week, and she'd even written a little diary of her thoughts and feelings. I was pleased to hear that on one day she'd thought about having sex with me. Most other days weren't so complimentary. She was mostly annoyed.

Deirdre: I think today has been quite illuminating, yeah. I think we've all learnt something, yeah, and I want us to do something a bit different this week. For the next seven days I need you to tell each other everything. Hold nothing back, yeah. Really let it all out there. Leave nothing behind and then next week, I want us to really pinpoint some key changes you can both make, yeah.

It's going to be a terrible week, I just know it. Emily and I haven't said much since we got back. I knew something was up with her dad. Let's hope he stays on the happy pills. If I'd known it was possible that he could be this happy, I'd have been slipping him some of the magic medication much earlier.

Saturday 14 September 6.30 p.m.

Camber Sands Holiday Park. Warmish. Drinking an interesting homemade beer from a caravan neighbour.

They've delayed the decision on the BBC job until Monday and so Steve is on tenterhooks. So to keep his mind off that and on something else, we're all at Camber Sands for the weekend. It's also been quite nice getting away from the house. William is all better now. His cold only lasted for a day. It was horrible seeing the little fella fussing and crying so much.

11.45 p.m.

Steve and Fiona stayed at the caravan with the kids so Emily and I could check out The Powerhouse! It was actually a lot of fun. Emily and I had a dance and drank quite a bit. It was nice to let our hair down and not worry about our marriage and whether we were going to make it or not. This is the trouble. I feel like when we don't think about it and we're just us, we're fine - like in Australia. However, when we start analysing it and talking about it then it all goes to shit. I said this to Emily when we were walking home, and she said that wasn't the problem at all. She said the problem is me and the way I deal with things. I didn't know what to say and so I didn't say anything. Then she got angry and accused me of closing up as per bloody usual and acting like typical bloody Harry. I didn't know what to say to this either. Emily said she didn't want to talk about it because I was too drunk. I said I wasn't too drunk and then Emily said I was denial, and so I asked if she was just talking about being drunk or something else, and she said, 'what do you think?' I didn't know what to say and so I didn't say anything else. These conversations are starting to wear me down. I honestly don't know what I think anymore. Maybe it is all my fault.

Sunday 15 September 8.30 p.m.

Emily and I had a proper conversation tonight. I don't know if it really helped or not, but at the end Emily said, 'Thank you for finally being honest with me.' Like I said, I don't know if this has helped or made it worse. We talked about Mark, and I apologised for punching him and for not trusting her. She said sorry too, but she didn't say what for.

Monday 16 September 8.45 p.m.

Steve got the job! Steve the Entertainer is going to be on the telly! He's completely over the moon and just keeps saying, 'OMG! OMG! OMG!' over and over again. Fiona can't quite believe it either. All the Js seemed a bit confused. The eldest, Jane said, 'You're going to be on CBeebies?' really emphasising the word 'You're'. We had a big takeaway from The Spice of Wimbledon and a few bottles of wine. He said he starts rehearsals in two weeks. The first show isn't going to air until December, but there's no doubt Steve is going to be a bona fide children's TV celebrity. I'm very proud of him. This is what can happen when you follow your dreams.

Wednesday 18 September 12.45 p.m.

At school. Eating a canteen lunch because I woke up too

late to make a packed lunch. Sunny.

There was an article in the newspaper this morning about the old weatherman. Apparently, he's joined a religious cult and is living on the Isle of Man. He was interviewed about his new lifestyle, and it seems he may have taken one too many magic mushrooms in the 90s.

He believes that all human life evolved from Martians that fled Mars two million years ago. He also said it's actually impossible to predict the weather, unless of course you can talk to the great Poompah Martian King who lives in Pembrokeshire. He also rambled on about how the government knows all about this and that it's a huge conspiracy. He also claimed that Elvis Presley is still alive and living in Dundee under the name Wally McManus.

Harry-son-ford

Harry, you big old bender. I hope all's well. We miss you here. It hasn't been the same without you and the gang. Just to let you know, I spoke to Katie, and we've agreed that when we have a kid, I'm going to stay at home and she's going to work. We just have to get pregnant now. I'm trying to persuade her to come back to Blighty for Christmas. We'll have to wait and see, but you might need to set another couple of places for Christmas day. What happened with your mum's results? Is she okay? Give her my love. Take care. Give big kisses to the wee man for me - and Emily too, of course.

Benzonimo x

Ben-d it like Beckham

Good to hear from you old boy. Mum is fine. She got

the all clear from the doctors and is now recovering from the radiotherapy. We would love to have you and Katie over for Christmas - it would be the best present in the world. You'd better let me know as soon as Katie is preggers. I can't believe you're going to be a dad! We had such an amazing time in OZ. I can't wait to come again.

Take care
Harry-Krishna x

Thursday 19 September 10.45 p.m.

Reasons why Harry is a bit of a shit husband by Emily Spencer:

He lied about going on a diet and quitting smoking
He is untrusting and irrational
He followed me and Mark and then punched him like a mental person
He constantly lets me down
He doesn't seem to realise that I'm fed up with always being let down
He says one thing, but then invariably does something else
He talks about change but is actually afraid of it
He was HOD and now isn't and didn't think to ask me if that's okay
Sexually things aren't great
Even though I forgave him for his almost affair last year with that slut Jamie, I don't think he realised how much it hurt our relationship
He seems to love kebabs more than me
And beer
And cigarettes

Emily brought this list to the session with Deirdre.

Deirdre asked how I wanted to respond, and I said that it was all true, except the last three. I love nothing more than Emily. Maybe William, but that's a different sort of love altogether. Deirdre asked us how we were going to fix our relationship and I said I had a plan. When Emily asked what the plan was, I said I couldn't tell her. Deirdre asked Emily the same question and Emily said that the only way we were ever going to work was if I stopped saying things like, 'I have a plan', when quite clearly I didn't have a plan. I really need a plan.

Saturday 21 September 9.45 a.m.

Home. Sunny. Emily at the gym. I wish I had her motivation. Playing Lego with William.

Disaster. My barber Dave is retiring. I've been going to Dave's for as long as I can remember - admittedly, being in my thirties, it isn't that long, but in my brain it is, and no one cuts my hair but Dave. I like going to see Dave. It's comfortable and familiar and I know exactly how the appointment's going to go and what haircut I'm going to get. I went early this morning and Dave was there as usual. We had our usual chat, he gave me my usual haircut, and just before I was about to leave, he dropped the bombshell.

'I'm retiring, Harry. Me and the family are moving to France.'

'Nooooo,' I said. 'Where am I going to get my hair cut now? I don't trust anyone else.'

'You could try John's or there's Franco's?'

'I like coming to you Dave.'

Dave explained that he'd been doing this for thirty years and had always dreamed of retiring to the south of France. Both his kids are at university and so he's off with his wife.

What am I going to do? When I left, Dave did his usual saying goodbye and thank you until I was out of earshot, and it brought a lump to my throat. 'Bye, thank you, cheers, see you later, bye then, take care, thanks so much, bye, bye, thanks, cheers …'

I got home, and Emily left for the gym. I started playing Lego with William and thinking about dreams. Apparently, everyone has a big life dream except for me. Steve is following his dream and Dave is following his. I need a plan, and I need a dream.

Thursday 26 September 9.45 p.m.

That was unexpected. We haven't seen Mark since the French restaurant incident. Tonight he showed up on our doorstep. His house has been on the market for a while, and I think Emily and I assumed we'd seen the last of the dirty dog.

'What do you want?' I said.

Emily overheard and came walking up behind me.

'I don't want any trouble, Harry,' said Mark. 'Hello, Em.'

'Mark,' said Emily standing next to me (a united front?).

'The house is sold and I'm leaving for New York next week. I got a job out there. A fresh start. I just wanted to come by and say goodbye and no hard feelings,' said Mark offering me his hand. A part of me wanted to tell him to fuck off and never blight our doorstep again, but I couldn't. If the truth be told, I sort of felt bad for him. He might have the money and the looks and that mysterious Colin Firth-ness, but he wasn't happy, and he didn't have Emily. He would never have Emily.

'No hard feelings,' I said shaking his hand.

'Bye,' Emily said and that was it, Mark was gone.

When we were back inside, Emily said she was proud of me for the way I handled Mark. She said it showed maturity. She gave me a nice smile and a kiss on the cheek. Definite progress.

Saturday 28 September 10.45 a.m.

Mum's cancer free party today. Emily is out running, and William is watching CBeebies while I'm reading the paper.

It's been okay since Mark came over. Emily and I were far more normal around each other this morning. We're both trying to put everything behind us and move on, but something is still missing. The missing link between slight weirdness and complete happiness. We need to evolve. We need to find the transitional link. Maybe the answer's in the newspaper.

11.05 a.m.

I think I've found the missing link and it was in the newspaper. I looked under the horoscopes first hoping to find some answers, but as usual all I found was complete and utter drivel (the moons in Uranus etc.). I was browsing the classifieds when I saw it and suddenly it all became clear. You know that moment in a film when the character has an epiphany? It was like that. I heard Emily's voice in my head.

'Part of the reason why I love you so much is that you're impulsive and reckless, and yes sometimes it needs controlling, but sometimes it's good.'

Emily said that in the VW campervan on the way to Devon. We had such fun on that trip. It was probably the last time I remember us being truly happy together. I wanted to recreate that again, and Emily had said she wanted to say yes more and be more impulsive. So when I saw the VW campervan for sale in the paper, I knew it was a sign. It was time to be reckless and impulsive. I gave them a call and I'm going to see it tomorrow. I have a dream!

11.45 p.m.

What a party. Loads of people turned up, we all got really drunk, ate lots of food, and Mum cried on average about every two minutes. I saw a few members of the Spencer family I haven't seen in years; old neighbours, new neighbours, old friends of the family and, of course, Derek and Pam. Derek was still in his happy place - he gave me a hug and said he was so happy that I was his son-in-law. A great, emotional night, but the highlight was at the end of the night.

It was just gone nine o'clock and the party was starting to wind down. However, before people started leaving, Dad turned the music off and ushered everyone into the lounge. He hadn't told me what was going on and so I was as confused as everyone else - including Mum.

'Thank you all for coming,' said Dad. 'As you know, Helen has been through a lot this year, but typically of her, she handled it with great aplomb and dignity. She never complained or got down about it. She picked herself up and marched on as she's always done. Helen, you are an incredible woman and an inspiration to us all.'

Mum was crying by now and we all thought Dad had finished so we started clapping, but Dad wasn't done. Not by a long chalk.

'When Helen got cancer, I was terrified and, of course, I thought she might die. But as time's gone on we've both sort of realised that it might have been a blessing in disguise. We weren't as happy as we could have been. We were drifting through life, but now we're focused, and we're going off travelling at the end of the year and we can't wait. However, before that I want us to do something else,' said Dad turning to Mum. 'If you'll have me, Helen, I'd like to walk down the aisle again.' Then Dad got down on one knee and Mum started crying even harder. 'You're the love of my life. The only one I need to be happy, and I can't wait to spend the rest of my life with you. Helen, will you marry me again?'

We were all overwhelmed and there wasn't a dry eye in the house.

'Yes! Yes! Yes!' said Mum, and Dad got up and they kissed. I held Emily's hand and she looked at me and smiled that smile again, and all I could think about was the missing link.

Sunday 29 September 11.45 a.m.

I did it. I lied to Emily and said I was going to the gym when I was actually going to see the VW campervan from the paper. I paid for it and I'm going to pick it up on Tuesday - Emily's birthday. It's going to be a surprise. I just hope it's a good one.

October

Tuesday 1 October 8.45 a.m.

Emily's Birthday

I've taken the day off work, and I've already made Emily a surprise breakfast in bed, and now I'm off to pick up the VW campervan.

'Where are you going again?' said Emily suspiciously.

'I have to pick something up.'

Emily was stood by the front door holding William.

'Umthin' up,' said William.

'That's right, little man,' I said. 'I won't be long.'

Off to follow my dreams or as they seem to say on every American reality competition show; it's time to go big or go home.

1.15 p.m.

'Are you angry? Em, please say something. Anything,' I said. 'This is the missing link. At least I think it is. I hope it is.' Emily was crying. In the street. Holding William. Looking at the VW campervan. And crying. 'I can sell it if you want. I just saw it in the paper, and I thought it could be our thing. You said yourself that sometimes my recklessness was good, and we had such a good time on that holiday that I thought this could be the thing that makes everything all right. Our missing link.'

'Oh, Harry,' said Emily finally. 'It's perfect.'

'Really? You don't think it will just sit on the driveway rusting away until after the twentieth argument you'll force me to sell it?'

'No, I don't think that at all,' said Emily and then she kissed me. Properly kissed me.

'Happy birthday,' I said when she pulled away.

'Pey irthdu,' said William.

'Thank you both,' said Emily. 'Now, where shall we take

her?'

One big happy family with a blue 1977 Volkswagen campervan called Bertie.

Wednesday 2 October 8.45 p.m.

A 'Sold' sign went up across the road today. Mark is officially gone. Let's hope the new neighbours are offensively ugly and as common as muck, or ideally two very gay men. We had dinner in Bertie tonight. We're going to take him somewhere this weekend.

I had a good chat with Steve earlier. He started rehearsing for his new TV show this week. It still feels strange to be writing that. Steve and his TV show. He's been at BBC HQ all week. He gave me the full rundown and told me which celebrities he'd seen in the canteen. I really can't believe Steve the accountant is now Steve the children's TV star. I also can't believe he saw Laurence Llewelyn-Bowen go back for seconds on dessert - he always looks in such good shape on the telly.

I also asked him if he'd had any marriage problems after they'd had their first J.

'Oh, definitely,' said Steve unexpectedly. I can't imagine Steve and Fiona ever having problems. 'The first year is always tough, Harry, very, you know, tense at times. Both tired, still trying to figure everything out, and Fiona's emotions were up and down like a bad balloonist.'

'So it's normal, then?'

'I don't know if it's normal, but it happens. Is everything okay with you and Emily?'

'We're getting there. We've had some problems and we've been seeing a counsellor. I'm hoping Bertie is the missing link.'

'Bertie?'

'Oh, the campervan. We named it Bertie.'

'Oh, yes, I saw the little devil outside. She's a beauty. You should bring her down to Camber. We'll have a ball.'

'Definitely,' I said and for the first time in a while, I saw light at the end of the tunnel.

Thursday 3 October 3rd 8.45 p.m.

Home. In bed. Emily in the shower. Nibbling on a flapjack. Raining - luckily I bought that cover for Bertie.

We had our last session with Deirdre tonight. Emily, Deirdre and I all agreed that things are going well and so we're going to see if we can 'navigate the relationship waves' ourselves without the 'help' of Deirdre St Cloud and her 'lifejackets'. I still don't know what will happen with Emily, but then again, who does? I think we're going to be fine. We're talking more than ever before, and Emily's been impressed with my recent maturity, and buying Bertie. Deirdre thought buying Bertie was a great idea and should, 'Bring us together as a family and promote that true family oneness, yeah'.

When we got back, we had a cuddle on the sofa and watched some TV. Emily mentioned sex for the first time in what feels like years. We might have sex tonight. Fingers crossed.

9.45 p.m.

Failure on the sex front. Emily got out of the shower and said her period had come. At least sex is back on the table and apparently Emily doesn't have to wear the Mega-Pants anymore – double bonus. Things are looking up in the Spencer house.

Friday 4 October 12.45 p.m.

Things are not looking up at school. Chris Bartlett is behaving like a dictator from East European hell and even Clive is getting pissed off about it. He slipped me a note during lunch in the canteen. He's organised a secret meeting in the stock cupboard with me, Eddie Collins and George Fothergill - who is back at school and not sick.

4.45 p.m.

Clive suggested a coup. He wants us to, 'Crush him beneath the weight of his own regime - much like Hitler.' Things are hotting up in the History department. Today Chris instigated a new mandate and is making us submit daily plans to him before school. Clive is outraged and said we must stand strong against the Bartlett machine.

Saturday 5 October 7.45 a.m.

Home. Packing up Bertie. Emily making sandwiches. William in the lounge dancing to Icky Artian. Sunny. The BBC weather girl looked a bit bigger than usual. I think she might be pregnant.

We're taking Bertie on a little road trip. We're driving up towards Cambridge. The weather is supposed to be nice. Let the campervanning begin. The only downside is that Emily seems to have put up some bunting inside Bertie. Poor Bertie.

9.12 p.m.

At a campsite near Cambridge.

There comes a point in every man's life when they realise something very important. Tonight was my moment. William had just gone down to sleep in Bertie, and I was outside, sitting with my feet up, eating a hot dog and drinking a beer, when I had a moment of clarity. This is it. This is who we are.

Part of the problem with Emily and I and the reason we keep having problems is that I've been fighting against the current. Since she announced we were having William, our life has been heading towards this - campervanning like proper middle-class parents. I've been fighting it though and swimming against the current. I always knew this was where we'd end up. It was inevitable, but for some reason I couldn't accept it.

I suppose it all comes back to the same thing. Fear. Having William meant giving up the possibility of weekend mini breaks to Stockholm at the drop of a hat. Being a parent meant accepting that I was no longer young and had to grow up and be responsible. Going on Emily's diet, quitting smoking, and joining the gym all meant the same thing - life in Wimbledon had changed and I had to change with it. The thing was I wasn't sure I was ready. Hence why I failed on so many levels this past year.

Then there was Mark. I wasn't really afraid of Emily cheating on me. I was more afraid that I would never be quite the man Mark was. He seemed so perfect, so together, and so grownup with his money, suits, job in The City, and working out as though he actually enjoyed it. However, as it turned out, he was probably more screwed up than me.

Tonight I realised I'd stopped fighting. I'd stopped trying to be something I no longer was. This is me, this is us, and you know what, I wouldn't change it for the world.

'So basically I'm sorry,' I said to Emily after I'd told her everything. 'I'm happy with you, with us, and the only thing I'm fighting for now is to make this work better than ever.'

'Harry,' said Emily looking across at me.

'Yes.'

'You do realise that you're completely crazy, don't you?'

'I'm a man. We're designed to be ridiculous.'

'You're definitely ridiculous.'

'I'm sure even Ben Fogle's wife gets annoyed with him sometimes. She's probably all like, 'You can row across the bloody Atlantic and yet you can't put your socks away in the right drawer,' I said, and Emily giggled.

'Come here.'

I leaned across and we kissed, and it was perfect, and I couldn't believe I'd spent so long fighting against it. I was happy. Emily was happy. William was asleep in Bertie and I'm not kidding you, but a shooting star shot across the sky and suddenly I had an idea. A really brilliant idea.

Tuesday 8 October 4.45 p.m.

At school. Eating a Twix. Sunny but cold - perfect.

I was in my room when Chris Bartlett came in looking all ruffled and annoyed.

'You didn't submit your plans today,' said Chris.

'Chris, you know we aren't going to do this. It's ridiculous.'

'What's ridiculous is you and the rest of your cronies thinking you can ignore my rules and get away with it. I know your game Spencer,' said Chris and then he left. I may need another stock cupboard meeting with my cronies.

7.45 p.m.

Derek rang me up tonight just to have a chat. It was very strange. His happy pills have taken our relationship to a new and very uncomfortable place. At the end of the conversation, he invited us over to their house on Saturday for the full Tenerife debriefing.

I was putting William to bed tonight and he said, 'wuv you,' and it melted my heart. I miss him being a baby because I used to love holding him in my arms and the moments when he would just lie on me and sleep, but it's pretty incredible now too because he can tell me he loves me all by himself. How brilliant is that?

Thursday 10 October 9.45 p.m.

I went to see Dad today. I had to run my idea by him.

The idea dawned on me when I was talking to Emily because, much like my parents, it feels like we're starting again. It sounds crazy when I think about it. We've been married for seven years, and we have William, but it feels like something new. Then I thought about my parents and how they're getting married again and it struck me. Why don't Emily and I renew our vows? If we're starting over again, then surely it makes sense to get married again too?

'I think it's a great idea,' said Dad over a few beers.

'And I'm not trying to steal your thunder, Dad. I know it's your day. You and Mum, but what if I surprised Emily after you get married? She'll be blown away.'

'Harry, I think it's perfect,' said Dad. 'We're getting married at the end of November and actually, I was hoping you'd be my best man. What do you say?'

'I'd be honoured,' I said, and we had a suitably uncomfortably long man-hug.

All I have to do now is tell Emily's parents too and write my new vows and it looks like Emily and I are getting married again. Ding dong the bells are going to chime.

Saturday 12 October 11.45 p.m.

Emily's parents' house. My parents asleep in the spare room. William asleep in our room. Derek and Pam asleep in their bed and Emily and I up talking and having a drink.

This was great. Mum and Dad are happier than I've ever seen them. Mum's almost like a born-again Christian without the annoying religious bit, while Dad can't do enough for her. Derek is tripping like a bastard on his happy pills and alcohol combination, while Emily and I are definitely hitting our stride again.

We drove Bertie here to show her off. We're going to sleep in her tonight. Pam made some homemade wine and it's going down a treat. It's pretty strong though. Emily's already pretty pissed and I'm getting there myself.

I don't remember much about the Tenerife planning, except that we're definitely going, we're staying at Derek and Pam's apartment, and it's during half-term - all the facts I knew before tonight. This wine really is strong.

Sunday 13 October 8.45 a.m.

What. The. Fuck. Happened? I literally feel as though I've been run over. What the fuck does Pam put in her homemade wine? Emily and I were crashed out in Bertie when there was a knock at the window. It was Mum and apparently it was time to get up.

'What the fuck happened?' said Emily.

'I have no idea,' I said. 'Although I think I know why your dad's been so happy recently.'

We're both still drunk and so we're going to stay here until much later.

3.45 p.m.

Much later. Still feel like death. Emily's parents have taken William to the park so Emily and I can rest.

'Did we have sex last night?' mumbled Emily. 'I remember having sex. I think.'

'I have no idea.'

'It may have been a dream.'

'I don't remember a thing, Em. I think I need to sleep.'
'Me too,' said Emily.

9.15 p.m.
Finally home. I feel as though I just had major surgery. Emily isn't doing any better. William asleep. Emily and I off to bed. Dreading school tomorrow. Ugh.

Monday 14 October 12.15 p.m.

At school. Raining. Eating a school canteen lunch because I slept through two alarms. Rory talking babies, Alan Hughes talking about the girl he shagged at the weekend, and all I'm thinking about is not throwing up. Why did I pick the meatloaf for lunch? Who knows what's in the school meatloaf? Definitely not meat. What the fuck was in that homemade wine?

I got to school this morning and Chris Bartlett called an emergency departmental meeting. It's the last week of school before half-term and I was hoping we could make it without any further drama, but it seems Chris is determined to continue his reign of terror. Clive, Eddie, George Fothergill and me all went to Chris's room, and he was waiting for us.

'Sit down,' said Chris pointing at the desks in front of him. We all sat down, and Chris went off on one. 'I don't know what you think this is, ladies, but I can tell you this for nothing - your little plan to undermine me is going to fail. I've already been to the Head, and he's given me permission to go ahead with the plans. You must submit your written plans for the day, every morning before school or there will be consequences,' said Chris slamming his fists down on the table. I think he's growing a little moustache too. Things are getting out of hand.

I got a message from Clive mid-morning. It just said, 'Meeting. Lunchtime. Stock cupboard. Tell no one'. I got to the stock cupboard not sure what to find, but inside all I found was Clive.

'Quick, come in,' said Clive in hushed tones. I quickly went in, and Clive closed the door and turned on the light. 'This stops now.'

'What does?' I said.

'Bartlett and his regime. We need to replace him. Coup d'état, Harry! Coup d'état!'

'Don't you think that's a bit strong?'

'He's gone too far. We need to find a way to undermine him, unsettle his position of power, and then we strike, and I know how.'

'How?'

'We need someone on the inside, Harry. You need to get close to him and then we can take him down from within.'

'I could just go and see the Head. Mr Jones is very reasonable—'

'No, Harry, it has to go down like this.'

Clive was very het up and I felt like I was dealing with a top-drawer Mafia sting instead of a middle-management disagreement at a secondary school in south-west London. I had little choice but to agree though. Clive can be very persuasive and maybe Chris had gone too far. We had to take him down - Wimbledon style. Or I could just try and talk to Chris teacher to teacher.

Tuesday 15 October 4.15 p.m.

At school. Eating an apple I found in my cupboard. It might be a bad apple.

I spoke to Chris Bartlett man to man, teacher to teacher, and I told him about the Mafia style Coup d'état and that he needed to treat us like equals instead of POWs. Chris responded thus.

'I know when you were Acting Head, Harry, you let things go. You didn't care because that's you, Harry. You're wishy-washy, you aren't a leader, you're beige, Harry, beige. You let people get away with murder because you think it's nice and people should just get along, but obviously that doesn't work. You failed and now I'm in charge. It's my way or the highway and be careful on the highway because you might get run over!' he said this and then gave me a sinister look as though I might meet a sudden and mysterious end.

I think Chris Bartlett may have gone a bit mental. I'm going to see Mr Jones to end this madness.

Wednesday 16 October 12.15 p.m.

At school. Raining. Eating lunch, small carrots, hummus, cottage cheese and grapes. When did lunch come to this? What happened to the good old-fashioned sandwich?

I went to see Mr Jones today and told him that Clive and Chris are heading towards their own version of the Cuban Missile Crisis. I explained that he had to do something otherwise he'd have blood on his hands.

'I feared this, Harry,' said Mr Jones. 'Chris cares deeply about the department, but maybe too deeply. I'll have a little talk with him.'

'Thank you.'

'But let's be clear, if I have to move Chris on, the only other person who can do the job is you. Would you be up for a second bash? Is everything okay at home?'

'We're doing much better. I found the missing link.'

'That's wonderful news. So, Harry, does that mean?'

'Let me talk to Emily first,' I said.

'Good answer,' said Mr Jones with a knowing smile.

8.45 p.m.

I told Emily about the whole Chris/Clive/Mafia/Coup d'état/meeting with Mr Jones thing, and she said I should be HOD again if that's what I wanted. I don't know if I do or not.

HOD Pros and Cons

Pros

More money

Sense of accomplishment and career progression

Being able to change things for the better

Chris Bartlett wouldn't be HOD

It would help prevent the end of days between Chris and Clive

Cons

The endless meetings

And the pre-meetings

The hours I'm away from Emily and William

The realisation that I can't actually change things for the better and that I'm basically a Whitehall puppet

The mountains of paperwork

More days not teaching (which I generally enjoy) and more days training (which I generally don't)

The pre-meeting pre-meetings

Norris Roker

The cons definitely have it.

Friday 18 October 4.55 p.m.

What a last day at school. At the end of the day Mr Jones called Chris Bartlett to his room. I joined Eddie and George Fothergill in Clive's room as we waited to see what would happen. It was tense. After about thirty minutes, Chris came storming into the room and for a moment there was a standoff. Chris looked at us and we looked at Chris.

'Mr Jones wants to see you, Harry,' said Chris eventually.

'Oh, right,' I said innocently.

I went to see Mr Jones, not really sure what to expect, but when I walked in it was obvious what had happened. Mr Jones is usually pretty composed, but he looked shaken.

'Sit down, Harry,' said Mr Jones. Then he did something unexpected. He reached into his desk drawer and pulled out a small bottle of Scotch. 'Something for the weekend?'

'Oh, sure,' I said.

'Mum's the word,' said Mr Jones passing me a shot of Scotch. 'Cheers.'

'Cheers,' I said and then we both took our shot.

'Arrrgh always gets the throat doesn't it, eh?'

'Sure does.'

'Chris is no longer the Head of Department. I tried to talk him around, but he called me a liberal, government fluffer and said that he couldn't work with his balls being shackled by Whitehall. I accepted his resignation, which means the position's open if you want it?'

Going into that room I had no idea what I was going to do if he offered me the job. The pros and cons were fairly conclusive, but suddenly, standing there, I wanted it. It was time I stopped treading water at school and if I could fix things with Emily, then maybe I could also be the best bloody Head of Department they'd ever had. And if not the best, then certainly better than Chris Bartlett.

'It doesn't look like I have any choice,' I said.

'That deserves another shot of Scotch,' said Mr Jones.

I'm HOD again, but this time I'm actually going to take it seriously. However, that can wait because I need to go home and pack for our week away to Tenerife with Mum, Dad, Pam and Derek. God help us all.

Sunday 20 October 10.55 a.m.

After Australia we really have this packing thing down. It's a piece of cake. Admittedly, Emily has a larger piece of the cake to deal with, but we're all packed and ready to go. Our flight is from Stansted at two o'clock. We leave in fifteen minutes.

It's time to go abroad, get pissed and behave like typical Brits in the sun. Give us two days and Mum will be as red as a lobster (factor 15 is fine, Harry. It works in England, I don't see why it won't work in Spain), Dad will spend the week shouting at everyone under the illusion that by shouting at people they will be able to understand him better (we're going to bloody Tenerife, Dad, not Borneo. They all speak English), Derek will no doubt argue with some unruly Germans about reserving spots by the pool, and before long 'The War' will get mentioned, and I'll get too drunk and throw up in the street. Brits on tour. How embarrassing and cliché, although for some reason I'm strangely excited about it. Maybe this is all part of the new me.

8.55 p.m.

Playa de las Americas, Tenerife. Hot.

We finally arrived after a very interesting flight. Apparently, big, brave, ex-copper Derek is terrified of flying. The only way he will fly is with medication and alcohol. So as soon as we all got to the airport, Derek was off to the bar and Dad, and I joined him while the girls and William got a cup of coffee at Costa. An hour later and we were boarding, and Derek was swaying backwards and forwards, talking nonsense, and then he told the stewardess she reminded him of Audrey Hepburn (compliment) in drag (insult).

The rest of the four-and-a-half-hour flight was mainly trying to keep Derek from A: Insulting any more stewardesses and B: Staggering around the plane like a drunken bastard.

'Is he always like this?' Mum said to Pam.

'It's worse with the medication, but yeah.'

Eventually we landed in Tenerife and got taxis to the apartment. It's super nice and has two bedrooms and a pull-out bed in the lounge/living area. Derek and Pam are in one room, Mum, Dad and William are in the second bedroom, and Emily and I are on the pull-out bed. Let the holidaying begin.

Monday 21 October 11.55 a.m.

We all woke up fairly early this morning. Actually William woke up early and so we were all awake too. The joy of being in the living room bed is that we have to wake up when everyone else does.

We left the apartment en-masse and went to the local English/Spanish cafe around the corner, Super Breakfast Cafe where for five Euros you can get the Super Breakfast Special (full English and a pint of lager). Obviously all the men ordered the Super Breakfast Special, while the girls and William went for the healthier choices. 'When in Spain,' said Dad taking a sip of his Carlsberg lager and eating a greasy banger with brown sauce - literally the most un-Spanish thing in Spain.

After breakfast we all went for a dip in the pool, which was lovely, and William had a blast. We brought along his little floats which we put on his arms, and he floated gently around the pool giggling. Mum's already starting to get a bit red (I don't understand it, Harry) and Dad is shouting at everyone as often as possible. Why does Dad suddenly turn into Del Boy as soon as he hits foreign shores? He also refuses to take off his vest (An Englishman never takes off his vest, Harry).

I'm writing this at the pool. Tonight Emily and I are going to stay in with William so the old folks can paint the town red. Tomorrow Derek and Pam will stay in, then Mum and Dad and so on. Although on Thursday it's Derek's birthday and so we're having a boys' night out. I'm already dreading it. Me, my dad and Derek living it large in Tenerife. It has disaster written all over it.

Tuesday 22 October 2.55 p.m.

Everyone back at the apartment taking a siesta. I wasn't tired and so I'm in The British Bulldog pub having a quiet pint and watching a repeat of a football match between Spurs and Arsenal from 1996.

Another relaxing morning. We got up, went to Super Breakfast Cafe and had the five Euro special again. I'm getting quite used to lager for breakfast and as Dad said again, 'When in Spain.' After breakfast we went to the beach and William made a sandcastle, while Mum got redder still and Derek got in a disagreement with a German couple about towels (oh, dear, it's started already), although no mention of 'The War' as yet. It seemed to end fairly peacefully.

This afternoon we're going to laze by the pool and then Emily and I are off out for the night with Mum and Dad. Should be interesting.

11.48 p.m.

Home. Drunk (ish). Emily slaughtered and falling all

over the place. Mum equally as slaughtered. She spent five minutes trying to get the key in the apartment door, while telling everyone to shh. She was shhing so loudly she consequently woke everybody up.

We had a great time with Mum and Dad. We ended up going out for a slap-up meal and drinking a lot of wine. Seeing Mum laughing again and joking around with Dad almost brought tears to my eyes. During a moment alone while the girls went off to powder their noses, Dad asked about me and Emily.

'Is everything all right now?' said Dad.

'Yeah, I think so. I know a big part of it was me. The way I reacted to things and dealt with stuff. Basically I was being a plonker,' I said, and Dad chuckled.

'I know what you mean. All that stuff with your mum and Eleanor.'

'Camel-toe?'

'Yeah,' said Dad smiling. 'It all happened because I was being an idiot. Your mum cheated with Larry, but only because I wasn't paying her the attention she deserved. I was too busy playing golf and being, well, a bit of a plonker.'

'Grandad once said to me when I asked his advice about something, 'We're men, Harry, it's in our DNA, and he was right. We're idiots and the reason we need women is to stop us from being idiots. Sometimes they fail and sometimes we fail, but we can't stop trying.'

'So you're still trying?'

'Every second, Dad. I love her too much not to.'

'I know,' said Dad and I saw tears bubbling around his eyes. Then the girls came back giggling about something. I saw Dad look across at Mum and he smiled. His face melted and all that was left was pure and unadulterated love.

Eventually, we stumbled out of the restaurant and headed home. I haven't been drunk with my parents for a long time, but I enjoyed every minute. Well, almost. When we got back Mum walked in on me having a wee and said, 'Ooo, I haven't seen that little fella for a long time.' Not the way to end the night.

Wednesday 23 October

Super Breakfast Café Special.
Pool
Drinks
Lunch
Siesta
Beach
Drinks
Pool
Dinner
Drinks
Pool
Drinks
TV
Drinks
Snack
Drinks
Shower
Bed

Thursday 24 October 4.55 p.m.

Derek's 60th Birthday

Another lovely day in Tenerife. Today we all went to a water park. We had a great time and William had so much fun. He kept saying, 'Gen Addy, gen Addy,' every time we got to the bottom of the kiddie's flume. I love spending all this time with him, but it makes me think even more about all the hours I'm going to be at work soon, and all the time I'm not going to see him. Small blessings, at least I'm a teacher and I get plenty of time off.

Tonight it's the boys' night out. I have no idea what's in store. Probably the pub, darts, food, beer, pool, possibly a celebratory cigar, and maybe we'll sing him 'happy birthday' over a few shots, and then back home before midnight.

Friday 25 October 1.15 a.m.

Oh my Christ! Derek's in jail!

The evening was going fine until Derek decided he wanted to hit the Scotch. I had sudden flashbacks to What Happened on the Landing, but I couldn't have imagined it happening again, and especially not in a busy, bustling club in Tenerife.

The night started well enough. We had a curry and a few beers. The plan was to visit a few different pubs and maybe, if we felt like it, a club. It was just after ten o'clock and we were all a bit drunk, especially Derek who is also on his medication for the rage. We were walking towards the last pub when we were stopped by a very attractive young woman, who insisted we try out her club. It was, apparently, the best, most pumping club in Tenerife, yeah, with the hottest, sexiest girls. She may have been attractive, but she obviously didn't know her clientele. There was sixty-yea-old Derek, fifty-nine-year-old Dad (who was wearing socks, brogue shoes and shorts) and me. We all had on wedding rings and hardly looked like the sort of men who needed the best club in Tenerife with the hottest, sexiest girls. And I'm fairly confident that none of us had 'pumped it' in a very long time. However, for some reason, Derek wanted to go in.

Fast forward an hour and Derek is sloshed, knocking

back the Scotch like it's going out of fashion, dancing with a group of young girls. I was sitting with Dad, trying to work out how we ended up there, when I looked over and all of a sudden, I saw it. Naked Derek! Then I heard screams. Girls were running in all directions. The bouncers were running towards Derek. Five minutes later, Derek was in the back of a police van, Dad was shouting at the policeman to try and find out where he was going, I was telling Dad to stop shouting before he got arrested too, and then Derek was gone and we had to come back and tell the girls what had happened. As they weren't drunk, Emily and Pam went to rescue Derek from a potentially perilous night in a Spanish jail.

9.55 a.m.

Derek finally came home this morning at nine o'clock. He was let off with a warning. Pam and Emily were there from about three o'clock. Pam called an old friend from the force, and they managed to pull some strings. Derek looked very embarrassed though and hasn't said much since his release.

Emily, Pam and Derek are all asleep. Today is our last full day here and I intend to enjoy it. I'm taking William to Super Breakfast Cafe for the five Euro special and then we're going to the pool for a swim. It's especially hot today. It's only ten o'clock and it's already stinking out there.

3.15 p.m.

Derek issued an official apology after lunch. We'd just finished, and Derek stood up.

'I'd just like to say how sorry I am for last night and the incident at the club. It was beyond reproach, and I feel absolutely awful. I hope you'll all bear with me while I work through this difficult time. Obviously I'm taking a break from the Scotch.'

He sat down, and I have to admit that a part of me (most of me, actually), did have a warm glow of satisfaction. After all my troubles with the Lamb family, my constantly getting into trouble, being accused of raping and being responsible for the death of Beatrice Lamb, it felt good to know that Derek had fucked up too. He'd also got naked and spent the night in jail - far worse than anything I've done.

9.45 p.m.

A meal out tonight. It's been quite an eye-opening holiday. The main thing though is that I got to spend some quality time with my parents, and Emily and I are back to normal. Life is back on an even keel again (definitely a different keel) but at least even.

Tomorrow we fly home. It's cold and wet in Wimbledon - brilliant. Off to bed in the living room. I am looking forward to our own bed again. Emily didn't want to do anything sexual here just in case someone walked in on us, and I can't blame her. We're just getting back into the sexy place, and nothing pours cold water on the possibility of sex than being caught fornicating by parents. It could set us back months.

Saturday 26 October 7.55 p.m.

Home. Wimbledon. Tired. William asleep. Raining. Cold.

Tenerife feels like a lifetime ago already. Derek flew home sans-alcohol and spent the whole flight strapped in, holding on like a white-knuckle ride at the funfair. The flight was a bit bumpy too which made him shriek like a little girl, which obviously made me happy. William loved the bumps and was shrieking and giggling. 'Or Addy, or Addy,' said William as the plane went up and down and Derek was as white as a sheet. I felt slightly guilty for enjoying it so much.

Sunday 27 October 10.55 p.m.

Home. In the shed. Eating a sausage roll and a packet of crisps. Still raining. The BBC weather girl (who I'm sure is pregnant) has predicted rain for another week. Brilliant.

Steve popped over this morning and gave me updates on his glittering new career at the BBC. He's loving every minute of his life and the first show airs in two weeks. They've already recorded five shows and apparently Steve the Entertainer has gone down a storm. According to Perry Pembroke (Steve's agent), he could be in line for a pay raise and maybe a bigger slot on the show - or maybe even his own show. Perry is excited. Steve is excited and I'm very excited. Life really is changing in Wimbledon.

I spoke with Dad about the wedding and it's going to be held at their local church. The vicar is a young, modern thinking bloke apparently and is more than happy to hold the ceremony there, and also for Emily and me to renew our vows too. I'm getting excited and nervous. If Bertie was the missing link, this is going to be final piece of the jigsaw. Mum and Dad are having a dance/disco in the church hall afterwards - a big piss-up and then they're off interrailing around Europe.

Wednesday 30 October 3.35 a.m.

Lying in bed. Emily asleep. Just got off the phone with Ben. I was sound asleep when my phone started buzzing and then the opening to Paperback Writer started playing.

'What the fuck is that?' said Emily.

I reached across and answered it. When your phone goes off during the night, a few things go through your mind. It's either A: Bad news. B: Good news or C: A wrong number. I was hoping for B or C.

'Hello,' I mumbled, rubbing my eyes.

'G'Day mate,' said Ben loudly.

'Ben, do you know what time it is?'

'Yeah, of course, I'm not an idiot.'

'So you're just an inconsiderate fool then?'

'No mate, I'm going to be a father. Katie's pregnant!'

I instantly sat up in bed.

'Oh, mate that's brilliant news. I'm so chuffed for you.'

'What's going on?' said Emily sleepily.

'Katie's preggers.'

'Oh, great, give them my best,' said Emily and went straight back to sleep.

'Emily sends her best.'

'Cheers,' said Ben. 'I had to tell you as soon as we knew. We haven't even told Karl and Sheila yet.'

'You'd better tell Karl, you bastard, otherwise he'll bloody chuck you out on the bloody streets you bloody no-hoper, bludging bastard.'

'They're next on the list you bastard,' said Ben.

I went downstairs and talked to Ben for a while about this and that. I told him about Derek getting arrested, which he found hilarious, and about Emily and me being good again. Ben is excited to be a dad and it's funny, I could never have imagined him being one even a year ago, but now I couldn't imagine him not.

I still can't sleep and so I'm just going to lie here and listen to Emily gently snoring and William on his monitor. Occasionally William will have a dream and he'll shout something out. It's mostly unintelligible, but he just shouted out something about me. I heard him say, 'Addy, Addy!'

It's crazy being a parent because it's overwhelming and fills me with more love and terror than I ever thought possible. Hearing him calling for me in his sleep, the fact that he dreams about me and thinks about me and relies on me for everything, is the most comforting thing in the world. I love it and yes, it's scary, but knowing that Ben is about to have this too fills me with even more happiness. I can't wait to share everything with him. It's then I realised I'm finally Steve. I've reached the pinnacle of parenting, Mount Parent, where nothing kid related is off limits. Where the desire to talk about them and share every detail of their life is not only encouraged but mandatory, where every single thing you do revolves around them and what they need, and nothing I need is that important anymore. I stuck my flag in the ground, claimed my place among the other parents who have clambered up this high, and declared this spot in the name of William Spencer - my son.

November

Friday 1 November 6.05 a.m.

Up early. The birds are singing, the sun is shining, and Emily and William are still asleep. Drinking coffee and eating Marmite toast.

Last night Emily asked me what I thought about during sex.

'What do you mean?' I said.

'When we're having sex, what do you think about?' said Emily again.

'Nothing, of course. Why? What do you think about?'

'Oh, just the usual stuff. Shopping lists, things I have to do around the house, shows I have to record on TV.'

'But that's mental. You have time to think during sex?'

'It's the only time I get to really just think with nothing else going on.'

'What do you mean, nothing else going on?'

'You know what I mean.'

'So while I'm due south giving you my best moves, taking you to the pinnacle of pleasure—'

'I wouldn't say pinnac—'

'Pinnacle of pleasure, you're thinking about recording EastEnders?'

'Sometimes, yes.'

'And you think other women do this?'

'Of course, we all do.'

'So you're saying that while I'm riding you like a prize-winning racehorse, you're wondering whether we should have porridge or Crunchy Nut Cornflakes for breakfast.'

'It's called multi-tasking, Harry.'

'But not during sex, Em. It almost feels, I don't know, blasphemous.'

'I don't think it is, Harry and besides, it's not like I'm not enjoying it. I love having sex with you, but if I can cross off a few things in my head while we're doing it, even better.'

And right there we have one of the fundamental differences between the sexes. Women think of sex in the same way they think of vacuuming, it's something else to cross off the list. Men just have a blank piece of paper with the word sex on and that's our list. And it never gets crossed out.

Saturday 2 November 3.45 p.m.

It's happened. We have new neighbours across the street. After the awful and racist disaster that was Mrs Crawley moved out last year, and then the snake in the grass that was Mark, I'm just hoping for someone nice and normal.

Emily and I were peeking through the blinds and it looks like there's a man about my age (slightly podgier, a tad greyer up top, tracksuit bottoms and jumper - all good signs), his pregnant wife (brown mousy hair, fairly short, anorak wearer - also good signs), and they have a little girl who looks about two years old (brown hair, cute, freckles). The good thing is that they weren't driving a fancy car (old Volvo) and none of them are that attractive. I mean that in the nicest possible way. They seem normal. Just like us.

Although knowing my luck they'll be born again Christians who wear Jesus creepers, make us say grace before having a cup of tea, and will force us to attend their church because it's actually really cool and not like church at all (even though it will be just like church, but with more guitars and lots of tambourines and a really young vicar called Dylan who will say 'groovy' a lot).

7.45 p.m.

I had a chat with Dad on the phone earlier.

'I want a stag party,' said Dad.

'Excuse me?'

'I want a proper stag party, Harry. When I married your mum, I didn't really have one. All I had was a couple of pints with Dad down the local. This time I want a real one.'

'You want a proper stag night? Lots of beer? Club? Strippers?'

'The whole nine yards and I want you to organise it. I've got a list of people I want you to invite. It's going to be on Saturday 23rd so you don't have long. I'm putting all my faith in you, Harry. Don't let me down.'

'No worries. If you want a proper stag party, then a proper stag party you shall have. Just email me the list and I'll get cracking.'

'Brilliant,' said Dad. 'Oh, your mum wants a quick word. Night, son.'

'Night, Dad.'

'Harry, it's your mother. I have something to ask you and you can say no if you want, of course, but since I'm getting married again and my own father is no longer around, I was hoping you'd do me the honour of giving me away. I know you're the best man too, but I'd love it if you'd do it for me,' Mum finished, but I was suddenly too choked up to speak. 'Hello? Harry, are you there? Hello? I think he's gone.'

'Sorry,' I said wiping tears from my face. 'I'd love to Mum.'

'Oh, brilliant,' said Mum. 'It will mean the world to me. Thank you, Harry.'

'Love you, Mum.'

'Oh, one last thing.'

'What's that?' I said sniffling up tears.

'Take care of your father on his stag. I don't want him tied naked to a lamp post in Skegness.'

'I don't think there's much chance of that.'

'And if you get a stripper, make sure she has big boobs. Your father likes them big, Harry. The bigger the better.'

Lordy!

Sunday 3 November 7.45 p.m.

I'm in love. We just met our new neighbours and they're perfect. They popped over to introduce themselves and we had a cup of tea, and within minutes the chemistry was buzzing all over the place.

The dad is Phil Gibson, thirty-five, originally from Billericay, Essex, an electrical engineer, and he likes First World War trivia (did my dissertation on that at university). He loves nineties music (check), enjoys a good shed (check), and best of all he makes his own home brew - in the shed (double check). He might become my new best friend. His wife Dawn is thirty-two and six months pregnant with their second. She's originally from Devon and is a stay-at-home Mum. She's lovely and immediately struck up a conversation with Emily, and within minutes they were the best of friends. They have a two-year-old called Stacey who started playing with William, and even he seemed over the moon. As soon as they left, I immediately turned to Emily, and she turned to me, and we both smiled.

'Perfect,' we said in unison.

9.45 p.m.

'I have to arrange Dad's stag do,' I said to Emily in bed.

'Oh, right, any ideas?'

'Some. He wants a proper stag night. The whole nine yards.'

'The whole nine yards?'

'He wants a stripper and according to Mum, he likes big boobs. The bigger the better.'

'Ooo, that's a bit …'

'Yeah, I know. Still it's what he wants and I'm the best man, I can't let him down.'

'And your mum's okay with this?'

'She's encouraging me.'

'Gross.'

'I know. And your dad's coming too. Let's hope he keeps his clothes on this time. The last thing this stag night needs is two strippers, especially if one's your dad.'

Emily didn't laugh at this. It's still a bit of a sensitive subject in the Lamb family.

Tuesday 5 November 9.15 p.m.

Guy Fawkes Night

Tonight was William's first proper fireworks night. He was barely out of the womb last year, but now he was properly excited. We told him all about it. The colours, the lights, and the loud bangs. We found a great fireworks show at a park nearby and we'd already arranged to walk there with Steve, Emily and the Js. We also invited our new neighbours, Phil, Dawn and Stacey, and so we all met up outside ready to go and see a wonderful fireworks display, eat hot dogs, drink hot chocolate and tea, and say 'ooh' and 'ahh' a lot.

It was the perfect night. It was cold but bearable after we'd wrapped up nice and warm. We put William in a big jacket with a nice, warm fur collar. He had on his woolly hat and gloves and looked absolutely adorable. The sky was dark and clear, so a thousand stars lit our way to the park.

We stood in the field with a few hundred other people. Children had sparklers and were racing them around in circles and William giggled with joy. The Js ran around, and little Stacey held William's hand. It was one of those nights that took me back to my own childhood. I stood with Emily who looked gorgeous all wrapped up with her scarf and gloves and we were happy. So happy. It was a wonderful night, until the fireworks started and William Freaked. The. Fuck. Out. He cried like he's never cried before. He was scared shitless. The firework had barely started, and I was running, and leaping across potholes, William clinging to my chest and wailing until we got home.

Wednesday 6 November 8.45 p.m.

Home. Eating a bowl of cereal. Damp. Emily watching TV - something American with a fat lady who keeps saying, 'Not on my watch,' and a black man who keeps talking about the streets man and getting very annoyed at another man (who isn't black but talks like he should be) and keeps saying things like, 'That ain't cool, man.' There's also another lady (who isn't fat but does have a lady mullet) and she keeps yelling at everyone and saying, 'That ain't real. You be playing me because that shit ain't real.' I literally have no idea what's going on, but something isn't cool, and something isn't real.

Friday 8 November 5.15 p.m.

At school. Cold. Eating a packet of crisps from the vending machine and a slightly old pork pie I had in the fridge. Emily and William having dinner with Stella from Kingston-upon-Thames.

Oh, the joys of being HOD again. At least my official title is now Head of Department, although Mr Jones did say that they're thinking of changing it to reflect a more modern approach to the complex structural integrity of the department. Apparently 'Head' sounds too much like I'm in charge, whereas they want something that gives a flavour of authority, but in less of an authoritative way, and with more emphasis that I'm their leader, charging them towards a better future together - as a team.

Today I had two pre-meetings, one actual meeting, and

then my departmental meeting, which went about as well as can be expected. Chris was fairly subdued, although he did manage to get in a few digs at me and the 'pussy liberal system that rewards mediocrity and conformity'. Clive is on my side now and seems to be using me as some sort of mouthpiece for his agenda, while Eddie has become a slightly annoying born-again hippy who is really 'relaxed and chilled' about everything, and George Fothergill was off sick again.

I'm just looking at Dad's list for his stag party. I'd better start planning it. I'm going to do the same day in the country we did for Ben's stag party. A day of adventure and manly pursuits before we head back into London for some drinks, a club, and strippers. Dad is going to get the real deal. I just need to contact everyone on the list. There's Uncle Pete, Dad's brother we never see because he lives in Bristol and is a bit weird. Frank Worthington, Dad's best friend from school (who is also my Godfather even though I don't know him, and I was about seven or eight when I last saw him), and Derek, obviously. I'm also going to invite Steve, who Dad's known for years, to keep me sane. Six men and one day to remember (hopefully for all the right reasons).

Sunday 10 November 9.15 a.m.

Home with William. Emily at the gym working out with Rocky. Sunny. Excited.

Phil's invited Steve, Fiona, the Js and us over this afternoon. He wants to show Steve and me the shed. I have to say I'm rather excited about it. Home brew, the shed, kids playing together, the wives nattering about whatever it is that women natter about (The X-Factor? The price of nappies? Ben Fogle?) and I intend to have fun and get a bit drunk on Phil's home brew.

11.55 p.m.

Home. Drunk. What a brilliant day. Phil and Dawn are brilliant. Phil's home brew is brilliant. All is brilliant in Wimbledon. Brilliant.

Wednesday 13 November 9.15 p.m.

'Fancy sex? We could bring out the costumes,' I said to Emily about eight o'clock with a sly wink.

'Not tonight, Harry. I'm not feeling well.'

'Are you okay?'

'Yeah, just a bit yuk.'

'Girls' problems?'

'Something like that.'

'Enough said.'

Harry-Kari

Hello mate. I hope all is well in wonderful Wimbledon. All good here. Katie is feeling okay at the moment, but it's still early. I have some bad news. I don't think we'll be able to make it over for Christmas. With Katie being pregnant and with lots to do here to get ready, I think we'll have to give it a miss this year. Maybe next? Miss you big fella. Karl and Sheila send their love. Actually, Sheila sends her love and Karl called you a Pommie bastard.

Love to all
Benjonimo x

I'm disappointed he won't be able to make it for Christmas. It would have been good to all be together on the most wonderful day of the year. It's still going to be an excellent Christmas. It's William's first proper one (I hope it goes better than fireworks night) and Mum and Dad will be back from their interrailing trip before heading off again in the new year. Derek and Pam will be over (hopefully fully clothed), and I have a few drinks with Rory lined up. Plus, we have Steve, Fiona and the Js next door, and now Phil, Dawn and Stacey across the road.

It's certainly been an up and down year with many highs and quite a few lows, but I must say that I'm looking forward to the next couple of months - especially the secret wedding with Emily. Let's hope there aren't any more surprises in store for us. For once, I just want everything to go as planned. Is that too much to ask?

Friday 15 November 5.15 p.m.

At school. Wet. Cold.

I'm off out with Rory for the night. I haven't seen much of him recently and now Miranda is a bit further along and not throwing up and blaming Rory for getting her pregnant, he's allowed out for a few beers.

'Ready?' said Rory appearing at my door.

'Definitely,' I said. 'And starving.'

We're off to The Alexandra for the night. We're going to have a proper dinner, quite a few pints, and we're going to talk absolute shit until we're too drunk, and then we'll plod home. This is the thirties equivalent of a blinding night out. We know our limits. I also have Dad's stag do next week which will no doubt be a bit messy.

11.50 p.m.

Home. A great night with Rory. Surprisingly, not that drunk. Maybe I'm getting a second wind of alcohol stamina or maybe it was because over the five hours we were in the pub we only drank six pints. We're now the old men who cuddle pints for forty-five minutes, sitting by the roaring fire eating pork scratchings. We had a lovely dinner and a really great chat.

'You were right,' said Rory.

'About what?'

'It does get better. At least at the moment it's brilliant.'

'Start of the second trimester things really pick up.'

'It's funny, when people used to talk about that glow pregnant women have, I never knew what they meant. What the fuck's a glow? But now I know, and I don't know about you, but I've never found her sexier. There's just something about her at the moment, it drives me wild,' said Rory.

'I know what you mean. When Emily was about six months gone, I couldn't keep my hands off her.'

'I'm the same with Miranda. I think she's getting a bit fed up with it to be honest.'

'They do get incredibly horny for a few months. My advice is to enjoy it while you can because like I said, it changes, and then before you know it you'll have a kid and sex will be the last thing on both your minds.'

'Are you and Emily getting back to normal again, you know, sexually?'

'Slowly,' I said. 'It took a while though.'

'But you also have William.'

'Yeah, they really do change everything. I know it's a bit cliché, but you'll never be the same again.'

Rory has really come around to being a dad. I suppose it always takes men a bit longer than women. It took me a while before I stopped being too scared to really enjoy being a parent. That's the thing though, once you relax and don't think about it too deeply, it's beautiful and as I'm discovering, that applies to a lot of things in this world, not just parenthood.

Wednesday 20 November 8.15 p.m.

Text from Phil.

Come over. In the shed. Use the side gate. Tell no one.

I really didn't know what to think, but I told Emily I was popping out and made my way over to Phil's. I let myself in through the side gate and crept down the side of the garden to the shed. There was a light inside. I knocked lightly on the door. After a moment, the door opened just enough for me to get inside, and Phil ushered me in.

'What's going on?' I said. 'What's with the covert operation?'

'Because of this,' said Phil with a big smile.

There was a table in the shed and it was covered by a grey blanket, but when Phil removed the blanket with a whip of his wrist, suddenly I saw it. The table wasn't just a table anymore, but a battle scene. Phil had recreated a battle from World War One. He had the trenches, the soldiers, tanks, little trees, barbed wire and everything else. It looked incredible.

'Fucking hell!' I said.

'What do you think?'

'I think it's fucking brilliant, mate. What battle?'

'The Somme. I used real photos.'

I had a look around and it was truly incredible. I've seen lots of photos of the Battle of the Somme myself and he'd done a great job. The detail was unbelievable.

'I'm really impressed.'

'Well, this one's done. It took me over a year in my spare time to get it just right, but like I said, it's done. So what I was thinking was, would you like to do one together?'

I felt a lump in my throat.

'Phil, I'd be honoured.'

'But we keep it between us, yeah?'

'Of course.'

'If the women get wind of this, there'll be questions. They won't understand.'

'Phil, enough said,' I said, and Phil poured me a home brew. World War One battle scene recreation and home brew in a shed - I was sure I'd crossed some sort of line, but I didn't care. I was all in.

Saturday 23 November 7.45 a.m.

Dad's Stag

Mum and Dad are already here. I instructed him to get here before everyone else as we're off to see Grandad. I thought it would be a nice way to start the day - have a quick beer together before we head off on the stag. Mum's going to spend the day and night with William and Emily. She doesn't like being home alone and we thought it would be nice for her to spend some time with William before she leaves to go interrailing.

'Where are we going so bloody early?' said Dad with a yawn.

'To see Grandad and you'll need this,' I said tossing him a cold can of lager.

'It's a bit early.'

'It's your stag, Dad, it's never too early.'

'Fair enough,' said Dad and off we went.

9.30 a.m.

Just back from seeing Grandad. Dad and I sat by his grave. It was bloody cold, but we drank a beer and told Grandad everything about the day. It still feels so strange that it was only just over a year ago since we had Grandad's stag and then his wedding. It's such a shame he couldn't be here for Dad's. He would have loved it. A day out on the lash with the boys.

Everyone else will be here soon and then we're going out for a slap-up breakfast, before we head into deepest, darkest Surrey for a day of archery, off-road three wheeling, and clay pigeon shooting, before we head into London for a night of debauchery. We've also booked a hotel in central London, so we don't have to try and make it back to Wimbledon.

Sunday 24 November 1.45 p.m.

I opened my eyes and a swirl of pain shot around my head, and for a moment I was confused and disorientated. Where was I? And what the fuck happened last night? I pulled my head up and looked around the room. I suddenly remembered I was in the hotel room, and it was Dad's stag, but what happened last night? More importantly, where was everybody? I'd booked the rooms and I was sharing with Dad and Steve. Uncle Pete, Frank and Derek were in the second room. However, looking around the room, it was empty except for me.

I slowly got up, rubbed my head, and walked off towards the bathroom. I needed a glass of water and a wee. I walked into the bathroom and that's when I saw him. Steve was lying fast asleep in the bathtub, trousers off (luckily underwear on - although green Y-fronts?), and shirt half unbuttoned. I quickly shook him awake. Steve stirred and rubbed his eyes.

'What happened?' said Steve.

'I have no idea,' I said. 'Do you know where Dad is?'

'No, isn't he with you?'

'No.'

I started to get worried. I wished I could remember something. Steve clambered out of the bath and got dressed. I grabbed a drink of water, and we headed next door to see the others. I knocked and knocked until eventually the door opened and a rather awful looking Derek answered the door.

'Oh, shit, fuck, bugger and fuck, what happened?' said Derek.

'We have no idea,' I said. 'Have you seen Dad?'

'No,' said Derek. 'Although we do have a nun in the spare bed and what looks like a couple of European backpackers on the floor. Frank is sleeping on the bathroom floor and your uncle Pete is sleeping completely naked on the bed.'

'So no one's seen Dad?'

'No,' said Derek.

'And when was the last time you saw him?'

'I have no idea,' said Derek. 'I also don't know why I'm wearing these trousers. They aren't mine.'

I started to get really worried. What if something terrible had happened to Dad? What if he had somehow lost his memory and was walking around London in a fog? What if he was so drunk he had somehow fallen in the Thames? What if something far more sinister had happened? We needed to find Dad and fast. My brain was working overtime and the thought of losing Dad scared me to my bones. Mum would never forgive me. I'd never forgive me.

I quickly rounded everybody up, including the nun and the European backpackers to try and see if anybody remembered anything about last night. Uncle Pete definitely remembered that Dad was with us at the strip club.

'He was with this busty blonde and she was giving him a lap dance.'

'Are you sure it was Dad?' I said.

'Sure,' said Uncle Pete. 'He has the moustache.'

'Dad doesn't have a moustache, Pete.'

'Oh.'

'I'm fairly sure he was with us afterwards. Remember we got those kebabs and then we went to that bar across the road?' said Frank.

'And then what happened?' I said, but no one remembered anything. Not even the nun or the European backpackers.

I tried calling Dad's mobile, but it went straight to voicemail. I was shafted. I had to go home and tell Mum the news. Derek could use his connections on the force if we had to. Dad was officially missing, and he was getting married to Mum in four days.

Me, Derek (still in mysterious trousers) and Steve (still in green Y-fronts) jumped in a taxi back to Wimbledon. We were going to have to tell Mum and start a search. Maybe she'd heard from him. I could only hope. Eventually, we got back home, paid the taxi driver, and dashed inside.

'Morning,' said Emily opening the door. 'You look absolutely terrible, you all do.'

'Have you heard from Dad?' I said in a panic. 'He's missing.'

'What?' said Emily.

'Dad's missing. We can't find him anywhere and we're really worried.'

'Harry,' said Emily. 'He's in there playing with William.'

'What?'

I went through into the lounge and there, sitting on the floor with a big smile on his face, was Dad.

'Dad?!' I said.

'Oh, hello,' said Dad.

'Where the fuck have you been?'

'Earmuffs,' said Emily.

'Uck bin,' said William.

Then Dad, who looked perfectly fine, went on to tell me what had happened.

Apparently, just after the strip club, he'd felt this sudden urge to see Mum. He realised he didn't need large breasted women and instead just wanted to cuddle up with Mum. He'd explained all this to me last night before he left (allegedly), but I must have forgotten.

'You were all so excited about getting a kebab and going

on to a late-night bar, but

I'd had enough, Harry. I just wanted to be at home with your mother. I missed her,' said Dad. 'But I had a great stag. A wonderful day. Especially the archery and off-roading, a real highlight, but I can't drink that much anymore. Lucky thing I knew when to stop, you three look terrible.'

And that was Dad's stag. I have no idea what happened to the nun and the European backpackers. We still don't know who Derek's trousers belonged to and where his actual trousers are and why Steve wears green Y-fronts. We got a text from Uncle Pete and Frank, they were heading off home and thanked me for a great night, and especially for the lap dances.

'What do they mean?' I said.

'You don't remember?' said Dad.

'Remember what?' I said.

'You paid for all our lap dances,' said Dad. 'It must have cost a fortune.'

'What?!' said Emily behind me.

'Oh, yeah, I remember now,' said Derek. 'You insisted.'

'Oh,' I said.

'I think even the nun had one,' said Steve. 'Although thinking about it now, I'm not sure she really was a nun.'

Tuesday 26 November 8.45 p.m.

Home. Watching TV with Emily. Just back from seeing Dad. Raining again.

I went to see Mum, Dad and the vicar tonight. We had to go over the details for the wedding. The vicar was a nice man. He's called Michael and was quite young for a vicar, and he wasn't too religious about everything (he even had on a pair of skinny jeans). The surprise is all set for Friday.

I'm so excited to see Emily's face.

At the end Dad took me aside and said he had an extra surprise for us. He wouldn't say anything else except that Mum was going to love it and it would be a really cool way to make the perfect day even more perfect. They say you can't teach old dogs' new tricks, but it seems in Dad's case, maybe you can.

Emily has been in a bit of a weird mood this week. I keep asking her if she's all right, but she just keeps saying that she doesn't feel good. I hope she's okay on Friday for the big day. You only get married for the second time once.

Friday 29 November 8.05 a.m.

Wedding Day

The sun isn't just shining, it's SHINING. We woke up this morning to glorious sun coming in through the window. Today's the day that Mum and Dad, and Emily and I renew our marriage vows. It's going to be a day none of us forgets for a very long time.

1.45 p.m.

We're just about to leave for the church. Emily's in the toilet. She's still feeling a bit under the weather. I hope today will cheer her up. William is wearing a little suit and I've literally never seen anything quite so cute in all my life. Steve, Fiona and the Js are driving down in an hour. We have to get there a bit early to get the church ready. Here comes Emily. She's looking gorgeous in a new dress, and she's had her hair done. She looks even more beautiful than the day I married her, and I almost choke up and start crying, but I need to keep myself together. I can't risk her getting a whiff that anything out of the ordinary is going on.

6.00 p.m.

At the church hall. Oh my goodness. What an afternoon. I'm not really sure where to begin. I suppose the beginning. Deep breaths, Harry.

We got to the church and Dad was already there, looking worried and agitated.

'What if she doesn't show up? What if something goes wrong? What if—'

'Dad, nothing is going to go wrong and I'm fairly sure Mum, your wife, is going to show up for her own wedding.'

'Fairly sure?' said Dad

'100% sure.'

After I calmed Dad down, Emily and I helped get the church ready, while William ran up and down the pews. William was loving church, while I was a bag of nerves because A: I had to give Mum away. B: I was Dad's best man. C: After they got married, I was going to surprise Emily and we were getting married again.

I met Mum outside, who was looking absolutely stunning in her original wedding

dress. 'I can't believe it still fits,' is the first thing she said to me with a giant smile. We waited outside while the last few stragglers filtered into the church. It was still warm outside, and leaves were falling around us. It was the perfect autumnal day.

The music started inside, and it was our cue to begin the walk down the aisle. 'Harry,' said Mum suddenly. 'Before we go in, I just wanted to say,' she started and then tears filled her eyes. She had her arm through mine, and I reached across my hand and gave hers a gentle squeeze. 'I can't think of anyone I'd rather have walk me down the aisle. I'm so proud of you son and I love you so much.'

'I love you too,' I said holding back my own tears. 'Ready?'

'Ready,' said Mum and we opened the doors and began

the walk down the aisle. The church was packed to the rafters, and everyone was smiling as we made our way towards Dad, who was stood up front by himself, eyes glazed over with emotion. I spotted Emily and William as I walked down, and I waved at them, and William got very excited. 'Addy! Addy!' he shouted, and everyone laughed.

I passed Mum off to Dad and then stood next to Dad with the ring in my suit jacket pocket. The ceremony went on and as it got near the end, I started getting more and more anxious about what was going to happen next. After Mum and Dad said, 'I do', the vicar was going to call Emily up, Steve was going to take William and then I was going to get down on one knee and ask Emily to marry me again. I was sweating buckets.

'Harry, the ring?' said Dad.

'Sorry?'

'The ring,' Dad said again.

'Oh, sorry,' I said and passed Dad the ring.

It was almost time. Eventually, Mum and Dad said their vows and there wasn't a dry eye in the house. They kissed, and the vicar pronounced them man and wife - still (which got a few giggles). Everyone clapped and cheered, and they probably thought that was it. Time to put the plan into action. The vicar looked at me and winked.

'Ladies and gentlemen. I'm sure you'll agree that it was a wonderful sight to see Greg and Helen getting married again and renewing their vows. Love like theirs that has endured so many years is something that should be celebrated and cherished. Through good times and bad, health and sickness, true love stays strong and lasts. So with that in mind, I'd like to invite Emily Spencer up here please,' said the Vicar.

I looked at Emily and she looked at me in complete shock. She stood up and all the heads in the church turned and watched her walk up towards me.

'I'll let you take it from here, Harry,' said the vicar to me.

Every eye in the church was on me, and Emily was giving

me a strange look. Eventually, she reached me, and I held her hands in mine. Then I got down on one knee in front of everyone.

'Emily. We've been married for seven years and there hasn't been a day when I haven't loved you more than the last. It's true we've had our ups and our downs, but through it all, we've always remained strong and stuck together. Today is about love and it's about Mum and Dad starting over and enjoying the next part of their lives together. We've had some difficult times over the past year and so I felt like it was the right time for us to begin the next chapter of our lives. You, me and William. I love you Em, always have, always will and if you'll have me, I'd love to renew our vows.'

Emily was in tears. Mum and Dad were in tears. I was in tears.

'Well, Emily, what do you say?' said the vicar after a moment.

All eyes were on Emily.

'There's just one thing,' said Emily through the tears. 'If this is a new start, the next chapter, then there's something you should know.'

'What?' I said suddenly terrified.

'One moment,' said Emily, who let go of my hands and walked back towards her seat. She got back and reached into her handbag. I had no idea what was going on, but then Emily stopped searching inside her bag and stood up, waving around a small, plastic, white stick.

'I'm pregnant, Harry,' said Emily. 'We're having another baby!'

I don't remember much about the next few minutes, but there were tears, hugs, congratulations, and I spent a great deal of time cuddling Emily and William and telling them how much I loved them. After we'd all calmed down, the vicar invited us back up again and Emily and I renewed our vows. Emily said it wasn't fair because I had time to do mine and she had to make hers up on the spot. Although to be fair, hers were definitely better than mine.

Then the cherry on the cake. Dad's surprise. Mum, Dad, Emily and I turned around and started the walk down the aisle when it happened. You know the wedding scene in Love Actually? Well, Dad did it. Apparently, it's Mum's favourite film and she loves the wedding scene. Before we'd even taken a few steps down the aisle, the faint singing of, 'Love, love, love,' began to emerge and then suddenly from the back of the church, a whole choir stood up and bellowed it out. 'Love, love, love.' Then just like in the film, a man emerged from behind the choir and started walking down the aisle. Although it wasn't just a man, it was Steve! 'There's nothing you can do that can't be done,' sang Steve in a surprisingly incredible voice. 'There's nothing you can sing that can't be sung. Nothing you can say, but you can learn how to play the game. It's easy.' Then suddenly someone started playing a cello, three men stood up and started playing trumpets and then three more with flutes, and then from behind us, the vicar started playing the electric guitar! Steve continued to sing, 'All you need is love. All you need is love. All you need is love.'

I looked at Dad and Mum, and then Emily and we all burst out laughing. Then I saw William and he had a huge smile on his face and was wiggling his hips. It was exactly as Dad said it would be. The most perfect end to the perfect day and among all the surprises, Emily had saved the best one for me.

December

Monday 2 December 7.55 p.m.

Home. Cold. William fast asleep. About to watch Love Actually with Emily. She's making the popcorn.

Mum and Dad left for their trip around Europe today. They're gone for three weeks and come back just before Christmas. They're visiting ten countries in twenty days. This is the warm-up for their bigger trip next year when they're planning on flying around the world. I still can't quite believe the change in my parents since the beginning of the year.

We saw them last night and they were very excited. It's been a bit crazy since the wedding and Emily's pregnancy announcement. We told William about the baby and that it's going to be in mummy's belly, and he keeps pointing at it and saying, 'Aaby! Aaby!'

Wednesday 4 December 3.55 p.m.

At school. Trying my best to tidy up and rush home because tonight's Steve's TV debut. It's on at four-thirty and we're all going to Steve's house to watch it.

I got a text from Mum today. They're in Paris and Dad has already managed to get in trouble by insulting a policeman. He thought he was asking for directions to the Eiffel Tower, but apparently he called the policeman a bag of shit. Luckily, the officer had a sense of humour.

8.15 p.m.

What a show. Steve the Entertainer was brilliant. We all crammed into Steve's front room. There was Steve, Fiona, the Js, Phil, Dawn, Stacey, Emily, William and me. Steve was only on for about five minutes, but he definitely stole the show. Steve ran a small shop where he sold all manner of instruments and magic tricks and so, obviously, when people came into the shop, Steve the Entertainer got to do what he does best ... entertain.

After the show finished we all clapped and cheered, and Fiona opened a bottle of champagne for the adults and apple juice for the kids, and we all celebrated a wonderful night in the career of Steve. He may well be my new hero. I was truly touched by Steve.

Saturday 7 December 2.40 p.m.

Christmas is officially here. We got our tree today and put-up decorations all over the lounge. William absolutely loves it. He's been sitting under the tree for the past hour just staring at it. Emily put on some classic Christmas music, and it feels really festive.

7.15 p.m.

Since I found out we're having a baby, there's been something I've been dying to do and tonight I did it. I rang Ben.

'Do you have any idea what time it is?' said Ben.

'Yes, it's three-forty in the morning.'

'So why the fuck are you calling me?'

'Because you called me in the middle of the night to tell me Katie was pregnant.'

'But I had news. Exciting news.'

'And so do I. Emily's pregnant!'

'What?!' said Ben.

'She's preggers. It looks like you and I are going to be having our babies very close together.'

'Oh, mate, I'm so chuffed,' said Ben.

'So you don't mind that I woke you up?'

'No, not at all,' said Ben.

'I fucking do,' said Katie in the background.

'Oh, sorry,' I said.
'Pommie bastard,' said Katie.
'She'll be right,' said Ben.

Sunday 8 December 4.00 p.m.

Phil and I went shopping today for our battle scene. We had a few discussions and debates about which battle to recreate, but eventually we decided on the Battle of Passchendaele. I'm quite excited. Phil's also talking about the possibility of going to France and doing a tour of the battlefields. I said we could take Bertie. It's all moving so fast with Phil, but we just click. There's just something about him. Our shared love of history and nineties music, and home brew beer in the shed. Emily's calling it a Bromance. Why is it that two men can't just hang out together, enjoy each other's company, plan holidays together and get on like a house on fire without it getting a label?

Tuesday 10 December 10.00 p.m.

'What if it's a girl?' I said.

'I don't know. Maybe Charlie, or how about India?' said Emily.

We were in bed debating names.

'I like India, but I don't want people to automatically assume that her parents were stoned, layabout hippies who thought India made her sound interesting. What about Caroline?'

'It's just so, I don't know, plain.'

'Exactly,' I said. 'No pressure. We're giving her a clean slate and she can decide exactly who she is and what she wants to be. If we go around calling our kid Tallulah Banana Skin Spencer, they're going to have to live up to that.'

'So you want to go completely traditional?'

'I do.'

'Then what about Beatrice?'

'After your grandmother who accused me of raping her and then died because I beat her at a game of Monopoly?'

'Exactly.'

'No thanks. How about Rachel?'

'I don't know. I quite like Rachel, but then what if she doesn't look like a Rachel and instead looks like a Primrose or a Wanda?'

'I don't think she's going to look like a Wanda, Em.' I said.

'She might, or she might be a Gemma or a Beatrix.'

'We could call her Trixie?'

'And she could go to work in strip clubs,' said Emily.

'Then we probably shouldn't call her Regina either. If you don't want your kid to work in the sex industry, don't give them a name that rhymes with vagina.'

'But Regina doesn't rhyme with vagina,' said Emily.

'It does if you pronounce it the right way.'

'What about boy's names?'

'Virgil?' I said.

'You're kidding me?'

'Yes. Although I do quite like Vince. It's edgy.'

'So is Vance.'

'Vance Spencer, he sounds like a rogue cop who does whatever he needs to do to get the job done.'

Emily giggled.

'We have no chance of picking out a suitable name, do we?' said Emily.

'I don't think so. Luckily, we have nine months to decide,' I said. 'And if nothing else comes up and it's a boy, I think we have to go with Vance.'

'Definitely and how about Trixie Regina for a girl?'

'Perfect,' I said.

It looked like we had our names. Vance Spencer for a

boy and Trixie Regina Spencer for a girl. One to be a rogue cop and the other a lap dancer at a sex club in Soho. Brilliant.

Friday 13 December 4.00 p.m.

At school. Nice and cold. The last Friday of term and so the last departmental meeting of the calendar year. Only three days of school left - plus the nativity play.

4.55 p.m.

Mr Jones came to our meeting today with some good news. I'm not sure his version of good news is the same as the rest of the English-speaking world though.

'Harry, we've finally decided on your job title, and I think this will really help define your role going forwards. So, from now on the title, Head of Department no longer exists. It's too Draconian in this enlightened age. So, in line with current trends and to make sure the team as a whole are considered, we've decided to call you, Curriculum Leader and Individual Team Supervisor,' said Mr Jones with a beaming smile.

'Or CLITS,' said Chris Bartlett with an even bigger smile.

Apparently, Friday the 13th is unlucky for some.

Wednesday 18 December 8.15 a.m.

The last day of school before Christmas and there's a party atmosphere in the halls and classrooms. The teachers are all wearing Santa hats and even the pupils are getting into the Christmas spirit, although Bradley Jenkinson took things a bit too far when he attached some mistletoe to his belt buckle and asked Miss Garibaldi for a kiss. The little scamp.

I intend to do no teaching today and instead we're going

to listen to Christmas songs, make Christmas cards, and eat the snacks I'm allowing them to bring in today. I will probably gain a good stone today with all the mince pies. Still it's only Christmas once a year and if I don't gain enough weight over the next few weeks, I'll have nothing to feel bad about in January.

Tonight is the school nativity play. Mr Fitzsimmons the drama teacher has apparently pulled out all the stops, although after last year's debacle, he didn't have much choice. Emily and William are going along, and it should be fun as long as the donkey doesn't escape again, and the three wise men remember to turn off their mobile phones.

9.15 p.m.

The nativity was a lot better than last year. The kids were brilliant and the one who played the octopus was particularly impressive, although not as good as the three wise owls. Mr Fitzsimmons took a little artistic license with the story of Jesus this year. The biggest leap (apart from the variety of animals) was probably the setting. Mr Fitzsimmons had foregone the usual Bethlehem and had Jesus born at a service station just off the M4. Mr Fitzsimmons said that the service station was the nearest modern equivalent, although he didn't explain the octopus or the flying monkeys. Still, an enjoyable night was had by all, especially at the end when the whole cast, joined by Mr Fitzsimmons and other game staff members, came on stage and performed 'Do They Know It's Christmas'. A blinding night.

Saturday 21 December 7.15 p.m.

Mum and Dad came home today and popped over with presents. Dad got me a string of French garlic. Emily got some clogs and William got some baby lederhosen - or babyhosen as Dad has been calling them. Mum and Dad stayed for dinner, opened the schnapps they'd bought in Germany and told us all about their holiday.

'Oh, it was wonderful,' said Mum. 'The trains were lovely, not like the trains here. And the people, so nice, even with your dad shouting at them so they'd understand him, you know what your dad's like. We really enjoyed Italy, Harry, the food and the countryside, just gorgeous. Oh, that reminds me, we saw a man in Rome who looked just like you, didn't we Greg? He was your exact double, although he was a bit taller, and Italian of course. And Switzerland, so beautiful, breath-taking wasn't it, Greg? I said at the time, it's breath-taking, like a postcard. You'd love it, Harry, you really would and oh, Germany, such wonderful people, even your dad was surprised. And the sausages, you'd love the sausages, Harry, really tasty and I'll have to show you the photos once I've got them developed. Your father thinks we should get one of those digital ones for next year. I don't know though, there's something about a physical picture isn't there, and I like going to Boots to pick them up, it's quite exciting,' Mum went on and I just smiled because she really was back - in more ways than one.

Tuesday 24 December 9.15 a.m.

Christmas Eve & My Birthday

There was a time in my life when the prospect of being 'mid-thirties' seemed literally decades away. Today I turn thirty-five and so it's here; I'm finally and officially 'mid-thirties', but I must say, it's not quite as terrifying as I thought. For a start, when I was eighteen, thirty-five seemed like the end of the line, middle-aged, decrepit, but now I'm here I don't feel that old. I'm not eighteen anymore, but that's okay. I'm happy. Content. I wish I didn't ache so much when I get out of bed in the morning and the unwanted hair that keeps appearing in unusual places would subside, but overall thirty-five isn't so bad.

William came in this morning with breakfast in bed. 'Appy Irthde,' he said, passing me a card with a big grin. The best birthday breakfast ever.

Today's also Christmas Eve and so we have to get ready for the big day. We have Mum, Dad, Derek and Pam coming over for dinner and I'm in charge of the turkey. I've ordered an organic free-range turkey from the butchers. I have to pick her up this morning. We're off to Steve and Fiona's tonight for drinks and I need to pop in and see Phil later - he picked up some more pieces for Passchendaele.

11.45 a.m.

The turkey is a beauty. She's in the fridge. Off to see Phil.

12.25 p.m.

Phil got us a couple of Brodie helmets to wear. I couldn't believe it. They were the first steel helmets introduced in 1915. He got them from eBay and so now we really look the part. No one must see what we're doing and how we look, especially Emily because she's already calling this a Bromance. If she knew about Passchendaele and now the helmets, she might start getting worried.

Harry,

Merry Christmas and happy birthday. I really wish I could be there to celebrate with you. Speak soon old man.

Love Ben, Katie and The Embryo x

1.05 p.m.

'Happy birthday,' said Mum. 'I thought I'd better call as

we aren't going to see you today. How are you feeling?'

'Fine, Mum,' I said.

'Are you sure, because I know thirty-five can be a difficult age? I remember your father, he had a bit of a freak out, didn't you Greg?'

'I did,' said Dad in the background.

'I'm fine, Mum, honestly.'

'I know, I know, just be careful and remember to take your cod liver oil, your father swears by it, don't you?'

'I do,' said Dad.

'Mum, I'm having a great day, I'm fine.'

'I just worry,' said Mum. 'Happy birthday and we'll see you tomorrow. Give William a big kiss and don't forget the cod liver oil. I'll bring some over tomorrow just to be on the safe side. Love you,' said Mum and then she was gone.

4.15 p.m.

Off to Steve and Fiona's. It's all getting very festive. We've been listening to Emily's Christmas classics album all afternoon. I've already had some mint Baileys, and William found the Christmas crackers and pulled two already. Emily just finished watching The Snowman and is crying her eyes out. 'It's Aled Jones, he gets me every time,' she said. 'He had such a lovely voice.'

The BBC weather girl has predicted snow tomorrow. Fingers crossed.

10.15 p.m.

Home. Slightly pissed. We had a great time at Steve and Fiona's. Phil, Dawn and Stacey came too, and they got me a birthday cake and a few small presents. A cracking night.

William is tucked up tight in bed and Emily is putting the presents under the tree. I'm enjoying a late-night mint Baileys, John Lennon and Yoko are cracking out their brilliant Happy Xmas (War is over), I'm looking out of the front window, and I'm sure I just saw a snowflake.

11.05 p.m.

It was the night before Christmas and all through the house not a creature was stirring not even a mouse - although to be fair, Emily's snoring like a bastard.

Wednesday 25 December 10.15 a.m.

Christmas Day

We woke up this morning to a blanket of white snow. I couldn't believe it. The BBC weather girl (who's definitely pregnant) was spot on again. We woke up William and took him outside. It was the first time he'd seen snow and he loved it. He wasn't sure at first and kept saying, 'Old Addy, old,' but after a while he got used to it and then he couldn't get enough. We built a little snowman and then Emily decided she wanted a snowball fight - is it wrong to use your child as a human shield during a snowball fight? Emily said yes, I said no.

William opened his stocking presents this morning. He was over the moon with his small selection of toys and hasn't stopped playing with them since. I can't wait for Emily to open the present I got for her. I found an old photo of us from when we first met, and I had it printed and mounted with a really cool frame. I also got her a really nice necklace. She's being really weird about my present and keeps saying it will be here soon. I have no idea what the daft old bat is playing at.

12.15 p.m.

Ben, Katie and The Embryo are here! The doorbell went at twelve o'clock and I knew something was going on because Emily was all excited and made me get it. I opened the door and there they were. It was emotional. I'm over the moon. They're staying with us over Christmas before they're off to his parents for a few days, and then they're back for our big New Year's Eve party. Best mate Ben is here. Christmas is complete.

Time to get the turkey out of the fridge and ready for the oven. I'm making herb butter to stuff under the skin (thanks Jamie Oliver).

2.45 p.m.

Mum, Dad, Derek, Pam, Ben and Katie are all here. The Christmas Mega-Mix is on, the turkey is in the oven, Mum is already half-pissed, Dad and Derek are playing Battleships, Pam is playing with William, Ben is helping in the kitchen (by drinking all the beer), Katie is lying down and watching Casablanca, and Emily is working on the potatoes. It's still snowing outside and there's a real party atmosphere in the house.

3.15 p.m.

Steve, Fiona and the Js are all over too. Their oven packed in just after the turkey went in. Steve is putting on a show for the kids and Emily is trying to find extra cutlery and plates. Dad just said that this is like a proper, old-fashioned Christmas (like during the war, apparently) and can't wait to play charades (Dad loves charades. I think it's his favourite thing about Christmas).

6.15 p.m.

The turkey was incredible.

'The best I've ever had' - Mum.

'So juicy you could almost drink it' - Derek.

'Gordon Ramsay is a pussy compared to you' - Ben.

'That was turkey?' - Dad.

'OMG!' - Steve.

We all squeezed in around the table, paper hats on, and Dad won the worst cracker joke of the day. What do you call a man with paper trousers? Russell. After we were all stuffed on turkey, it was time to crack open the board games, play charades, and start the serious drinking.

10.15 p.m.

The party is in full swing. Phil, Dawn and Stacey have joined us too after getting back from his parents' house in Billericay. All the kids are upstairs, some asleep, some not. Dad and Derek are sitting on the sofa like a couple of old men talking about proper old men stuff and drinking brandy. Mum, Pam and Fiona are going at the vodka and dancing around the lounge and trying to get everyone to do the conga. Emily, Dawn and Katie (the pregnant trio) are drinking alcohol free sparkling apple juice and eating as much dessert as they can because they can't bloody drink, all right! Steve and Phil are playing Guess Who? and Ben and I are drinking, talking and laughing like the good old days. A proper Christmas. And it's still snowing.

Tuesday 31 December 8.15 p.m.

New Year's Eve

Another year gone, only this one feels a little bit different. I suppose it's having William. Life isn't just twelve months in our life anymore, but twelve months in his and he's changed so much - we all have. Mum got cancer, but recovered, and now she and Dad are better than ever. I almost lost Emily again but didn't. I became AHOD/ASM, but then wasn't. I became HOD again, but then it was changed to CLITS. We bought a VW campervan called Bertie and it's proven to be the missing link. We have the best new neighbours we could have hoped for (especially after the snake in the grass that was Mark) and Phil and I are now heavily into a secret recreation of the Battle of Passchendaele. Steve is now a celebrity children's entertainer on CBeebies, and I couldn't be prouder of him (although he still owes me a big slice of thank you for making him change his name from the Kid Fiddler/ Touched by Steve). Best mate Ben is having his first child, Rory and Miranda are having their first. Phil and Dawn are having their second, and Emily is pregnant with our second. A year from now four new lives will be here, kicking and screaming, and causing us heartache, pain, stress, worry, anxiety, and more love, happiness and joy than any of us could have hoped for.

All in all, it's been a brilliant year. A few lows, but also a lot of highs, and unlike last year, the highs definitely outweigh the lows. I wonder what next year will bring.

Tonight's our big New Year's Eve party. We figured after last year's in bed by ten-thirty debacle, we needed to do something positive and reclaim our youth, or more correctly, reclaim our life. We may be older, with kids, but that doesn't mean we can't have a good time. Tonight all of our friends and family will be here celebrating with us, and we'll definitely make it to midnight.

Life is properly back on track. It may be a different life than the one we used to have, but you know what, this one is better. It's older, wiser, fuller and happier than I ever imagined. Of course, tomorrow is going to be a nightmare - I'll be hungover to hell and whether I want to or not, the kids won't be, and they'll want to play. They'll need their nappies changing, and they'll demand I get off the sofa and stop complaining about my head.

Still, that's tomorrow. Tonight we sing, we dance, we drink, and we watch Jools Holland's Hootenanny. This year William will turn two, another kid will be delivered and turn our life upside down, and I'll turn thirty-six. I'm not scared anymore though. I have no reason to be because I know I can do it. This is what I am now, and I don't think I've ever been happier.

11.59 p.m.

In William's bedroom with Emily and William. Everyone else downstairs.

'Ten.'

'Nine.'

'Eight.'

'Seven.'

'Six.'

'Five.'

'Four.'

'Three.'

'Two.'

'One.'

'Happy New Year, Em.'

'Happy New Year, Harry.'

'Happy New Year,' we both say to William who is in Emily's lap. He's semi-awake.

'Happy New Year Vance Spencer or Trixie Regina Spencer,' I say putting my hand on Emily's belly. I look across at Emily and smile, and then down at William, who opens his eyes and smiles at me. My family. Then William does something really awful in his nappy. I don't need to look because he farts, and then comes the noise that can only mean one thing. And then the smell hits us.

'This one has your name written all over it,' says Emily.

'No, no, I'm too drunk,' I say putting my hand over my nose. It smells like hell. It has all the early signs of a nuclear poo.

'William, who do you want to change your nappy?' says Emily.

William looks at us both and then he smiles and says, 'Daddy.'

What else can I say? He's my son. I love him unconditionally.

'Flip a coin, best of three?'

Be sure to follow Jon on Twitter *@JRance75,* on Facebook *@JonRanceauthor*, and check out his website *www.jonrance.co.uk* for all the updates on his latest work.

Thank you for reading. I hope you enjoyed *This Family Life*. Do leave a review if so on all your preferred platforms to help spread the word!

Thank you!

Printed in Great Britain
by Amazon

22165251R00179